THE WITCH OF THE PROPHECY

VICTORIA JAYNE

Happy Reading

Vim Jayne

Connect with Victoria,
twitter.com/@authorvictoriaj
AuthorVictoriaJayne@gmail.com
authorvictoriajayne.com

CHAPTER 1

The fruity fragrance of the potted primrose tangled with the hints of sweat and fresh sex. The pillows and duvet coiled into a heap on the bed. However, the couple responsible for the disheveled state was no longer there.

The glow from the moon shone through the large window, causing her ebony waves to shimmer, while he stroked his pale, slender fingers through her hair. He couldn't recall another time in his life when he had felt as content as he did at that moment. His whole world was in this oversized chair.

Her plump body curved in just the right places; her olive-toned, bare form lounged across his much paler lap. As she flipped through the leather-bound text, Rori leaned in, burying his nose in her hair and inhaling deeply. He savored the raw scent of the woman who had captured his formerly still heart. He couldn't help but smile.

Turning the page of the old leather-bound book, she read while resting her head against his chest. She was warmer than he was. She had far more life than he did. Perhaps his desire to possess her was something other than infatuation.

Pressing his lips to the top of her head, he didn't care the cause; he only wished to have her.

How long had they sat there? How long had it been since he'd been inside her? How long had it been since she screamed his name?

Having lost the concept of time long ago, he found it worse when with her. When she shifted her position even slightly, the stimulus stirred his hunger for her again.

"I can't believe this stuff is so hidden." She broke through his thoughts.

He smiled. There was much about the world he wanted to show Divina before reality set in.

"Humans would not be able to handle such information." He stroked her arm with his fingertips. "Or perhaps I should say, they didn't, so we had to take it away and hide it. The world would be a much more violent place if humans knew."

With a furrowed brow, she turned her glacier-colored eyes that burned his soul, toward him. "You trust me?"

"You're not fully human," he reminded her, while playfully booping her nose before giving her a soft kiss on the forehead.

Her innocence drew him in like ants to sugar. He cherished her. These intimate moments with her were more valuable to him than any jewel or treasure.

"So you keep saying," she grumbled, and once more shifted her hips, eliciting a groan from him.

He wondered if she knew how those full hips affected him.

Her smirk told him all he needed to know about that.

"In all my years, I have yet to be wrong," he whispered in her ear.

Rolling her eyes before turning them back to the book, she sighed.

"I'm not sure I can handle the responsibility," she admitted.

There: her vulnerability. Sure, she was mortal, therefore vulnerable. That wasn't the vulnerability Rori liked. No, the uninhibited honesty she offered him showed her trust in him. How she offered him her true self without concern for self-preservation.

Naivety.

He loved her for it and hated himself for what he had to do with it.

Closing his own eyes, he took in a deep breath of her beautiful scent. Relishing the moment, he pushed the future from his mind.

In the end, the right now, would be all he had. There was no need to rush it. Right now could end at any moment, and he'd only have the memory to comfort him.

"You are so much stronger than you know, Divina. I will show you," he said.

Those wide, innocent blue eyes pinned him once more. He hated the Ember Witches at that moment. He hated prophecies. He hated the world for what it was making him do.

"You've shown me so much already," she said with wonder in her eyes.

He forced a smile on his face. "There is so much more."

Three Years Later

Rori awoke from his daytime slumber with longing in his heart. Sometimes memories were the worst form of torture. When he let her go, he'd made peace with not having Divina.

Forced to walk away from her, avoiding her for three years, had helped in achieving that peace. With the prophecy set in motion, he no longer had that luxury. They sent him back to her.

CHAPTER 2

From the shadow of the tent, Rori stepped into the artificially lit fairgrounds. Using the tips of his thumb and forefinger, he cleaned blood from the corners of his mouth that had caught in his trimmed chestnut-colored goatee. The abundance of prey in this setting was a temptation he couldn't avoid. With his hunger sated, he continued to hunt for Divina through the people overindulging in socially acceptable gluttony and gambling.

Stalking through the crowd, he curled his finger to his cherub-like, rounded nose while his palm covered his mouth. Attempting to block the nauseating odors of sugary cotton candy and salted popcorn, Rori feared he'd lose his dinner. The melodic repetition of the carousel, joyful cries of children, and the calls of the game vendors impaired his enhanced hearing. Dressed in a charcoal vest over a crisp, white shirt tucked into his jeans, the dark-short-haired Rori didn't particularly fit in with the crowd. He detested carnivals.

As Rori rounded the corner of a ring toss, his target came into view. The hand over his deceivingly youthful face dropped, unveiling a sinister grin of triumph. On the fringe of the festival sat a brightly painted, handcrafted, wooden vardo. His cognac gaze fixated on the chalk sandwich board proclaiming five dollars for palm readings and fifteen dollar tarot card readings. Snorting, he rolled his eyes.

The sounds of glee faded as Rori approached the bottom of the four stairs leading to the entrance of the reading wagon style vardo. Overhearing the muffled conversation within, he grinned delighted to hear her voice once more. Not wanting to interrupt her session with a client since he planned to request her assistance, his pale, slender digit trailed along the intricate carvings on the wagon.

It didn't take long for a frail, sickly looking woman clutching a tissue to her nose to exit and descend the stairs. Once at the bottom, she turned to repeat her thanks to the woman remaining at the opened entrance of the vardo. Smiling at Rori, the woman passed him and disappeared around the corner heading into the crowded carnival.

Hands in his pockets, he lifted his attention to face his prey and was awestruck. Candles flickered behind her and offered a soft, golden glow, flattering her sun-kissed skin. The peasant blouse and flowing skirt hid her curvy body, but Rori remembered it. A breeze sent strands of her thick, wavy, ebony mane across her oblong face accented by angular cheeks. Memories of their time together danced through his mind, and he couldn't help but grin fondly, longing for different circumstances.

"No." The quick and curt response cut through Rori's thoughts.

The object of his lust gathered the colorful linen of her ankle-length skirt as she descended the stairs toward her sandwich board.

Rori's smile remained, always appreciating a challenge. "I haven't asked anything."

"The answer is still no," she asserted closing the sign.

"Oh good, you're done for the night." He strolled closer to her ignoring her negative response to him.

Rori's nose wrinkled when she stomped past him, lugging the cumbersome sign. The scent of patchouli, sage, and myrrh clung to her. The incense covered her natural, earthy scent. He wanted to scrub the artificial aromas from her. Instead, he plucked the sign from her grasp effortlessly.

"You'll cost me business," she growled and tried to yank the sign back from him.

He admired her fire. He missed it. It had been too long.

"If it weren't for me, you wouldn't have a business," he said as he relented and released her sign.

Thump. With the sign clutched in Divina's hands, she fell back onto her behind. Rori chuckled.

Flushing red, his raven-haired beauty glowered at Rori from the ground. Abandoning the sign, she clamored to her feet. Divina dusted herself off. "Won't let me forget that, will you?" Rage flashed in her narrowed, icy blue eyes. "I'm not helping you!"

Pointing an accusatory finger at him, she jabbed it as if to accentuate her point. That long slender digit had once been used to tease him. Was it possible to be attracted to a finger? He grinned.

With a twitch to her reddened cheeks, she huffed. Lowering her hands, she balled the two into white knuckled fists at her sides. The natural beauty before him glowed when she was angry, and it only stirred more need for her.

Attempting a neutral expression, he diverted his gaze and cleared his throat. "Can we move past your futile attempts at denying me the request—" When Divina's mouth opened to interrupt him, he held up a hand. "That I have yet to make, and get to the point where I make it?"

"You... you are—" She stammered with shaking fists.

"Charming? Devastatingly handsome? Sexy?" He waggled his brows suggestively. His appreciative gaze swept over her. Licking his plump lower lip, he remembered her flavor. It had been too long since he tasted her.

"Dangerous," she spat. She bent to grab her sign. With purpose, she ascended the short staircase. "And an asshole," she shot over her shoulder.

"You seem mad," he said while cheerily following behind her.

"You seem not to understand the word no." She dumped the sign inside the heavily adorned yet sparsely decorated vardo and turned to him. With her back to the inside of her wagon, Divina's arm's outstretched to take hold of the door-frame. Her curvaceous form, hidden by the loose, almost costume-like clothing she wore, blocked his entrance to her tiny home.

"Dreadful word." Remaining at the bottom step, forced to look up at her, Rori had to admit, it wasn't a bad angle. Doubting there were any bad angles for this fiery witch, he took the opportunity to appreicate her features.

Once again her effortless beauty stole his breath. How he wished he could comb his fingers through the tangled mass of dark hair. How he wished to bury his nose in the crook of her neck once more. His gaze lingered on the pulsing jugular vein, and his mouth watered.

"I hate you," she declared bringing him back to the present.

Holding a hand to his barely beating heart, Rori gasped. "Why?" feigning shock. "I'm lovely."

"I trusted you." Her anger seemed to waver, replaced with hurt and a crack to her voice.

Momentarily, the pang of guilt stung. However, Rori's mouth was quicker, and he said, "Well then, you can't exactly blame me, can you? That was your mistake."

Silence.

Shit. Guilt and regret swirled within Rori's chest immediately raising his temperature, if that were possible. He bit his lip as if that could somehow pull back his words. Sucking in a breath through his tightly clenched teeth he braced himself for her reaction.

Slowly, she shook her head back and forth, her jaw tight. Yep, hurt reflected in those eyes. It seemed she remembered, too. He focused on a particularly intricate rose carving in the vardo, unable to keep his gaze on her. He felt something. He wasn't used to that. She had done that to him before, caused him to feel things. Maybe things were better this way.

He was a vampire. A vampire with feelings was weak. Feelings could be exploited and used against him. He couldn't be weak anymore.

He shoved his hands back into the pockets of his dark washed, cuffed, blue jeans and looked toward the sky. He had gone too far with that last quip. It wasn't fun anymore.

"Can we put a pin in that hate?" he asked before actually looking at her. "I really do have something I need to discuss with you."

CHAPTER 3

D ivina could spit nails at the way Rori spoke so casually to her, so nonchalantly, so flippantly. As if they didn't have a history together; had he forgotten what he put her through last time?

Folding her arms over her chest, she tried to hide her flipping from fury at his mere presence to pain at having him show up in her life once more. The thump bump of her heart thundered in her ears just from seeing him. Seeming to race, she vibrated where she stood. Battling with her fight or flight instincts, she glared at the man with the deceiving babyface.

With fingers twitching, she held back the urge to punch him. Barely restraining the desire to ram her knee into his groin, she scowled at him. As her ire festered within her, the prickle of nature coursed through her, and her mind ran through a short catalogue of spells to hobble him.

Yet, the more she glowered into his youthful features with the alabaster skin and plump lips, a warmth blossomed in her chest. She wanted to hurt him, but if she was honest with herself, a small part of her wanted to kiss him. Fuck! She had loved him once. He threw that away.

He took one more step up, joining her on the landing, just in front of her door. The button of his tailored vest grazed her arm, and it felt like lightening rocketing her heart. Sucking in an audible breath as he closed in on her, trapping her on the landing, Divina felt like a gazelle cornered by a lion.

Holding her ground, attempting to appear stronger than she felt, Divina's arms fell and she flexed her fingers, balling them into fists and relaxing. The thought of summoning the wind, to throw him back away from her had her fingertips itching. A hint of cool pine, what was left of his cologne, twirled in the air wafting its way to her nose and brought back memories of snuggling with him and the comfort he had once given her.

Crowding her as if he belonged there, he took ownership of that tiny platform, made smaller by his presence in her space. Placing his soft hands on her upper arms, Divina jolted and her eyes snapped open. Narrowing them, she scanned his face again, for something, an intention. Why was he there? What did he want?

"Divina, I wouldn't be here if I didn't feel it necessary," he said with tenderness. The softness in his large, brown eyes reminded her of a puppy begging for food.

Ill prepared for the conflict of emotions triggered by his touch, she wriggled out of his grasp. Glaring at him, she took half a step back and hit the door of her wagon. The warmth in his touch evidenced he'd fed recently, and as much as she warred with the idea of the old romance they once had, his lips had touched someone else. If she could focus on that, she'd be able to hold onto the anger she desperately needed not to succumb to his charm.

Seeing no avenue of escape without the use of spells, which would be ill-advised with the amount of humans lingering about, she sighed in resignation. Hearing him out would be the only way to get him out of her hair. Reaching behind her, while keeping her eye on him, she turned the knob and pushed the door in.

Stepping inside her wagon gave her some space to breathe freely again. Though the space was tight, the few feet between her and Rori released the tether he seemed to have around her. Making her way inside, Divina sat behind the small, foldable, wall table upon a pillowed couch which doubled as a bed. With a wave of her hand, she gestured for him to take a seat opposite her.

Though she had just backed herself into a corner in a sense, the table offered a barrier between them. Preventing him from invading her personal space, she hoped it would keep her head clear.

He nodded in acceptance and entered her narrow and compact home. As he moved she couldn't help but notice his grace, the smoothness of his gait. He had a way of gliding when he walked. No one should be able to move that smoothly through life.

As she assessed him, her gaze landed on the rolled sleeves of his collared shirt. They strained over his biceps. Memories of how those arms had once held her tenderly crept into her mind.

Divina tore her gaze away. She couldn't get lost on memory lane. Once he sat, she demanded coolly, "What trouble have you gotten into now?"

Rori wasn't a man who rushed anything. He moved as though he had all the time in the world, and in reality, he did. Confidence one mastered after the first one hundred years of life. It came from the knowledge that the next hundred or the hundred after that wouldn't be as hard.

Divina, on the other hand, was mortal. "I'm not agreeing to anything," she added as if that would somehow convince him to get on with it.

Rori shifted his attention from her to run his fingers over the threadbare fabric covering the seat cushion of the chair she used for clients. He frowned in disapproval. Rori was accustomed to more extravagance than she could afford. He reluctantly took a seat.

Clearing his throat, crossing his legs under the table, he interlaced his fingers, then took a relaxed hold of his knee as he sat upon the wooden chair opposite her. "There are rumors—"

"There are always rumors. You never troubled yourself with gossip before." She cut him off, still annoyed that he dared come to her.

He arched a brow. "If you insist on interrupting me, this will take longer."

She sat back, arms folded over her chest. Heat rose through her face and her eye twitched. The prickle of annoyance danced up her neck. As much as it galled her to admit it, Rori had a point.

"As I said." He paused as if waiting for her to interrupt again. She waved a hand for him to continue uninterrupted. He nodded. "There are rumors. As you know, with Klaus accepting the sun, there is a vacant seat on the council, a vacant vampire seat."

She nodded.

"The princes are rumbling about who will be the next emperor and thus take that seat. Which, of course, is causing an uproar with the dukes."

"Rori, as much as I enjoy the little lesson in vampire politics, I don't see how this concerns me."

Rori, always her teacher, often explained the supernatural world to her. At one time, she valued those lessons. She had needed them to know who and what she really was, but not today. He gave up his role as her teacher when he gave up on their love. Now Divina just wanted him to say his piece. Then, she could deny him, and they both could move on.

"I'm getting there."

She sighed.

He took a moment to smooth his pants. Was he stalling? "There is going to be a coup."

She arched a brow.

"I have your attention now?"

"I'm waiting for you to get to the part where I care. I'm practically human."

"But you're not," he said.

"Isn't the sun about to come up?" Divina snapped impatiently.

"You keep interrupting. This is taking longer than expected." He sat back. "I might have to spend the night." He had that sly grin that used to make her melt. At one time, she adored that grin. The lopsided half smile used to have her stomach in knots and her heart fluttering. But not today, not anymore.

"Try it, and you'll burn," she growled back when narrowed eyes.

Once more, he covered his heart as if wounded by her words. "Divina."

"Get on with it, Rori."

"Percival Hohenzollern."

Divina waited. Rori said nothing. They stared at one another stubbornly.

"I don't know what that is," she finally said after a continued silence.

He groaned. "Do you really exist in a world where you don't pay attention to what is around you?"

"I try to keep myself out of trouble." She glared at him.

He frowned, his never-ending confidence appeared to

waver. "If you don't pay attention, trouble comes to your door."

She raised her brows and gestured toward him. "Case in point." She stood up and smoothed her off-the-shoulder, white, peasant-style blouse. "I'll do better next time," she assured him. "So, trouble, why don't you take your Percy Honey-whatever and get on with your night."

With the unexpected thud of his fist against the table, Divina recoiled as a gasp left her lips.

"You're not taking this seriously. You cannot be this foolish." He rose, his full height a good six foot and change, five inches over her. Thankfully, she still had the reprieve of the small table between them.

"I don't involve myself in vampire poli—"

"Goddamn it, Divina." Rounding the small table with preternatural speed, he took away what little defense she had. He seemed enormous towering over her with an ominous glint in his eye she'd never seen before.

Fear closed her throat, paralyzing her to the soft pillows of her couch leaving her vulnerable, when he gripped her upper arms pinning them to her sides. His gaze bore into hers. Like a deer caught in the headlights, she couldn't move.

"The prophecy is in motion, and you want to play fucking games!" he growled.

As the initial shock at his outburst subsided, Divina rolled her eyes. Rori had preached to her about the prophecy since he told her she was a witch. Having been raised in foster homes, she never had a clue about her background. When Rori strolled into her life, he came with more than just clues to her heritage, he came with a prophecy.

While he never told her the exact wording of the prophecy, she had heard more than enough about it impacting his and her lives. As far as Divina was concerned, the prophecy was just another manipulation tool Rori had used against her to get what he needed from her.

Her impatience at his mentioning of the prophecy only served to spur his outrage. He released her and turned his back to her. Letting out an animalistic cry of frustration with his arms flailing, he narrowly missed her spice cabinet.

Divina leaned forward, her hand out, prepared to catch anything he could knock off a shelf. With little room in her wagon, there wasn't much space for Rori to have his little hissy fit. When his fingers grazed the curtains of the window, he paused his movements, as if suddenly aware of the cramped space.

Rori mumbled to himself. Eventually, he folded his arms. She couldn't see his face. Suspecting he held his chin in an attempt to regroup after his child-like tantrum, Divina lost some tension in her own body with the sound of Rori's deep breaths.

Sitting back onto the multi-colored cushions, she returned to the sanctuary she had behind the table. Waiting for Rori to collect his thoughts once more, she studied his tight posture. The length of time it took him gave Divina pause. Perhaps, she should take his visit a bit more seriously.

Rori sighed and turned toward her. The lines on his face were deeper than before as if he had aged ten years in the last five minutes. His hands fell to his sides when he asked, "Have you joined a coven as I requested?" The sound of defeat in his voice all but crushed Divina.

CHAPTER 4

"**N**o."

Rori barely heard her. The look of guilt in Divina's eyes, was the look of a child given a chore that wasn't done. It reminded him of how he had mentored her.

Divina had been innocent then. She had no idea what the world had in store for her. Rori hated himself to this day for being the one to show it to her. He hated having done the Ember Witches' bidding. He hated how he had tainted her.

Sitting back down in the distasteful wooden chair, Rori suddenly felt weary. "You need a coven," he said trying to implore her in a voice typical of a father toward his daughter and not the tone of a man speaking to his ex-lover.

She didn't say anything. She lowered her gaze as if caught cheating on a test. Divina busied her fingers with the fringe dangling from the scarf covering the table. It was all Rori could do not to scoop her up and settle her in his lap. He fought the urge to cuddle her, to stroke her hair, and tell her he'd protect her, that things would be okay.

He should have been delighted Divina hadn't aligned with a coven. It lent credence to the prophecy, and to what he'd been told he needed to do. Though, a part of him wished she had. A coven would have offered her protection, a protection he yearned to give her.

"I don't see how it's any business of yours." Divina's voice was weak. An attempt at defiance. Maybe, even a jab at him for how they had left things. However, it lacked the conviction she displayed earlier.

Gods help him, Rori had to exploit it. For the sake of all beings walking this earth, he needed Divina on his side. Telling himself using her this last time was a means to an end, Rori took a deep breath. "I've always wanted what was best for you. I wanted you to find a coven, not just because you are powerful and need to learn how to harness it, but because it will keep you safe." He had never spoken truer words in his long life. It helped that the truth served his cause in this instance.

Looking up at him with large, doe-like, eyes brimming with tears, Divina questioned him without words. The pain reflected in them belonged to Rori. It pierced his heart when her voice hitched with her reply. "You have never once concerned yourself with my safety."

It was all Rori could do to keep his hand down and not cover the metaphorical wound. Instead, he looked away, unable to hold her gaze any longer. There wasn't much he could say to that. He had kept her safe, the only way he could, while simultaneously getting what he and the witches needed from her.

Rori clenched his jaw. Fucking witches. Fucking fate. Fucking prophecy. He yearned for different circumstances.

Rori's gaze fixated on the table. Divina's tear splattered onto the table and drew Rori's attention. The ache in his chest increased. He never wanted to see her in pain, but he had caused it, over and over. He had dealt her pain all because of some prophecy.

Longing for the days when he'd first entered her life, when the two of them were happy, Rori's jaw tightened. He fingered the table and winced at the memory of when he had been instructed to leave her behind, that she had done what was needed. A palm over his chest, he gently rubbed at his sternum. Per the witches, the lazy beat of his heart was all Divina had been meant to do when he first met her. Once he had the heartbeat, he had to break hers.

"Do you feel guilty? At all?" she asked waking him from the memories.

Without looking up at her, he said, "I don't have time to feel guilty, and neither do you."

"You're a monster, Rori." She swiped at the tears falling down her cheeks.

At that, he looked up at her with an irrational ire flourishing in his chest. Only he could beat himself up over the mistakes of his past. He loved Divina, but he could only handle so much.

Keeping his face neutral, despite knowing he'd wronged Divina, but he chose not dwell on that. "You think I want this?" he asked as a challenge, getting to his feet kicking the tacky chair out from behind him. "You think I wanted to come here? You think I wanted to be at your door? Of all the doors in all the world, I wanted to go to yours?" Rori scoffed as the warmth of building anger blossomed on his cheeks.

Gaping at him with wide-eyed shock, Divina leaned back.

"Powerful witches sprinkled about the world." He pinched his fingers and mimed adding spice to a metaphorical globe. "And yet I came to you? I. Have. To." With his chest heaving, he took a moment to breathe. "Our fates are twined together. You felt it yourself. You know I have to be here." He all but vibrated with anger at her. "So suck it the fuck up, put on your big-girl panties, and step up to the goddamn plate. You can't wallow in that pain forever." His chest heaved.

Frozen in place, Divina's mouth hung open as she stared at him.

Fuck.

Shifting gears, his unexpected rage-filled outburst had gotten her attention as expected and was necessary, he needed to rein it in to really hammer it home. Closing his eyes a moment, he drew in long breaths until the heat receded. Lowering his voice, he displayed the empathy he truly felt while opening his expression and meeting her gaze. "I'm no fool. I know I destroyed what we had. I had to."

Divina blinked at him. Her hands rested in her lap and tears slipped down her cheeks. Had he gone too far?

With her stunned expression, she sat on that awful couch strewn with cushions, which lined the back wall of the wagon and doubled as her bed. Rori stood opposite her with a table between them, gut knotting with conflict. Neither one spoke for what felt like eons.

"How did you get so empty?" Her voice cracked.

Hesitating at the rawness of the question, Rori took a moment to gather his thoughts. Empty. A word he'd never thought could be used to describe him. The woman he'd felt the most for, and she thought him empty because of his own actions. The weight of the accusation caused his shoulders to slump.

He turned toward the window, checking the night for how much time he had. The darkness of the night had lightened from pitch black to a navy blue. The sun would make an appearance sooner than he would like.

He sighed before he answered. "With time, you learn to turn it off." Rori wouldn't look at her. "Sort of, anyway. The pain of losing the best thing you ever had, it gets dull the more times you lose it." He looked over his shoulder at Divina. "You call it empty. Maybe I am. I just think I am surviving."

"That's no way to live," she whispered.

"Then it's a good thing I'm dead," he quipped and returned to studying the brightening skies.

Amid her silence, he glanced over his shoulder toward Divina seated amongst cheap decorative pillows wearing the costume of a fortune teller. The intensity of her gaze upon Rori sent a wave of regret crashing into him. Despite the years that had passed since he'd crushed their hearts and left her, she still looked upon him with trust. Watching her internal debate play out on her features, Rori shifted.

"What do you need from me, Rori?" Divina sounded defeated.

He hated that tone coming from her. He hated that he had manipulated Divina again. He hated that he knew how to get her to do what he needed.

She was stronger than she knew. The ease with which Rori conquered her was always an unpleasant surprise. Longing for the day she'd beat him at his own manipulative game, he wished he could strengthen her defenses. He wished his purpose was to build her up. He wanted so much for her to be free of vulnerability. She deserved so much more than his purpose.

He sighed. "Tonight?" He turned his body to face hers. "I need a place to stay. The sun will be up soon, and I'm too far from my hotel."

She frowned at him.

Holding up his palms, he couldn't stop the smile crossing his lips. "Platonic. Tomorrow, or well, later today, we can discuss the details."

Divina reached behind her and tossed a pillow to the floor. "Don't you even think of getting up here. And, I snore."

He half smiled as he closed the shutters preventing any light from coming in. "You always have." While he responded playfully, his disappointment in her grew. He wanted her to be stronger against his manipulations.

Floop. A pillow struck him in the face distracting him from the moment. Taking him away from his sorrowful thoughts, he decided to just enjoy being in her presence again.

Rori gazed upon Divina while holding the pillow. How he missed her playful nature. It only made him hate himself that much more.

CHAPTER 5

Careful not to utilize too much effort, Aric turned the wrench to ensure the plumbing fixture secured tightly. He hated working on his kitchen sink. The space under it was cramped for his broad frame. He should update the whole setup. The thing clogged more than any sink he had ever worked on.

With his leg against the can of powdered cleaner, Aric realized he should have placed the cleaning products on the table when he emptied them from under the sink. Now, he had to inch his way out like creeping around a sleeping and hungry lion. The perfect way to end a sink repair.

Mid-wiggle, he paused. That scent. It wasn't his. It wasn't his pack's. Jasmine. Honeysuckles. That scent was female, an unknown female. Interesting. He was pretty far out for anyone to find him.

A knock on the door sounded before he could finish his escape from under the sink. *Thunk.* The scent of cleaner filled his nostrils blocking out anything else. Blue crystals and powder covered his pants. "Motherfucker!" he growled.

Aric stalked toward the door and yanked it open. "What?"

He snarled swatting at his crotch; he attempted to rid himself of the spilled cleaner.

A scantily clad, voluptuous blond with large brown eyes looked up at him. The unknown female said nothing. The female merely swept her gaze over him. Aric couldn't help but notice when her eyes lingered on his blue powder-covered crotch.

Aric's brow rose. "You lost?" he asked.

Looking past her, behind her, Aric scanned the lot of land he called home. Observing nothing visually out of the ordinary, his hackles rose in suspicion. Sniffing the air, not even his pack's scent was in the air. Nothing but that blasted cleaning powder.

"Aric Braun," she spoke in a sensual whisper.

"Yeah?" Her voice drew Aric's attention back to the curvy woman. Leaning against the doorframe with his arms over his bare, tattooed chest, he narrowed his gaze upon her. The blue cleaning crystals were now a distant concern.

She ascended the two stairs, and Aric stepped back confused. Slithering past him, she entered his home, his den. Balking at the idea, his inner beast snapped. Opening his mouth to protest, he paused as her warm skin grazed his, and he swore it tingled like a small electric shock. Recoiling, Aric swung around offering her a wide berth in the cramped space that was his trailer.

Curling his lip, his wolf pacing within him, Aric rubbed at the spot where their skin touched. Who did this woman think she was entering his domain uninvited. Following her fluid, sensual movements with his predatory gaze, he studied her in an attempt to ascertain her intentions.

The woman walked the remaining five steps as if she were a runway model until she reached his couch. She twirled and lowered herself to a seated position. Temporarily distracted,

Aric couldn't help but appreciate the grace and poise as she crossed her long legs.

Aric, the human and the side half in control, remained standing with a good distance between them despite his wolf's distrust. It wasn't every day an attractive woman sought him out. So, he'd give her a chance to explain.

"Would you mind telling me who you are and what you're doing here?" he asked politely. No point in getting all bent out of shape over a pretty woman stumbling upon his home.

Canting her head to the side, she wore a blank expression.

For a full minute, she and Aric stared at one another. The intense eye contact had his wolf on edge but not pouncing. His human skin itched at the awkward, unnatural lack of interaction. He didn't care how fine she was, staring at him like that cost her some attractiveness points.

Typically, if someone stared at him in such a fashion, Aric's wolf would take it as a sign of aggression and push him toward attack. His wolf paced within him letting his distrust be known without the urge for violence. While the wolf was wary of the female, he seemed curious as well.

Patience was not Aric's wolf's forte. His wolf was more a take-action-ask-questions-later type beast. What was it about this woman that felt so off?

The woman offered no response to him. She just looked through him.

"Well?" He broke the silence.

"Selene." The name trickled off her tongue.

He waited.

Nothing more came. Aric had asked two questions and gotten only one answer. Sighing in frustration, he ran a hand through his tangled, shoulder-length, multi-toned brown hair. "Right." Aric clapped his hands together. "So, good talk." He waved a hand to the door. "On your way then."

She lifted herself like a ballerina. With movements so

fluid, Aric swore she rehearsed them. He couldn't help but be captivated by them.

Perhaps that was the reason for the delay in his reaction when her hand shot toward him. With wide eyes, his wolf growled, and it rumbled from his chest. Her fingers curled around his wrist before he could pull his arm away.

It burned in a way. It tingled like a million tiny pins pricked Aric's skin. Her touch felt as though he had sat on his hand for an hour and the blood was returning to it. Snapping his jaws, his wolf howled in discomfort. Aric, the human, froze in confusion.

Selene held him tighter. It took Aric what felt like an eternity before he found the ability to yank his arm back. With a little twist, his arm came back to him. Her hand lowered.

Aric rubbed his wrist glaring at her. "The fuck?"

"Don't you recognize me?" Her features shifted into a wounded expression.

"No." Aric stepped back from her again. The cramped trailer didn't offer much in the way of room to separate them but Aric needed all he could get. It wasn't that he was afraid of her. He just wanted to be out of her grasp. Everything about it was wrong. Sizzling pain at first now lingered like a bad sunburn. With his wolf scratching at his insides to be released, Aric grit his teeth forcing the animal down.

She took a small step forward.

"Stop!" Aric held up his hands. "Don't."

She jolted. "But—"

"I don't know what you are. I don't know who you are. But I do know I want you out of my house."

"You don't mean that," she suggested in a whimper. Again her hand came toward him.

The rumble in his chest was his wolf's warning to the female.

When her hand snapped back, Selene practically pouted.

Though, she did step away from him. "I thought wolves knew their mates when they saw them."

"Lady—"

"Selene," she whined. "I know I'm not a wolf. I know I must be a disappointment." Were those tears in her eyes? "But we *are* mates. Didn't you feel it? I didn't believe it. When I touched you, I felt it. Didn't you feel it?" The words spilled past her lips in such rapid succession Aric almost couldn't follow her.

"I felt something." He couldn't deny that.

"The mate bond," she urged.

Scrubbing the back of his neck with his left hand, he considered her statement. He had never been mated before. Though, he understood how it worked. He'd seen it enough. Others had explained a physical feeling when mates touched for the first time. However, he was hard-pressed to believe it felt that uncomfortable. He was pretty sure it should be euphoric. Why would anyone keep going back to what he had just felt?

"I'm a witch, a seer," she confessed, interrupting his thoughts. "So I'm not just some human who knows about wolves. Have you met a seer before? Have they told you of your mate? I can't see my future. I can see others', though."

He eyed her skeptically.

"I grabbed your arm, and... wow." She smiled then. "I mean, *wow*. The zing, you felt it right?"

Zing? Would he call that a zing? Maybe? It was pretty electrifying. He continued to rub his wrist.

"When I touched your arm, I saw—"

"I thought you couldn't see your future," he barked, interrupting her because he was not buying her bullshit. If she was a witch, she could do spells. The tingling lingered. He needed to talk to his pack. He needed to know more about what it felt like to meet a mate. It didn't feel right.

"I can't." Again the injured expression spread across her face.

Shouldn't he feel something when she looked like that? Shouldn't he want to comfort her? Shouldn't his wolf be drawn to her? She repelled the wolf. Aric just felt annoyed. She felt wrong.

"I can see yours though." She tempted him as though offering some kind of forbidden fruit.

"I have done well for myself without a seer," he countered. As his skin crawled in her presence, he sensed a buzz in the air causing him to twitch.

First, her gaze lowered, then her chin followed. "The vampire emperor has met the sun. The prophecy is in motion." Her voice became monotone. "There is a vampire whose heart beats for a witch, but she belongs to a wolf. That vampire shall take the seat."

He gaped at her. "You think I'm the wolf in some prophecy?" He blinked.

It started slowly, with a tickle in the back of his throat. However, it wasn't long before his laughter grew in both volume and liveliness. Aric let out an overexcited belly laugh. Doubling over with one hand covering his stomach, he used the other to slap his knee.

"What?" The ceremony in her voice was lost, replaced with annoyance.

His eyes watered as he continued to laugh so hard he had trouble breathing. Coughing, he shook his head and waved a hand trying to rein it in.

"What?" Selene demanded with a stomp of her foot.

Finally, catching his breath, Aric answered, "I don't know who has been feeding you this, lady."

"Selene," she growled with a glare.

Uncontrollably, the chuckles bubbled up again. Now he felt joy around the woman. She was batshit crazy. Inhaling deeply, he regained his composure easier this time. "I'm sorry," he said half-breathless. "I'm sorry."

Selene balled her fists and gritted her teeth.

The jovial moment passed, and Aric straightened. He had to admit; she was actually kind of cute. Even more so when she was angry, he mused.

"I'm not some prophetic wolf," he sighed. "I'm just a simple guy." He looked around his shabby 1970's trailer. It had threadbare, mustard yellow upholstery, shag carpet, and a slight stink of a wolf. "You're looking for some sort of King Arthur type knight, sweetheart."

"Selene!" she corrected him again.

"Selene," he repeated with a sheepish grin. "I'm not your wolf."

Her eyes clouded. Aric's wolf shot up within him. Gone was the laughter. Her pale hand reached for him. Aric found he couldn't move away. Gripping him again, the pain shot up his arm and through his wolf, quelling his beast. Aric bellowed in pain and fell to his knees. What was she doing to him?

"I have seen the prophecy. I have seen the wolf," she roared, staring down at the man on his knees. "You are the wolf of the prophecy; you will give Perci his rightful place."

Crippled by his inability to call his wolf forward, Aric gawked up at the woman from his knees while shocks radiated from her touch through him. Snapping his human jaws at her felt like his only recourse. Attempting to use the strength of the wolf to get out of her vice-like hold proved futile. His wolf was nowhere to be found. Nothing worked.

"Selene." A masculine voice called from Aric's door.

Aric's head whipped to see who beckoned the woman. A man stood with his hands behind his back. He was clad in a three-piece suit and had impeccably combed, black hair.

"We might have to go with plan B," Selene informed the man.

The surge of whatever she did to him pulsed through their touch, and Aric's throat closed. His muscles taut in an attempt to fight it off were ineffective. Choking on energy she forced through their joined skin, Aric's vision blurred. His lids fluttered closed before weakness conquered him.

Collapsing to the thick carpeting with a thud, Aric's world went black.

CHAPTER 6

Lying on Divina's floor, Rori interlaced his fingers on his chest, closed his eyes, and drifted off to sleep, reliving the events of the previous night.

Rori sat on the corner of the hotel room bed staring at the spinning card in his fingers. Any human, or well anything, watching him would see a man staring off into space holding what looked like a wedding invitation. However, what he held was much more than that.

A vampire summoned by the Ember Witches was a pretty big deal. A vampire summoned by the Ember Witches twice in one lifetime was unheard of. Yet, Rori held the black card in his hand. The silver calligraphy taunted him. He'd done the bidding of the Ember Witches before. He wasn't sure he wanted to do it again.

Who was he kidding? It had nothing to do with want. It had to do with strength. Rori wasn't sure he could do it again. The last time he did as they asked, it nearly broke him. He couldn't handle that again.

They would only summon him for one reason. The only matter the witches had in common with him was nothing he

wanted to discuss. Rori twirled the card and sighed in resignation. With his left hand, he scrubbed his face. He could sit
there for a millennia telling himself he wasn't going to accept
their invitation. In reality, when the Ember Witches
summoned, you went.

The hand-drawn filigree along the edges of the card were
meant to disguise enchantments to keep the message of the
card hidden from all but the intended recipient. The gothic
romance of the card called to times long since passed and
would remind the recipient not only of the age of the coven
but the power. As with most supernatural beings, with age
came strength.

Despite the ornate design hiding the spell, the card held a
simple message. The invitation didn't need to be addressed to
anyone in particular. It just needed to tell the intended recipient where to go and when.

Ursuline Convent

1 a.m.

Amusement had filled Rori the first time he'd received an
invitation. Awaking to its appearance one evening at his
bedside had offered a bit of excitement. With no sign anyone
had been in his room aside from the card laid upon the unoc-
cupied pillow, Rori fell for the mystique of it all.

Not this time. For all he knew, it was the same bloody
card again, holding the same message. Why waste cards when
they can just keep using the same one over and over?

The reappearance of an invitation to meet with the
Ember Witches lacked the mysterious aura the second time
around. There was a cost to helping the witches—a debt he
had paid tenfold in his opinion.

While Rori wished he was strong enough to rebuke them,
to refuse to attend their meeting, a flicker of hope lit within

him. He'd be able to see her again. It would be the only reason they called him. They needed them together and while Rori was no weak vampire, emotionally, when it came to her, he had no defenses.

No one met him at the gate when arrived the second time. Rori walked alone as if he had been there a million times before. No one appeared to help navigate the small maze of hedges for him. He walked through the grounds. No one was at the door to usher him through the dark museum.

With the dimmest of lighting casting shadows and a sinister feel, marble statues depicting historical Catholic lore were protected behind fancy iron gates or plexiglass cases. The ornate floral and bejeweled robes of religious leaders displayed upon the walls with plaques describing the deeds of their former wearers were yellowed from age. Old oil paintings hung from the wall with only small accent lights upon them giving the subjects evil expressions and the appearance that their eyes followed Rori as he walked through the halls. A chill ran through him as he passed a bust of someone he did not recognize.

Making his way through the halls like this was his home, and he wasn't a guest, he wondered over the intention of the witches this time. He wasn't sure if they trusted him or if they trusted the fact he knew just how powerful they were.

On a sublevel below the basement, in a clichéd hidden-from-human's room, Rori found them. The same place he had met them previously. Though he'd only been there one time before, this place left an impression.

It wasn't the whole coven. There was no way to fit the entire coven in one room. No, what was before him, seated at a large horseshoe-shaped table, were the thirteen male and female witches dressed in linen ceremonial robes. These were the ones in charge of different factions of the coven, the Ember Liderii.

With the flickering of torchlight that lined the lower room, Rori observed the room of witches. They varied in age and abilities, gender and race, but their power pulsed through the air like a beating heart. The hoods of their robes were down, revealing their differences. It seemed the youngest were seated toward the opening of the half-oval table. Their appeared ages increasing the closer they sat toward the center.

Each witch sat with their hands clasped upon the table and backs straight. Their gazes were intent upon Rori as he entered. Of course, they had been expecting him, and he was only a little late. Though, not one witch showed a hint of emotion in their expressions. Each blank slate stared at him while he made his way toward them.

Taking a deep breath, incense filled his nose and did nothing to calm his nerves. Rori entered the horseshoe of their table bracing himself for what they'd demand of him. A lone chair waited for him at the center. Tugging at the bottom of his pinstripe vest laid over a crisp, white shirt with sleeves he had rolled to the elbow, Rori lifted his chin. Once he took his seat, he crossed his jean-clad legs and clasped his hand over his knee. He steeled himself mentally for what was about to come, while maintaining a calm facade.

Despite the number of witches present, the room was silent. Wafting through the air, as if carried upon the scents of burning sweet spices and flickering flames, was the promise of magic held in the gathering of witches. Similar to the air during an electrical storm, their power filled the room. They offered no greetings or introductions. They'd be unnecessary. Rori may not have known all their names, but reputations preceded them.

The witch at the center, a gaunt, older woman with waves of ashen hair cascading down her back, Esmine, was the one who represented the witches of the Council of Others. She was the head of all the witches in the country. However, witches didn't have jurisdiction over vampires. Rori's respect for her was solely due to the sheer power the woman harnessed.

Esmine spoke first. "Roricus Fromm." She announced his full name in a somber, formal tone. "You have been summoned before the Ember Witches to further your role in the prophecy."

Rori rolled his eyes. This was too much ceremony for him. He let out a heavy sigh. "I have an appointment. Can we cut through the pomp and circumstance stuff and just get to what you are asking of me?"

Silence.

With a groan he folded his arms over his chest preparing for a long night. The one thing that irked him about witches was that everything with them was a big formality. They had a million steps and had to say a poem before anything could get done.

Esmine continued as though he had said nothing. "The prophecy has been set into motion."

Rori stiffened, lowered his crossed leg to fold his arms over his chest. The prophecy was a sore subject with the vampires. Not only did it call for the death of their oldest and most powerful representative, but also laid blame on Rori's kind for the humans' discovery of all that goes bump in the night.

"I am aware" was all Rori offered to the conversation.

Though, it wasn't a conversation so much as a sentence being handed down to him. The witches before him were similar to judges offering their ruling. Rori internally snorted as the idea crossed his mind. The witches had no authority over him. However, he wasn't eager to discover the penalties for ignoring the Ember Witches.

"You did very well with the first portion of this," Esmine said in praise.

Rori clenched his jaw. The "first portion of this" had changed him in a way he had never thought imaginable. A man walking the earth for over 350 years should have had better defenses for such things.

Esmine nodded when Rori remained silent. "We understand it was difficult for you."

"Fuck you," Rori spat. He knew fake empathy when he saw it.

To the left of Esmine sat a much younger, dark-haired woman, Florence. Rori had seen her around before, outside of the convent. She kept to herself, but her large, empathetic eyes filled with sorrow often followed him. Esmine was the leader of the coven; she was the mouthpiece, so it surprised Rori when Florence spoke.

"She was never meant for you Rori," she said with compassion clear in her voice leaving Rori questioning her authenticity.

Rori didn't need their empathy. "That wasn't what you said last time."

To Esmine's right, a blond woman spoke. "We told you that you would find the one who would let your heart beat again and that you were to introduce her to the ways of the witch." She said in a monotone voice. There were no offers of condolences; fact-checking only.

Rori found an odd sense of comfort in that. It felt less manipulative with information presented straightforward and truthfully, rather than with all the riddles they typically used. He was a vampire, dammit; they didn't need to handle him with kid gloves.

"Your heart beat again, didn't it, Roricus?" Esmine asked with an arched brow.

Glaring at her, he wouldn't dignify that with a response. His heartbeat wasn't the point.

Vampires were essentially dead. Their hearts stopped beating in most cases. True love could revive a heart to beat again. However, it wasn't going to bring life back or make them mortal. It only allowed the heart to beat subtly. Rori didn't understand why it happened. What he did know, was that when his heart beat again, it was the most glorious feeling he had experienced since he had been turned. As though the slight beating amplified everything it was to be a vampire.

Esmine nodded. "The vampire whose heart beats for a witch that belongs to a wolf shall save us all. He shall take his throne and rule over all kinds."

"I'm not some prophetic, self-sacrificing hero." Rori's arms fell to his sides, and he used them to push himself up. He wasn't going to sit for this. "I will plead guilty to all my crimes but being a hero isn't one of them," he said to the court with contempt.

Esmine cracked a smile. "Roricus, you are many things but a hero." She shook her head.

Why did that assertion bother Rori? He had just made the same point himself. She didn't need to agree with him.

Emptiness spawned in Rori's gut. Was that disappointment at their lack of belief in him? What had these witches done to him? He lowered his gaze in an attempt to process Esmine's words.

Florence spoke up. "Sometimes, the world doesn't need another hero, Roricus." She folded her hands over the intricately carved table. "There are times when the monster has more morals than the supposed heroes."

"Keep your spells and your morals away from me," Rori said and raised his gaze to the center witch. Locking his ire directly onto Esmine when he spoke. "I'm not doing anything else for you."

Rori had had enough of these witches and their games. They spoke in half-truths, giving him hope before, but he knew better this time around. He wasn't some toy with whom they could play.

"You have no power over me," he declared.

Esmine was the first to chuckle. Followed by the blond, then Florence. It didn't take long for the entire panel to join the laughter.

Rori's lip curled into a snarl. His canines extended. Heat rose through his chest, up into his face. His fists clenched tightly and he shook. He couldn't take on all thirteen witches. They'd get him in the end but not before he took out Esmine.

"My apologies." Esmine held a hand to her chest as her laughter subsided. She waved her hands in both directions so the witches would do the same. "It was just that you seemed so adamant about it."

His restraint was only as strong as his self-preservation instinct. "I don't answer to your coven, or any witch for that matter," Rori said with his fangs still visible.

"You think you have a choice," Esmine said with a tilted head. The exaggerated pleasantness of her tone signaled her sarcasm. "How very sweet of you." She folded her arms on the table and leaned toward him. "But Roricus, the time has come for you to take your place. It is time for you to step up and be what you were created to be."

"And if I don't?" Rori countered. The temptation to walk away from the table, from the witches, from the prophecy, grew the longer he stood there. The witches had proven before that they promised great things but with them came suffering. He'd done their bidding before and while he was given a beating heart, leaving his emotions more intense and raw, he had to give up the person who had given it to him.

From where he stood, their price wasn't worth the reward and the witches were not beings he could trust.

"The vampire who belongs to the witch will end your kind, our kind, and all other kinds," the blond offered without emotion. A knot of discomfort grew in his chest, not just from how the witch spoke but from what she had said.

The witches collectively shifted in their seats. It seemed they were not comfortable with that portion of the prophecy. Rori wasn't either. He had grown fond of existing. But that anyone thought that he was some savior was laughable at best.

"Perhaps looking at it a different way would help." Florence sounded hopeful. All attention shifted upon her. She glanced at her sisters and brothers before she addressed Rori. "She returned the rhythm to your heart. Don't you owe it to her to find the one to whom she belongs? Don't you want her to live and to find true happiness?"

"And what of me?" Rori was selfish. The years had made him bitter, and the demands these witches had only added to it.

The thirteen witches surrounding Rori gasped. Florence hadn't expected that answer. She frowned and sat back looking to her fellow witches for support. Esmine brooded. The blond sat with a blank expression. The others whispered among themselves.

At the end of the table, almost behind Rori, a young witch, not more than eighteen stood up. Her auburn locks were pulled back, pinned loosely in a bun. Her pale blue eyes were on Rori when she spoke. "You get something men of all kinds have spent lifetimes attempting to acquire."

Rori turned to face her fully. Wasn't that love? Wasn't that supposed to be the be all end all? Wasn't everyone in every lifetime chasing their heart's desire?

They had told him Divina wasn't meant for him. They had

told him his heart would only beat for her and yet he would never have her. What was this infant witch attempting to tell him?

When she didn't immediately offer up the answer, Rori turned to the other witches. Perhaps one of them knew what the ginger-haired witch meant. None spoke. They appeared as befuddled as Rori. So he shifted his attention back toward her.

"Well?" Rori asked impatiently.

The young witch furrowed her brow. "I thought it was obvious."

Rori let out a cry of exasperation. "What is it with you witches?" He turned around, attempting to get a good look at every one of them. "Why must you speak in circles and poems? Just come out with it! Not one of you is immortal, yet you waste time as if you will live forever!"

"Power," the blond announced.

The weight of the silence that filled the room had Rori sitting again. Not that he could see, but the red-haired witch sat as well, her point made.

Rori blinked a few times before he regained his ability to speak. "Emperor?"

"What good would it do you to be given a mortal?" Esmine asked while Rori pondered the gravity of what laid at his feet. "She has served her purpose in your life. She has quickened your heart. She has taken the numbness of existing beyond death away. With your ability to feel once more, you have now reached your full potential and can serve on the council properly." Manipulation and coercion laced her voice.

Florence chimed in, "It is time for you to let her go, let her be with the one for whom she is meant. Her finding her purpose should give you the freedom to pursue your own."

The words of the witches were distant to him. He barely heard them. He focused on what they had just promised him.

Ultimate power over all of his kind and the ability to lay down laws over anything that wasn't human.

"Emperor," Rori repeated in utter fascination.

His heart fluttered at the thought. His hand covered his chest. The feeling he had all but forgotten: hope.

He swallowed and looked to the Ember Witches with new eyes. "What is it I have to do?"

CHAPTER 7

"Hmmm?" The rocking lulled Rori in and out of sleep. Just as his consciousness returned, he drifted off again. Sleeping on a floor with a bunch of pillows had turned out quite nicely. Then again, the sleep a vampire had during the day was most akin to a coma. The only thing that could wake him was the sun.

However, after nightfall, the thump of his head bouncing on and off the pillows jarred him awake. He blinked a few times. Shifting his gaze around the small, hand-carved enclosure, it took him a moment gain his bearings.

"Divina," he whispered in recognition. The night before came back to him in a flash.

Rori groaned and dragged his palm over his face. He had agreed to do what the Ember Witches requested of him. Well, maybe not requested—demanded was a better word. They were known for their ability to see into the future, and their predictions were usually accurate.

Kicking the blanket off himself, he attempted to get to his feet. With the vardo in motion, it wasn't an easy task. These things weren't equipped with the best suspension. Finding his balance, he gripped the wall. Divina had folded the table flat, so using that to hold himself steady wasn't an option. Stumbling, he made his way to the couch. The world got a whole lot more stable after he sat down.

Removing his phone from his pocket, Rori checked the time. Just after eight. He sighed. So early. His stomach knotted, reminding him that he hadn't eaten since early last night. Sometimes, he hated being a vampire. The hunger could drive a lesser man insane and often did. Not every human could cut it.

Rori knew from experience. When he was younger, a newly turned vampire, Rori often struggled. He had to get over his distaste for violence quickly if he wanted to survive. Animals tasted like shit once a vampire had eaten human blood. But in a pinch, a good rat could stave off the famished sensation, preventing a murderous rampage when he went out to hunt.

Murder was never good for vampires, and a rampage even less so. The risk of being found out would be too high if Rori killed a human. No, it was best to take a little from many sources rather than take your fill from one. He had learned that early. Taking sips and not having a dead body were easier. Take a drink, heal the wound, go about his business.

He scanned the interior. On one wall was a small kitchenette, or rather, a microwave and a hot plate on top of a mini fridge. A tall cabinet was on the left of that, bungee corded in place. From the looks of things, she was a decent housekeeper; no rats were along for the ride either.

A small TV hung on the wall opposite the couch. He smiled, remembering Divina's love for movies made in the 1980s. How many times had she made him watch that film with the man in black and the giant? He couldn't remember.

With a quick shake of his head, Rori cleared the extraneous thoughts from his mind. He needed to stay out of the past. He had been told she wasn't meant for him. He had to use her to fulfill his destiny. Going down memory lane would only make the task more difficult.

After tapping a few icons on his phone, Rori placed it to his ear.

"Evening moonshine," Divina said, in an unexpectedly cheery voice.

He smiled. They had created that particular phrase when they were happier. Perhaps a sign of her mood, he hoped. Getting her to do what he wanted was easier when she was in a good mood.

"I don't have my passport. You can't kidnap me too far," Rori mused.

"I don't think one is required for the borders we're crossing."

"We're crossing borders?" he asked in surprise.

As he attempted to stand, she hit a bump causing him to fall back on the cushions with a groan.

"Yep." The laughter in her voice didn't sound right.

He rolled his eyes. There were times when her playfulness irked him. "When I fell asleep we were in a field in Alabama."

"You are very observant," Divina quipped.

"You know this thing isn't meant for highways?" Rori said in exasperation. "These wooden wheels can't take the beating of modern speeds."

"Then it's a good thing we aren't on a highway and that I have it on a trailer," Divina said.

Rori went to the window and pulled back the curtain. The stalks of green passed by surprisingly slow. Perhaps that was why he felt every godforsaken divot into which she drove.

"Where are we going?" he asked.

"I took the liberty of searching your pockets while you were asleep," Divina said.

He hissed.

"Don't worry, I checked you out of the hotel where you were staying." He heard her confident smile through the phone.

"That was kind of you," Rori gritted out.

"What can I say? I am a giver." He imagined her shrug.

Her sarcasm and the way her cheerful words did not match the tone of her voice sent the message loud and clear: Divina was not, in fact, in a good mood, which left Rori wondering what he had left in his pockets.

"So what was in Louisiana?" she asked. "You were in the French Quarter."

He couldn't have been that stupid. "Fine gumbo," he retorted.

"I doubt you went to New Orleans for gumbo."

"You're right." He put the phone on his shoulder and dug into his pockets. "It was the beignets."

"I miss when you didn't lie," Divina said with a hint of sadness laced in her voice.

That stung. Rori cleared his throat. "I am not lying, merely being evasive and a bit cheeky," he corrected. "I miss when you didn't kidnap me," he said.

Quiet.

Rori heard the wind rushing past. The blinker chimed. He braced himself for the turn, and everything went left.

"Where are we going, Divina?" he asked more sternly.

Nothing.

Though Rori could still hear the jingle of Divina's keys swinging from the ignition. Divina hadn't hung up. Curious.

He was a patient man. He could wait her out. Rori had lived hundreds of years. He had learned how to wait. Holding onto the small sink, Rori peered out the window.

44

That was the thing about the United States—or, well, the world in general. Most back roads were nondescript. They all looked the same once you traveled enough of them. They were on a paved road between two giant fields. They could be anywhere.

"They summoned you again," her voice broke into his thoughts.

"Yes." Pinching the bridge of his nose, closing his eyes and hanging his head, Rori answered as simply as he could.

No use in denying it. Only one person in the whole world knew about his involvement with the Ember Witches: Divina. Granted, he had told her because he felt they were the best coven for her. In retrospect, perhaps that hadn't been a wise idea.

Telling her they had sent him to introduce her to her purpose hadn't been a lie. It had only been a way to show they cared for her wellbeing. The way he had left her, his abrupt departure from her life, must have soured them to her. Perhaps it was her reason for not pursuing a coven, that particular coven, since they had sent him and he broke her heart.

"That's why you came back," she said pulling him from his thoughts.

"The prophecy is why I came back."

He wasn't lying, it was partly true. He didn't want her to know about the extent of the witches' involvement just yet. Some things needed to be put into play before he could tell her the full extent of her role in the prophecy. Though, it might not be wise to tell her about it.

"You won't find the answers in New Orleans," he said.

The phone went silent before a beep sounded in his ear.

Rori had done it that time. Divina had had enough. He lowered the phone and attempted to stand. Like he'd just discovered his legs, Rori wobbled until he fell back on the couch again. There wasn't much else he could do.

Rori needed to stick with Divina. She was a huge piece of this journey to get him on the throne and the vampire council.

He needed her to find the wolf. Once he had the wolf, he would use the wolf army.

Pack? They call themselves a pack, right? They would help him defeat Percival, Perci, the Duke of the territory, who was next in line for the throne. Once Perci was out of the way, he would take Perci's place and the council would have no choice but to crown him emperor.

Rori would get the throne. Divina would find true love. The wolf would get to kill things. Everyone would win. They would all live happily ever after, so the prophecy went. Then why didn't it feel right?

The plan seemed simple enough. Sure, some of the details could've used some fine-tuning. It had only been a few days, and he didn't have the time to work out all the kinks yet. When they found the wolf, then Rori would flesh out the plan. Simple as that.

To distract himself, Rori decided to nose through Divina's belongings. He told himself it was to find out if she had been practicing. While he mentored her, she had caught on quick. She was a natural. Rori was curious to find out what progress she had made on her own since she chose to disregard his request to join a coven.

At first, he had been delighted to see how hungry she was to master the spells, to cultivate her strength as a witch. However, the more powerful she became, and the speed with which it happened, the more concerned Rori had been with her going it alone.

Divina was a powerful tool. As far as he knew, he and the

Ember Witches were the only ones who knew that. The risk of her continuing to practice was not only that she would gain strength and the ability to cast more spells, but she would also have the power to cast spells beyond her maturity as a witch. He hoped he wouldn't find—

There it is.

Traditional little witch. He smirked. He found it deep in the bottom of a trunk, under scarves and old photos, the leather-bound text from the Ember Witches that he'd given her to introduce her to the world. As he flipped through the pages, something slipped out.

Rori frowned. The book was ancient; it had held up for centuries. Now that he gave it to Divina, pages fell out? He bent down and plucked the page off the floor. Finding it to be thicker than that of the pages of the book, it didn't register immediately that it didn't belong bound to the text. Turning it over, he paused.

Two faces, frozen midlaugh, stared back at him. Their mouths opened wide with blue tongues clearly on display. Vampires didn't need to eat food to survive. They needed blood to survive. When attempting to blend in and appear human, a vampire could consume food to keep up the illusion of life. Unless a cute little gypsy swears you will like the flavor of some blue lollipop with gum in it.

The lollipop had been horrible. Too sugary. The color simply from chemicals. But it had made Divina laugh, which made Rori laugh. Divina had such an infectious laugh. He ran his finger down the side of the photograph. They had been happy once.

With a sigh, Rori tucked the picture back in the book. He had no idea which page it dropped out from where she was using it as a book mark. She would know he had found the book. The bottom of a trunk, wrapped in scarves wasn't an ingenious hiding spot. So there was no point in attempting to find the picture's original place in an attempt to mask his snooping.

Thumbing through the pages some more, he found what he had hoped he wouldn't. One of the pages had some handwriting on it. Fresh. Divina's. He turned the book to see she had written all along the side margins. She had attempted to adjust some spell, to add to it.

Rori wasn't a witch. He didn't know what these things meant. He had learned enough to start Divina on her journey; his purpose, according to the Ember Witches. He couldn't cast spells or anything, but he did know the steps and the words. However, based on the book's alterations Divina had been studying. She had already surpassed what little he knew.

He looked to the front of the vardo. "What have you gotten yourself into?"

Divina shouted at the phone before tossing it to the passenger seat of the beat-up pick-up she drove. The phone bounced off the bench seat and landed somewhere up against the passenger side door. "Great!" she groaned. "Exactly what I needed."

Rori had already put a giant wrinkle in her day. Not only did she have to cut her work short and risk losing some income, now she was going out of her way to find out exactly what he was after. It was the only way she'd rid herself of him and then the game would be over.

She would no longer be blinded by his charm. She'd be a step of ahead of him, instead of the other way around, and this time she'd be the one to walk away. She'd be the one to disappear while he slept, while he'd be the one left with questions and she'd move on with her life for good.

She had let him stay in her home and had even covered him with six blankets when she had to leave the vardo to do some laundry, just to protect him from the sun. The least he could do was to be forthcoming about what he wanted, why he showed up. But, no, he didn't. He had to be all mysterious. So, of course, she had to go through his things and make her own connections. It was really all his fault she had to be so intrusive.

Maybe the time had come for her to meet those Ember Witches. Tired of them going through Rori to get to her, she'd make him take her to them. She was an adult, goddamn it, they needed to treat her like one. She could speak for her damn self. She would march right up to them and demand they stop this ridiculousness.

There was just one problem: Divina had no idea where they were. Sure, Rori had told her about them, saying they had sent him to guide her with nothing but good intentions. He had encouraged her to join them. However, he had neglected to tell her their location. Pretty hard to go to them if she didn't know how to find them.

Then again, he'd taught her the locator spell. When he waltzed into her life all sly charisma and charm, she'd fallen for him far too easily. She hadn't a clue about witches or vampires or wolves before she met him. In the year they'd spent together, he'd patiently shown her the possibilities of her own potential while introducing her to the world of the supernatural she never knew existed all around her. A world of wonder opened up around her, she hadn't a prayer in the world against falling in love with him then. When he left, without so much as a post-it explaining why, he damaged them. Maybe his coming back and not telling her what he really wanted was some sort of test, which she had failed. Instead of using spells, she'd relied on her human skills and only used magic when he jammed it in her face again.

From the little bit of snooping she did, she at least narrowed them down to a city in the United States. She really should have known, however. Where else would the most powerful coven be located? So she packed everything up and set off for New Orleans.

CHAPTER 8

T he pitch-black sky above sparkled with the bevy of
stars. Midnight approached and the waning crescent
moon offered little light when Divina pulled the truck into
the rest stop. There was no way to be inconspicuous when
traveling with a brightly painted, intricately carved, wooden
wagon. So, in an attempt to limit the curiosity of others,
Divina parked the rust bucket and the vardo in the back, far
away from the restaurant and gas station.

After retrieving her phone from the pit of napkins and
empty water bottles, Divina exited the cab of her truck and
moseyed her way to the vardo. She expected Rori to leap out
and complain about her driving.

She paused at the door of the wagon, waiting. Nothing
happened. That couldn't be good. What was he up to?

Yanking the door open, Divina charged in. She looked to
her right, nothing out of place. Her gaze swept left and found
Rori. He was sprawled across her couch with his legs crossed
at the ankle. A book blocked his face from her view.

Heat rose in Divina's cheeks. Balling her fists at her sides, she marched up to him and snatched the leather-bound journal from his hands, she gawked at his intrusion.

"Have you no sense of a person's privacy?" she growled.

With his hands in the same position, as though he still had the book in them, he turned his head ever so slightly to face her. Miming as though looking around the book, he regarded her. Struck with his pale appearance, concern doused her ire slightly. He was too pale.

"This, from the woman who frisked a man while he slept?" he said with a wry smile.

Divina lifted her chin and held the journal to her chest. "This is private."

Slowly, Rori lowered his hands. Turning his body, with deliberate movements, his feet swung to the floor. He never broke his intense gaze on her.

"I wasn't aware my pockets were public domain," he said.

Walking across the cramped space to the cabinet which held her herbs, dry goods, and other things she may need, Divina found room to breathe. Undoing the bungee cord holding it all in place, she opened the cabinet. She pressed her lips to the journal before placing it between a box of macaroni and a jar of sage sprigs.

"You've been a very busy girl," Rori whispered in her ear from behind her.

She whirled around, surprised at his proximity. Having not heard his footsteps or sensed his approach left Divina startled, so she glared at him once she regained her composure.

"That is none of your business," she snapped.

"I told you to join a coven." Rori frowned. "You're meddling with things beyond your comprehension."

Outstretching his arms, Rori filled her personal space. Her pulse ticked up as an unexpected uneasiness spread in her chest. Caging her in with the open cabinet to her back and him to her front, the coolness of his body contributed to her unexplained discomfort.

She had once found the closeness of his body to hers intoxicating. At one point in time, it had made her knees weak. However, things had changed.

"Wasn't it you who said I was one of the great powers of the world?" she asked, annoyed.

Reaching behind her she fumbled with the jars. Believing she had the right one, she shoved it between them. With tight lips she kept her gaze locked on him to witness his reaction.

Silver, probably the most powerful substance known to supernatural creatures, was an excellent repellant for things that lurked in the night. Rori's brown gaze trickled down to the jar and the smirk upon his face fell. He stepped back a few paces before lifting his wounded eyes toward her.

While no words were exchanged about what she produced, the message, she hoped was clear. Divina wasn't going to be manipulated so easily. She had learned things and would fight back this time.

Replacing the jar of silver powder, Divina closed the cabinet. She reattached the bungee. She waved, curled, and twirled her fingers while mumbling an incantation.

Locked.

Now Rori wouldn't be able to go through that cabinet again. She turned back to him and gave him a triumphant smile.

"All the more reason you need proper guidance," Rori responded smugly.

Divina narrowed her eyes at him unsure if her irritation was with his invasion of her privacy or because he was right.

Looking around her meager abode, she took inventory. There were nooks and crannies for storage everywhere. Having meant to cast spells to make it so snoops couldn't get in—another thing to put on her list of things to do once Rori was asleep again, she had no excuses to procrastinate anymore.

In her sweep of the place, she caught Rori's eye roll. "If you think I haven't already searched your little hiding spots, you underestimate me."

Divina grumbled about nosy vampires before she moved past him and flopped on the couch. "So why are we going to New Orleans?" she asked.

Rori stayed on the other side of the one-room wagon. He leaned against the now spellbound cabinet with his arms crossed.

"You tell me, kidnapper," he teased.

"I'm just trying to figure out what you want," she said.

"I told you what I want. I want your help to save the world." He grinned.

Divina noticed the strain in his expression. The smile didn't reach his eyes. The lines around his features seemed deeper than when she last saw him. His coloring was paler than it should be.

Rori wasn't the oldest vampire in existence, but he was up there, having seen his share of centuries. In her time of knowing him, and learning about vampires, Divina had discovered that the older a vampire got, the more manageable the hunger became and the better their ability to manage it. She had seen Rori hungry before; this was beyond just hunger. Something weighed on Rori's mind. Why wouldn't he tell her?

"How, exactly, am I supposed to help you save the world?" she queried.

Rori shifted his posture. He looked away from her toward the window. Something caught his attention a moment before he looked back at her. "Do you see that woman out there?" He pointed.

Divina groaned, pushing herself from the couch. Why couldn't he just tell her?

Outside the window a woman smoked a cigarette. She had loose skin and should have worn a dress a size bigger. Her wavy, bleached, stringy hair was an awful shade of blond with dark roots. The heels she wore were not practical for the gravel pavement she was on.

"Why am I looking at a hooker?" Divina asked.

"She is a lady of the night, show some respect," Rori admonished from behind her.

He pressed his body against her back. The coolness trickled up her spine. She couldn't remember the last time he had felt that cold. She was pinned again, this time between the small sink and Rori.

Divina shivered. He needed to eat. She needed space from him. It nagged at her that his presence still affected her. She cursed silently at the thought.

"She is here to seduce men, to lure them into her den, and to give them pleasure in exchange for cash. Don't belittle her skills, Divina. Not many can perform them," he whispered into her ear in a sensual voice that still made her knees weak.

Gods help her.

Divina tilted her head away offering him her neck. For a brief moment, Divina lost herself in his charm. She allowed herself to bask in the memory of how good being in his presence had once been.

Shaking her head to try to get the fog out, Divina scurried away from Rori. She folded her arms over her chest and looked anywhere but at him. "Did you just imply that I should be a prostitute?"

Rori's attention remained on the woman outside. He didn't respond immediately, rather he seemed to study the hooker.

"I'm starving," he said. Rori walked past her, toward

the door.

"Wait!" Divina reached out to grab his arm.

Once she had a hold of him, Rori inhaled audibly and deeply. He froze in place with eyes closed.

Divina furrowed her brow at him. What was that about?

"Rori?" she asked.

"No," he whispered. He moved his arm slightly, in a twitch motion. It felt like he wanted to flick Divina's touch off him.

Divina released him.

"What just happened?" she asked.

Rori straightened his vest and rolled his shoulders back. Finally, his eyes opened. He turned them on her.

"I'm a very hungry vampire, and you are getting between me and my next meal. Do you wish to become it?" he said through gritted teeth.

Divina gaped at him. Rori had never threatened her before. As stupid as it sounded, Rori was a predator, and to him Divina was just prey, though she had never feared him. He had never given her reason. Something was seriously wrong.

～

Zapped with a thousand volts of electricity. When she grabbed his arm, he had to use all his restraint to not writhe on the floor in pain.

Was it pain, though? Pain wasn't the right word. No. He didn't have the right word.

Relief flowed through Rori when she released him, and it took him a moment to gather himself while the last of the prickles faded. Her touch had always aroused a tingle in him. Naturally, for she was the reason his heart beat again. However, Divina's touch had never felt as intense as it did at that moment. He made a note to avoid it in the future.

Exiting the wagon, he inhaled a lungful of the cool autumn air—something he needed after that surprise. He sensed her eyes boring into his back. He wouldn't turn back, though. He needed to eat, and that hooker would be a nice combination of amenability and discretion. She would probably taste like an ashtray and who knew what sort of chemicals she had flowing through her system. All things Rori would gladly deal with over what was going on inside that wagon.

It wasn't until Rori had taken a few steps away from the vardo that he heard the click of the door closing. He breathed a sigh of relief. When she showed him the silver, he realized his Divina had learned a few things and wouldn't be so easy get on board with his flimsy plan. He still hadn't worked out exactly how he'd ask her for what he needed. How does one go about telling the woman he loves that she is meant for another? How does he introduce them and watch them fall in love?

Rori shook his head. Not a thought for right now. He could think about that once he took the edge off. Another thing that irritated him at the moment; since when was Rori so edgy at night? He felt like a mere hundred-year-old, the way his hunger taunted him.

Why was he so out of sorts? What did those witches do to him in that stupid convent, anyway? He shouldn't feel the effects of Divina if she weren't meant for him. That's what they said. She wasn't meant for him. Perhaps, if he repeated that statement often enough, he'd believe it.

"Well, hello there," he greeted the lot lizard with a sly smile.

Time to switch focus, if for no other reason than so he could do just that: focus. Once he had some blood in his system, he'd have a clearer head.

CHAPTER 9

G roaning, Aric brought his hand to his temple in an attempt to stop the pounding. The bright sunlight seeping through the blinds caused him to squint. It wasn't long before the gently whistled breathing of a female caught his attention. A look to his left revealed a blond, fast asleep, with her back to him.

From what he could tell, she was, at the very least, topless. That realization brought awareness to his own state of undress.

She stirred when Aric attempted to reach for his boxers. He froze. Thankfully, the woman just shifted her position and seemed to remain asleep.

Who was this woman? How did she wind up in his bed? He looked around the room for clues. His trailer was in its typical disheveled state. He wasn't much for cleaning up.

His eyes landed on the empty bottle of Jameson. Perhaps he had blacked out? When was the last time he blacked out? He peered at the woman again. Where did he meet her?

Women typically didn't appear from under his kitchen sink. The last thing he remembered was clearing a clog from his kitchen sink. He remembered spilling the cleaner and the smell of jasmine.

Aric inhaled. Okay, he remembered smelling her. Or, did he? No. He had smelled her before. Why was everything so unclear? She smelled pretty good though. Pushing his sheets toward her, he exposed his bare body to the cool morning air. Careful not to shake the bed too much, he inched off it and grabbed his boxers.

Once standing, he made a quick motion, pulling them up to cover himself. He didn't want to wake the woman until he had a better sense of what had happened last night.

Aric tiptoed away from the bed and closed the small curtain. It separated his bedroom area from the rest of his trailer. He attempted to make as little a sound as possible. The irony that he crept around his own home was not lost on him.

He sighed in relief once there was a barrier between them. For some reason, he found that with her out of sight he would be able to concentrate better.

Time for some context clues; Aric decided to take stock. His jeans were in a ball on the ground. He picked them up and inhaled. Cleaner soap. He unballed them, and the fuzzy memory of knocking over the container came back to him. He looked to the sink. Okay, so at least he had finished the repair.

Strewn over his couch was a small, pink crop top. Aric held it up and sniffed it. He arched his brow. Along with the scent of the female, there was another. The additional scent was extremely faint. Any human nose would never have picked it up. It smelled of rotting meat. He threw it over his shoulder as his stomach churned. He wasn't sure if it was the whiskey or the smell.

He continued his investigation. Sticking out from between the cushions of his couch, Aric spotted some denim.

Once he pulled it free, he found a yellow G-string inside the pants, laced with the scent of arousal. His cock enjoyed that smell perhaps a bit too much.

He furrowed his brow in intrigue. She had been naked in his home. He had been naked. But there was no sex smell.

The crinkle of the curtain caught Aric's attention. Spinning on the spot toward the sound, he held the pair of panties in one hand and the jeans in the other. He shouldn't have been surprised when his gaze landed on a very naked and very beautiful blond with curves for days.

The gods themselves proportioned the woman. Heavy chested, thick thighed, and he had the sudden urge to nip at her luscious curves. The chubby he sported got closer to full mast. She rewarded him with a seductive smile.

"Oh good, I was afraid I'd have to leave naked," she said with erotic intent lacing her voice.

The animal within him clawed and growled. The beast urged Aric into action. Into what action, Aric wasn't sure, but his human was tempted to indulge in the woman. Something hindered their ability to do the deed the previous evening, and he wasn't about to let that mistake occur twice. The wolf snapped within him at the thoughts, but Aric dismissed the beast.

She bit her lower lip staring at him. The heat of her gaze washed over him. She did not attempt to hide the fact that she drank in his muscular physique.

Aric rolled his shoulders back and added a slight flex. He might as well give her something to look at.

"Who said you were leaving?" he asked in a playful challenge. Abandoning her clothing, Aric stalked toward the female.

It took him four short strides before he wrapped his arm around her waist and pulled her against him. His heavy erection, peaking from the slit in his boxers, pressed against her soft belly. His free hand fisted the hair at her nape before his mouth joined with hers.

"I guess I'm staying then." She teased him with a smile and unsaid intent.

It wasn't every day the world blessed a wolf with a beautiful, naked blond. Aric would be a fool if he didn't take her up on the nonverbal offer. Again, his beast howled his disagreement with the human's decision.

Once he was past the taste of sleep, otherwise known as morning breath, he got a sample of her true taste. Hungrily he chased her tongue lapping at the honey flavor that was hers and hers alone. He tugged at her hair to send the message that she was to open herself to him.

She rewarded him with a moan. Her tongue eagerly danced with his, and her leg sought to slip between his thighs.

He allowed her leg between his own. Her hands tickled up and down his arms. The subtle tingle of her touch sent waves of pleasure straight to his groin.

This female was well practiced in the art of pleasure. Aric growled when he pulled his mouth from hers. He grinned hearing her gasp for breath. Good, the reaction he wanted.

He dove in and kissed her neck. She tilted her head offering him better access. The sign of submission got him even harder, if that were possible.

Gently, Aric nibbled at the juncture between her shoulder and her throat. As his tongue laved the area, he felt an odd ridge. Before he could think to question it, her hand reached into his waistband and gripped the root of his cock.

Now it was his turn to moan. She coiled her fingers around his stiff erection. As the female squeezed him, he nipped her neck a bit harder. He had no intentions of claiming the female, whose name he had forgotten. However, he did want her to get the message that he enjoyed what she did.

It only took a few strokes for Aric to take action. Sliding his hands down her body, delighting in the flair of her hips, he found the glorious globes of her ass. He dug his fingers in before lifting her.

As he had hoped, she brought her legs up over his hips and hooked her ankles behind him. Her arms looped around his neck. He returned to kissing her mouth. His teeth grazed her bottom lip. His tongue speared into her mouth. He may not want to claim her officially, but at that moment, she belonged to him.

What he planned for this female was no lovemaking session. He didn't know this woman. He intended to fuck her and would give and take pleasure from her. With each step down the short hall toward his bedroom, he groped her behind and nipped at her bottom lip.

Once he felt the edge of his bed at his shins, he broke the greedy kiss and was breathless. His eyes flashed gold; his wolf charged inside him attempting to push forward, to stop Aric. He could feel the burn of the beast over his skin. He strained to keep the confused animal down.

She shivered. She must have seen it in him too.

He threw her back onto his bed. She let out a squeal of either fright or excitement—at this point, Aric didn't care. He throbbed and needed a release. He tugged down his boxers and kicked them off to the side, crawling onto the bed.

Aric kissed up her right leg. He trailed his tongue over her kneecap and toward her thigh. He offered sweet bites to the soft skin, and her whimpering sounds told him he tortured her in the best way possible.

The musky aroma of female arousal filled his nostrils. The rumble of his wolf's disapproval thundered from him. He licked at the glistening, shaved, and swollen slit. He wanted to sample her nectar before driving into her.

Her legs parted wider, offering him full access to her. He reached over her belly and gripped as much of her breasts as he could in both hands. Her hard nipples were between the knuckles of his middle and index finger as he kneaded her flesh.

At first, Aric slid his tongue over the outer lips. She rewarded him with a slight hint of the spicy tang that was a flavor all her own. However, once his tongue dove in fully, flicking against the hardened bead that was her clit, she gave a more rewarding taste of her arousal.

He only briefly tongued at her before making his way up her belly. He just needed her primed for him. His right hand moved off her breast and teased her entrance. He circled the opening with his finger, and she whimpered. Her fingers ran through his hair.

Aric took the abandoned nipple into his mouth in time with his finger pressing into her. He watched as her eyes rolled back, and she sucked in a deep breath. Her back arched and her body pressed further against his. The look of being lost in lust fueled his passion.

"More?" he whispered before flicking his tongue against the darkened nub atop her breast.

"Yes!" she nodded, biting her lower lip.

Another finger plunged into her. She cried out, and her leg muscles tightened. Aric pumped in and out a few times before curling his fingers in a come-hither movement.

Her walls pulsed around his digits. She writhed beneath him as he searched for that sensitive spot he wanted to exploit. He wanted to see her get to the edge.

Her body stiffened. Her eyes widened. Her chest stopped moving, and Aric realized the woman had stopped breathing. He pressed further into her and spread his fingers. She thrust her hips up to meet him.

The slick opening of her sex gripped his fingers. The pulse

of her need squeezed around him rhythmically. Aric groaned in pleasure.

Perfect. That was exactly where Aric wanted her to be. He removed his fingers. In a swift movement, helped by his unnatural speed as a shifter, Aric climbed up her wanton body and slid his erection into her. His arms on either side of her he buried himself to the hilt.

As she was not his mate, there was no need to worry about impregnating her. As he was a shifter, possessing advanced healing, there was no threat of contracting any sort of disease. Condoms weren't necessary, he could enjoy the raw feel of her satin walls around his cock without worry.

Her legs pulled up around him, and she screamed. The first hint of impending orgasm rippled around Aric's cock. Oh, this was a responsive female. He would have to thank whoever sent her to his trailer. He slowed down, allowing her a moment to back off from her impending orgasm.

As much as Aric enjoyed pleasing a woman, if she came too soon, he wouldn't enjoy it as much. Part of his enjoyment was the back and forth. Will he push her over? How close to the edge could he take her?

She whimpered, reached down his body, and gripped his ass. She dug her heels into him and urged him to move.

He growled, lowering his head to her neck again. He bit down, not hard enough to break her skin. No. He would not claim this female. He just wanted her to know who was in charge, that he was in control of her pleasure.

Once she got the message, her hands relaxed. Her heels no longer dug into Aric's back. He moved his hips going slowly at first, really dragging out the tension and the pleasure. He wanted her needy and begging.

He withdrew carefully, keeping the tip of his cock at the female's opening, and studied her expression. She kept her eyes sealed, her face contorted.

64

"More," she begged.

"Patience," he whispered back.

He thrust forward with all his might, bouncing her up farther on the bed. She shrieked and raked her nails down his back. He withdrew again only to bury himself against the opening of her womb. This woman was tight but not too tight. She could handle the force he planned to use with her.

He repeated the slow withdrawal, the violent thrust back in her. It pleased him to hear her whimpers and her need for him. However, doing this wasn't going to do it for him. His attempt to tease her, to extend her denial, resulted in teasing himself at the same time. He would take his pleasure from her.

Shifting on his knees, Aric pulled her legs up. He closed and straightened them, nearly folding the woman in half, and used his chest to press her legs against her. The position changed the angle of his entrance. He had learned where that delightful spot was and he intended to assault it until the woman forgot her name. Hell, Aric had, it was only fair.

As he hammered into her, he knew he hit the right spot. Her breathing had shifted from panting to short gasps. Her legs tightened. Her pussy clamped around him. It wouldn't be much longer before she went over. His balls tightened, but he needed to hold off; he would not blow before she did.

Pulsing spasms rippled around his erection. The wave of wetness that soaked Aric's cock and dripped down Aric's balls told him all he needed to know. Soon her cries of pleasure filled his trailer. He released her legs and gripped her shoulders. It was his turn.

While she rode her orgasm, he plowed into her with reckless abandon. Each thrust forward meant he would pull her back against him. He gritted his teeth as he grew that much thicker. He was right there. He threw his head back and let out a howl as his orgasm hit.

His cock pulsed deep into the female. Rope after rope of his seed sprayed inside her. Her moan was distant to him. He got lost in his orgasm.

He collapsed over her. Both their bodies glistened with sweat from their exertion. Aric breathed erratically. He kissed her softly on her swollen mouth. She purred in response and stroked his back. Each twitch of her pussy walls around his cock sent another shock through his system.

He tingled all over while he laid atop her. After a moment, he rolled over onto his back. He didn't know who she was, but he was quite pleased she had knocked on his door.

"With all the drinking we did last night," Aric said, "I apologize, but I can't remember your name." Aric felt an obligation to ask since he had just been inside her.

She laughed as she rolled toward him. She placed her head on his chest. Instinctively, his arm came up and cupped her to him.

"Selene," she whispered.

Why did that sound familiar?

CHAPTER 10

The night grew blacker as Divina busied herself with enchanting her hiding place. The crescent moon moved through the sky while she worked on spelling, snacking, and checking the time on her phone. The longer Rori was gone, the more impatient Divina became.

She ground her teeth in aggravation when she texted him and got no response. She left the vardo and roamed the parking lot looking for him. Her jaw set and her eyes scanning, she blocked out the catcalls of the truck drivers while she searched.

Three hours had passed. Three hours Rori had been gone. The last hour of which, she'd spent looking for him out in the woods and calling his cell which went to voicemail. Had he uprooted her from the carnival, from her livelihood, to ditch her at some rest stop? She seethed with anger at his thoughtlessness.

The idea that something might have happened to Rori tickled her mind. *He's immortal*, Divina told herself, dismissing the thought. What could happen to him? Returning inside her vardo, she sat on her couch, thumbing through the book

Rori had given her when they first met. She had all but memorized it, which meant she wasn't actually reading it. It served as a connection to him, a bit of a security blanket. Staring at the book, Divina's mind volleyed back and forth between extreme anger at Rori and worrying about him.

Divina tossed the book onto the couch. "Fuck this shit," she growled and pushed up to a standing position.

Grumbling a string of obscenities, Divina gave the inside of the vardo the once-over. She tested the bungee cords to ensure her items were secured and stowed safely. Once satisfied she exited it, locked the door, and went toward the cab of her pick-up.

"Bastard thinks he can just waltz in and drop some bomb on me so that I leave the fairgrounds." She shook her head while mumbling to herself. "Well, he's got another thing coming."

"What sort of asshole would do that?" Rori's charming reply came from behind her.

Relief. No, anger. Back to relief. Nope, this was fury. Divina spun and charged at him. "What the fuck, Rori?"

Rori held up his hands defensively and laughed. Divina's fists collided with Rori's chest in a flurry. It did nothing to stop his joy.

Divina stepped back and tugged at her floral linen shirt. Rori pulled at his tailored sleeve while rolling back his shoulders, unfazed by her assault aside from how it had impacted his impeccable attire. How did he look so put together after sleeping on a floor?

"Where were you?" she demanded.

Rori arched an eyebrow. He cleared his throat then patted his belly. "Had a nice satisfying meal."

She groaned and rolled her eyes. "It doesn't take you that long unless you did more than just feed." The pang of jealousy in her quip surprised Divina. She had no claim on Rori, nor any sort of expectation of any sort of fidelity, it had been years since they were together. The idea that he may have been intimate with the prostitute shouldn't have stirred any sort of negative feelings in her. Yet, she stood there angry that he might have.

"It does when I want to be discreet." Rori waved a finger at her. "And when I can't just have one." He winked.

"AARRRRGGG." Divina shook her fists at him. "Why are we here?"

Rori's face slipped into a neutral expression. The flatness of his features lacked emotion. He was the epitome of calm.

"I don't know. I was kidnapped and brought to this humble establishment," he said.

Divina let out another exasperated cry. Clearly, Rori wanted nothing to do with being forthcoming. He seemed content to waste her time.

She balled her fists so hard her nails dug into the palms of her hands.

"Fine," she growled.

She finished her walk to the truck and climbed in.

"Stay here. Do whatever. I don't care," Divina said from inside the cab, reaching to close the door.

Rori was hot on her heels. His hand clamped down on the door handle of the truck preventing her from closing it.

"Where are you going?" he asked.

She smirked. "I didn't have a satisfying meal."

He frowned. "Well, at least take me with you."

She pulled at the door. Rori was a three-hundred-plus-year-old vampire. There was no way she'd close that door if Rori didn't want her to.

"Let go!" she demanded.

"Not until you agree to let me come with you," he bargained.

She rolled her eyes. "You came here with me. That didn't work out."

"I told you that it wouldn't. It's not my fault you didn't listen to me," Rori said, releasing the door.

Divina yanked it shut in time to feel the bench seat sink under Rori's weight. She clenched her jaw while jabbing the key in the ignition.

"I brought you here because, for some reason, I thought you would take me to the Ember Witches. They keep sending you to me, and I figured it was time to cut out the middleman," she said.

Divina figured she might as well lay it all out on there since all other tactics had failed. Why not try the truth? What's the worst that could happen?

Rori's face fell. He looked out the window and paused.

"They don't want to speak with you," he said softly.

"That doesn't make sense. They keep sending you as a messenger to get me to do stuff. Why can't they just talk to me about things?" she asked.

Rori kept his gaze on the lot. "I think we should try Florida."

Divina touched his arm at the elbow. Rori jumped and recoiled. He curled his body defensively against the passenger side door. He looked down at his arm and then at her hand as if they were alien to him. He brought his opposite hand to his elbow and rubbed it with a frown.

"What just happened?" Divina asked with a touch of skepticism.

She had touched Rori countless times in the past. He had never pulled away from her. Historically, Rori had the opposite reaction when they touched. Something was seriously wrong.

"I don't know." Rori's voice sounded weak.

He continued to stare at his elbow. He kept it covered protectively with his opposite hand.

"Would the witches know?" she asked.

Rori slowly lifted his gaze to her face. For a split second, Divina was sure she saw the old Rori in there. The Rori she had once snuggled. The man whose heart shouldn't beat, but she heard the subtle thump bump of it after their first time together.

However, it didn't last. It took merely a second for the coldness to return. Rori frowned.

"I'm sure they would know, but they aren't exactly up for chatter," he said.

The tension in him released. Rori settled back into a more typical posture on the passenger side of the truck cab. However, he kept as much of a distance from Divina as possible.

Rori took out his phone and turned his focus to that. The glow of the screen illuminated his face in an eerie blue. He had eaten, so he wasn't as pale as before. The lighting, however, seemed to highlight the lines of his face. Rori didn't look as young as he once did.

In a matter of seconds, the feminine robotic voice of his phone announced that it was starting its route.

"We're not going to Florida," Divina said and turned the keys in the ignition.

"But the phone said we have to go this way." Rori turned the screen toward her. He protruded his bottom lip in a pout.

"No. We came here for a reason," Divina insisted.

"No 'we' didn't." Rori lowered the phone. "You came here on a mission"—he pointed toward her chest—"and kidnapped me. I am here against my will."

His hand flattened against his chest. He regarded her with a wounded expression all wide and doe eyed.

"Gah!" Divina slammed her hands against the steering

wheel. "Can you for once, just once, think of me and my needs?"

Rori's face went blank again. Soon, his eyes narrowed at her.

"Fine!" he growled.

He tapped his screen a few times.

"If I do this, you can't throw that lie in my face anymore," he said.

"It's not a lie," Divina insisted.

He held up a finger near her lips. He wouldn't touch them. Instead, his finger hovered just in front of her.

"You have no idea of my intentions. You've never understood. There are greater things at play than you know. So you cannot, and I will not allow you, to insult me about my intentions with you any further."

She gaped at him. Upon closer inspection of him, it dawned on her. Divina had not only insulted him; she had hurt Rori. She blinked a few times as if unable to process this revelation.

"Make a left out of the lot," Rori grumped, interrupting her thoughts. "I'll get you to the Ember Witches, but I can't guarantee they'll see you. Hell, I doubt they just hang out there – it's a meeting place. But I'll show you what I know. On one condition."

Divina eased the truck towing the wagon out of the lot.

"What is it?" she asked as she made the turn.

"We're going to Florida after this, and you won't question me again," he said.

"Wha—"

"Tut." Rori held his hand up once more. "No questions. Against my better judgment, I'm doing what you asked me. I'm getting you to the Ember Witches, so I would say you owe me."

Divina sighed.

He lowered his hand.

She looked out at the road. "I would say *you* owe *me*."

"I did. Didn't you hear me? I said 'you owe me.' Really, Divina, you need to pay more attention if you're going to see the big picture," Rori replied looking at his phone. "Make a right at the third light."

CHAPTER 11

After parking the vardo in a lot and disconnecting it from the pick-up truck, they rode in near silence. Rori begrudgingly gave directions as they drove.

Divina would think he was fucking with her if they weren't there. And if for some reason, they were there, Rori wasn't sure what sort of reception they would receive.

He couldn't shake the bad vibe crawling up his spine. The closer they got to the convent the more intense the vibe became.

Finding no cars on Charles Street allowed Rori to breathe a bit easier. Maybe they wouldn't be there.

Divina pulled over and turned off the engine. Rori turned off his phone. Divina looked past him, out the window, to the large white cement wall.

"What is it?" she asked.

He turned to regard the large, moonlit, neoclassical French colonial stucco-covered brick building with the white cross over the front. The completely unremarkable yet asymmetrical building lacked the typical ornamental nature of most houses of worship.

"The Old Ursuline Convent," Rori answered.

Divina leaned closer to him. Rori pulled back as much as he could. He crammed his body against the door. He couldn't risk them touching again. Her touch was too much for him. It had never been that intense before. Something told him that it was because he wasn't taking her as his own anymore. He suspected the world fucked with him for going against the natural order or some shit.

"Why a convent?" she asked, clearly in awe of the rather ordinary building.

Rori opened the door to get some air.

"I'm not exactly familiar with all their history, but I would imagine that it was easy to hide in plain sight if you called yourself a convent. No one questioned a gathering of women praying if they wore habits," he said with a grin.

She tightened her lips, not taking her gaze off the building.

"I guess," she said and climbed out of the truck from her side.

Divina and Rori stood outside the closed gate. Beyond it were neatly trimmed hedges lining a small, maze-like path to the grand entrance of the building.

Rori studied Divina as she seemed mesmerized by the building.

"I can feel it," she whispered.

Rori took a step away from her cautiously. Had he been too close? Did she feel the sparks as he had?

"The power," she added as she raised her hands.

She spread her fingers and bowed her head.

"There is so much of it surging from this one building," she said with joy.

"Oh." Rori stuffed his hands in his pockets disappointed that she wasn't talking about their connection. Was it one-sided?

The weather turned a bit chilly. While he had fed, the hooker hadn't been a proper meal. Rather, her chemical-laced system proved to be too vile for Rori to enjoy. So, he had only eaten enough to stave off the urge so he wouldn't attack Divina. Even with additional sips from other sources, he hadn't really sated his hunger.

"They're calling to me," Divina said gleefully.

Rori forced a smile. "Goodie." His sarcasm reflected his lack of enthusiasm.

The heavy, ecru gate creaked and slowly swung open.

Rori sighed. He wasn't in the mood for the witches and their riddles. However, one look at Divina's hopeful face, and he wasn't about to pretend he would stay behind.

Divina took two hesitant steps toward the small parking lot before looking back at Rori. She smiled wide with excitement, but her eyes reflected caution.

Rori lowered his head and walked past her to take the lead. He resigned himself to the fact there was little he wouldn't do for that woman. It unnerved him.

The entrance of the convent opened as they approached the step. Florence stood with a welcoming grin. Divina reached out to Rori, grabbed his arm, and held him tight.

Rori grit his teeth as the sensation radiated from his arm and spread throughout him. His fists tightened to the point they were white knuckled.

The intense heat flowed from his arm, over his chest, and down to his crotch. Rori kept his eyes on the Ember Witch in an attempt to ground himself. He didn't want to show any signs of Divina having an impact on him. He couldn't accept it. He had made his choice when he last saw them.

Florence's gaze landed on him. Her smile faltered. She offered him a nod. A very subtle flick of her wrist, accompanied with a wiggle of her fingers and the hotness receded.

Rori frowned. While tingles lingered in place of the intensity of Divina's touch, Rori wondered what the witch had taken away. Was it their connection? Did she know what the intense electric bolt feeling was all about?

"I'm Divina," she introduced herself as they came closer to Florence.

"Yes," Florence nodded. "I know. I'm so glad Roricus brought you here. We have been waiting for you."

Divina released Rori's arm. "Why didn't you just come and get me yourself?" Divina demanded like a petulant child.

Florence chuckled. She reached out to Divina, seeking to wrap her arm around her.

Divina hesitated, stepping back from the woman. She folded her arms over her chest. Divina stole a glance at Rori who furrowed his brow.

"She's not going to talk to you about that out here," Rori said motioning for her to go along with Florence. "You have to meet the elders of the coven."

As skeptical of the witches as Rori was, she wouldn't get any of the answers she needed if she didn't play along with them, and knowing her, she'd need Rori's blessing to do just that. So, he had to play the supportive part.

Divina eyed the two suspiciously.

Florence kept her expression positive, delightful, and overall nonthreatening.

Rori kept his face neutral, which was easier to do without the shooting heat from Divina's touch. He had wanted her to join the Ember Witches. They were the only ones who could handle the potential within her.

He nodded toward Divina and gave her the go-ahead she sought. Essentially, he gave her permission to find out about the Ember Witches. No matter how much he doubted their intentions, Rori couldn't deny they were right for Divina. She would learn the most from them. He would be a fool to prevent her from reaching her potential.

Divina hesitated a moment longer before she went along with Florence. Rori looked away, pretending there was something wrong with the sleeve of his shirt. The two women made their way through the museum. Rori kept a few paces behind them. He wasn't about to abandon her to the witches.

The walk through the halls was quiet save for the sound of their footsteps on the marble floor. Rori used the time to brood. As they rode the elevator, he promised himself that it was worth giving up Divina to be Emperor.

He'd get to rule over his kind. He'd get prestige. He'd have a say over all kinds as being the emperor would put him on the Council of Others. Who didn't want that? The Ember Witches had told him as much. He was immortal. She was not. Their mating was ill-fated from the start. Loving a mortal was fleeting. Being an emperor was forever.

Sure, he could turn her. But if he did, she would lose a part of herself. The connection to Earth, the part of her that was a witch would die with her when she died to become a vampire. She would come back a changed woman. She would be empty.

No. Rori could not sacrifice Divina's nature for himself. Rori was a selfish ass, but even he had limits. Right?

Rori had seen the delight in her eyes when she cast her first spell that worked. He saw how eager she was to learn more. She had thrived since then, despite not having a coven. To take her magic away from her, no matter how much he loved her wasn't right.

No. Emperorship was his future. He sighed. The Ember Witches and some wolf were Divina's. His expression soured the moment the thought of the wolf entered his mind. The thought of a low-class mongrel with Divina, his Divina, had his blood boiling.

The doors opened to the subbasement. Rori followed behind and entered the all too familiar room. He watched

Florence lead Divina into the center of the horseshoe table. He surprised himself when a smile crept across his lips, observing how maternal Florence appeared in her handling of Divina.

He wiped the smile off his face with his hand remembering how the witches had manipulated him. Perhaps this was all a manipulation; all a ruse to get Divina.

He remained close just outside the ring, protective, prepared to spring into action if needed. Though, he wasn't too sure what protection he could offer against the most powerful witches of the largest coven in the U.S.

~

The thrum of energy between Divina and Rori had stopped. Divina had watched the hand motion from the dark-haired witch who had greeted them. However, Divina hadn't had much time to wonder about it.

They had pulled up to this rather blank-looking building with a wall around it. Power radiated off it. There was no doubt the building belonged to the Ember Witches. There was also the nagging feeling of them pulling her.

Then the gates opened as if to confirm the sensation. The woman appeared, then they were in an elevator. Divina's head spun. Maybe the lack of sensation between she and Rori had nothing to do with the hand motion of the dark-haired witch. Perhaps, the bombardment of the powerful auras of the thirteen witches seated at the curved table drowned out their connection.

The woman guided Divina toward the center of the table. Essentially, the witches wrapped around her in the same way the waves of magic coming off them did.

Once the woman patted her arm and turned to take her seat, Divina looked back toward Rori. He was her safe zone.

Rori stood back, out of the open circle of witches. He held himself in a loose hug. His gaze fixated on her. When their eyes met, he offered her a nod.

Calmness washed over her when she received his nonverbal blessing in this. Divina took a deep breath, raised her chin and rolled her shoulders back. She could handle this. Rori had wanted her to join them before. She could do this. She was meant to do this.

"Divina Bahari," the woman at the center of the horse-shoe table announced to the room of witches.

Divina's head snapped back, and she took in the older, frail-looking woman with the cascade of gray hair.

"Yes?" she said. Her voice shook slightly.

"We are the leaders of the Ember Witch Coven." The woman opened her arms gesturing to the women who surrounded Divina.

Divina swallowed and looked around at each woman's face. They were of varying ages, appearances, and from what she could tell, power. Divina nervously shifted her weight from one foot to the other.

Did she belong there? Could she measure up to them? The feeling of inadequacy bloomed in her chest and sought to take root within her.

"As the most powerful coven throughout this country, we have branches in each state but the thirteen witches before you are the leaders," the woman explained.

Divina nodded. She studied the woman speaking. The lines around her eyes and the deep creases at the corners of her mouth told the story of a woman who had seen much. Divina wondered what kind of person she was.

"I am Esmine Richart," she introduced herself with a bit of a curtsy. "I am the witch designee for the Council of Others," she said.

Divina's eyes widened. Her mouth fell open. Esmine, she

was Esmine. Divina was in the presence of Esmine, the most powerful witch on this side of the world.

Esmine grinned pleased with Divina's response to her. Esmine waved a hand to her right. "This is Florence Beaumont."

The dark haired woman who had brought Divina through the convent nodded. "We are delighted to finally have you here, Divina. We have been waiting for you," she said.

The warm, welcoming tone Florence used washed over Divina. Florence's words doused the flames of intimidation she felt. A smile crept on her face, and Divina felt soothed. The woman projected the power of a strong empath.

Esmine waved a hand to her left. "This is Jessa Soleil."

A blond woman closed her eyes and nodded her head.

"These two women are considered my advisors, though every witch at this table advises me. As my seat on the council is to represent the best interest of the witches of this territory not just my own."

Divina tucked some hair behind her ear and cleared her throat. Not about to forget she had come there for a reason, she steeled her resolve.

Looking over her shoulder for Rori gave her encouragement. His gaze remained trained on her. Nodding in his direction, acknowledging his support, she turned back to Esmine with her courage fortified. While she focused on the lead witch, she was addressing them as a whole.

"You could've summoned me if you wanted me here. I don't understand why you kept sending Rori," she said.

She attempted to sound confident, but the crack of her voice surely ruined that façade. Though, she told herself it didn't matter how it came out. All that mattered was that she stood up to them.

CHAPTER 12

W hile Rori hung back, he watched Divina engage with
the witches. He remained silent as they introduced
themselves to her. He scoffed at their self-importance and
hoped Divina would see through that.

The intention had always been to introduce her to the
Ember Witches. Rori knew they were the most powerful
witches in the country. The strength within Divina remained
untapped. There was more power in her than any other witch
he'd met. It would take the power of all the Ember Witches
to harness that which was inside Divina if she were to go
rogue. It only made sense that they'd want to control her for
their purposes rather than risk having to fight against her.

He glanced around the U-shaped table of witches. From
what he had seen last time, every seat contained a witch. He
wondered whose seat Divina would overtake.

Then his eyes landed on the farthest seat. The seat, if he
remembered correctly, belonged to the young redhead. The
one witch who had tapped into what motivated Rori. The
seat was now empty. He arched a brow in curiosity.

Rori scanned the others again; perhaps she had moved

seats. He had assumed they were assigned a seat in designation of hierarchy. Maybe he was wrong.

Nope. She wasn't at the table, and to the best of Rori's recollection everyone seemed to be in their previous locations.

Had she been cast out for her comments? Surely she had helped their cause. Rori shook his head. No. If she wasn't there, it had nothing to do with him or Divina. He didn't know the witch's story. He condemned the narcissism within him at the thought the missing witch had anything to do with him or Divina.

The pang of hunger twisted Rori's stomach and surprised him. The hooker and the trucker he had at the rest stop weren't enough to sustain him. He couldn't take his fill of them.

He thought he had perfected the right amount to keep the hunger away. The cracking sensation of him being dried out without a full complement of blood told him that he'd guessed wrong in the amount he took that night.

Rori's hand went to his belly, and he sighed. His mouth watered as he watched Divina. She had been the most decadent flavor ever to grace his tongue. What wouldn't he give to lap at her vein once more. Feeding from strangers, or people he didn't care about, sparked no emotions within him. They were merely food. However, with Divina, the combination of their connection and her witch blood, had been addicting. Even the thought of her blood sent shivers through him.

His focus on the night, the witches, and Divina faded. He fixated on Divina's throat. He studied the pulsing blue vein in her neck. He had tapped into that vein many times before. His mouth watered at the thought of sampling her once again.

"You look a bit peckish," a familiar feminine voice broke into his thoughts.

Rori refocused.

"Are you offering to remedy the situation?" he asked of the redhead.

He wouldn't deny the state of his hunger. It was written all over his face. And peckish, well that was an understatement. He turned his attention on the young witch.

The redhead blushed and shook her head while simultaneously looking away from him.

"I was merely going to suggest that you have time to feed properly, while we speak with Divina," she said.

"And leave her here? With you?" he asked.

He lifted nodded his chin in the direction of the conversation he could no longer follow due to his hunger.

The redhead offered him a knowing smile. "There is no safer place for a witch than with her coven," she said.

Rori scoffed. "She hasn't accepted your coven."

The redhead laughed. "You and I both know she will. It is her place. It is why we sent you to her; to start her on her right and true path, freeing you, for yours."

Rori hesitated. Freeing him? From what? Divina? Why did he need to be freed? The word "free" didn't seem right.

The young witch furrowed her brow at him.

"You are famished," she said.

"I'm old," Rori flicked his gaze toward Divina. This whole thing didn't feel right.

"You're not that old."

Rori clenched his jaw. Why was the witch trying to get rid of him? He turned his ire-filled gaze upon her.

With having so little blood in his system, his emotions tended to be exacerbated by the hunger.

"I'm old enough that if I wish to oversee my Divina, I will," he said through clenched teeth.

The redhead's face went unreadable. Her jaw twitched while she eyed him.

"You're meant for power, not Divina," the witch reminded him rather coolly.

Rori clenched his fists in defeat. The Throne. Did the witch believe he'd forgotten about the throne? Did she have to keep bringing it up?

His gaze slowly rose to Divina at the center of the witch coven. A coven. Her coven? Divina needed a coven. She needed the proper guidance to grow her strength. He could never be the mentor she needed in that, no matter how much he wanted to be. He wasn't a witch.

His expression softened, and he lowered his gaze. He couldn't look at Divina without feeling the hunger intensify. He felt the lure of her blood like a knife to the gut. The hunger for her flesh ached as much as his need for her blood. Both tugged at him so hard it was all he could do to stand in place.

Rori released his fists. The faint trickle of blood on his palms indicated he had tightened his fists to the point his nails had cut into his flesh. The slight sting brought awareness to it.

The hand that patted his forearm drew his attention. The redhead gazed at him with sheer empathy.

"We will keep her safe. You go feed," she urged him. "It is what is best. When you return, you won't look at her like a starving man looks upon a perfectly prepared steak."

The sparkle in her eye unnerved Rori.

However, as much as he wanted to, he couldn't argue. He needed a clear head. In his state, he wouldn't be able to think rationally. He hadn't been this hungry in a long time. There was something about Divina, about being around her that took all his energy.

Rori put it out of his mind. He turned away from the redheaded witch without so much as a word. He stalked his way down the corridors and through the museum. He would get some blood. He would come back. He would continue his mission to become Emperor.

~

The pink and purple hued sky signified the end of a long day. The night would be upon them soon. Aric said his goodbyes to his pack mates/employees. Chuck and Ted were trusted to close up the work site.

Sex with Selene had washed away the previous night's questions. Aric chalked it up to the Jameson. He made a mental note not consume so much of it next time. He just needed to figure out exactly how much he had consumed.

As he pulled his pickup out of the yard, his phone vibrated on the seat beside him. He furrowed his brow as he read the message.

I took the liberty of giving myself your number.

Selene had entered herself into his phone. Aric wasn't sure how he felt about that. He responded. **Nothing stalker-ish about that at all.**

His wolf responded with unease, pacing within Aric. Something wasn't sitting right with him regarding this Selene.

I planned on coming back for seconds. Her quick and flirty text said.

Well, that got Aric's attention. His downstairs even twitched a bit. His wolf, on the other hand, wasn't as intrigued. If Aric didn't know better, his wolf was against the idea. Aric, though, couldn't resist the stroke to his ego.

No whiskey this time. Aric fired back a response despite his wolf's misgivings. The animal within him rarely was at odds with him regarding meeting such primal needs.

Does that go for me as well?

Aric snorted. She was funny. Why was his wolf acting so

weird? How often did a funny, sexy, willing woman show up naked in his bed?

Absolutely not. You can drink mine. He responded in defiance to his wolf.

The following text was just a location and a time. Aric smiled while shifting in his seat. His human side looked forward to meeting up with Selene again. He wished he knew how to get to the bottom of why his animal side was against it. It wasn't like the beast could talk.

Perhaps he would need some whiskey to quiet the animal. The disconnection of his wolf and his human sides regarding getting laid was out of character for his wolf. It ate at Aric. It was usually his wolf that was the driving force behind his pursuits of females.

As he pulled onto his land, he made it a point to leave a voicemail for a pack elder. They were good for this sort of thing. Bruce had been around a few hundred years or so; he'd seen a thing or two. If anyone knew about a wolf being at odds with his human regarding a female, it would be him. If not, Aric had no idea who else to ask.

CHAPTER 13

Having walked to the block behind the convent, Rori found a strip of bars bustling with tourists. The sound of carnival jazz boomed from the band on stage. The crowd of people, mostly humans, congregated toward the performers. It allowed for a brief reprieve between the stage and the bar.

The smell of colognes, alcohol, and sweat permeated Rori's nose. The bar was an ideal place for hunting. It was New Orleans. There wasn't a place in the world that was more supernatural friendly than New Orleans. For this reason, not all romance novels about witches and vampires set there were works of fiction.

Rori's gaze panned the crowd of mostly human patrons, the majority of which looked as though they were on vacation. Tourists tended to dress in bolder fashions, matching their indulgent attitudes. They tended to be freer, more risk-taking, and very accommodating. Tourists could sustain a vampire in any region.

While Rori's ideal meal was a holistic vegan who ate organic, he doubted he would find such a tasty morsel in a dimly lit and overcrowded bar. He had resigned himself to sampling several drunken co-eds and the second-hand buzz that would accompany such a late night snack.

That was until he spotted her.

Their eyes locked from across the bar. The tight, azure crop top left little to the imagination. Her long, flowing blond hair perfectly accentuated her heart-shaped face and was held back by a tie-dye scarf. The long, chunky earrings drew Rori's eyes to her neck.

His mouth watered at the sight of her; even more so when he saw the telltale sign of healed puncture marks. She was someone's pet, or had been. Someone had fed from her frequently enough to leave a mark.

The way she looked at him, gave him the impression she either wasn't someone's any more or it wasn't an exclusive sort of thing. That was okay with Rori. His fangs had already distended, and he had a hell of a time keeping his mouth closed to hide them.

Rori stalked through the crowd, eyes on his prey. He delighted in the fact that she returned his intensity. The heat between them was static through the air. To his surprise, Rori's groin seemed to be paying attention as well. Only one other female had elicited such a visceral reaction from him, and now he wasn't only curious about her taste but also her intentions.

Was she something more than a potential snack to him? He didn't recall the prophecy mentioning another woman. Perhaps the prophecy didn't know all.

He sidled up to her at the bar. Another gratuitous once-over had him swooning. The curvaceous woman was a treat for the eyes. The two drank in each other's appearance. Rori did his best to hide his fangs when he licked his lips.

"You are familiar," Rori said as he curled a lock of her hair around his finger.

The sensual smile grew on her painted lips. "You're thirsty."

"I am," Rori whispered bringing his mouth closer to her ear. "But this," Rori reached to stroke the puckered flesh. With his thumb poised to graze over the slightly raised bite marks, his remaining fingers collared her neck.

Rori jolted. He recoiled, stepping back from the female. The sharp shock from their touch was familiar. It was the same one he had felt when he touched Divina. How was that possible?

Her gaze remained intent upon him.

"You have permission," she crooned before stepping away from the bar curling her finger at him. "Come," she beckoned. "Not here."

Confused, Rori hesitated. He glanced down at his hand, expecting to see a burn. Nothing. His fingers were fine. He looked back at her, but she wasn't there.

Frantically, Rori scanned the crowds of people. He couldn't lose her. He had too many questions. It took a moment to spot her again.

Rori snaked through the crowd following her. Though she kept a few paces ahead of him, she never looked back to ensure he followed. Rather, she kept going until she reached the side exit, then she was out the door.

Rori found her in the alley. She had her back to the brick wall of the club. If he weren't so intrigued by the sensation, which still had him rubbing his fingers together, he would scoff at the cliché of a vampire intending to feed in an alley in the streets of New Orleans.

When he approached, he kept his distance from her. He didn't want another unpleasant experience. Her chin tucked down a bit so she could eye him from beneath her brow.

"You haven't lost your thirst have you?" she asked with a pout meant to entice him.

"What was that?" Rori demanded, sure she knew of what he spoke.

She chuckled in amusement. "That couldn't have been your first time."

Rori eyed her skeptically. "Who are you?" he asked.

"Selene," she said. She lifted her hands, so the palms were up, and gave him an innocent shrug.

Rori lifted his hand. He extended it, intent on gripping her arm, to jostle her. To show her that she shouldn't be fucking with him.

But, he didn't. In an exasperated cry, he lowered his hands. Unable to bring himself to make contact with her again, for fear of the shock, Rori snarled at himself and her.

"What was..." He paused, frustrated he couldn't find the right word. "That?" he repeated.

She canted her head, smile still there.

"When two fates cross paths, it can manifest itself in quite a sensation. Especially, if the two paths cross in a manner that is not intended," she said, as though he should have known that already.

Rori narrowed his eyes. "You're a fucking witch."

No one else spoke in riddles like that.

Once again, the innocent shrug. "Guilty as charged," she snickered playfully.

His gaze flicked to the marks on her throat. Not uncommon for witches to feed vampires. Their blood was laced with indescribable power. On a vampires tongue, the power was a unique flavor specific to the witch. Rori had fed from a few witches in his time. From the look of those marks, she was well sampled.

"Drink from me, Roricus," she urged extending her arm, wrist up.

Rori's eyes landed on her offered wrist, his fangs still

distended as though they had a will of their own. The blue veins called to him.

"That." Rori couldn't bring himself to label that feeling. It hurt. It burned. It felt as if electricity blazed through him. If she were to be believed, he felt that feeling with her and Divina, because it was wrong. He went against what was intended. What was intended for him and this witch? What was intended for her and his Divina?

He looked to Selene for answers like she could hear his thoughts.

She smiled at him, only moving to jut her wrist toward him again.

"Once the blood flows, it won't be as bad."

Rori salivated at the thought of witch blood. His willpower was at a hundred year low. He took her wrist in his hand and gritted his teeth as jolt went up to his arm. His entire body stiffened.

It took more strength than he thought he had to lower his head slightly, keeping his eyes on her. He struggled to position his mouth to meet the wide, blue vein on the inside of her forearm.

Selene whimpered, and her eyes rolled back into her head when his teeth pierced her skin. As he sucked in the spicy flavor that was Selene, the witch, the pulsing electricity raged on. He attempted to block it out while she moaned in the ecstasy of his bite.

Rori had dealt with quite a few familiars, or exclusive vampire food sources, who seemed to get off on being bitten. Though he had to admit, Selene was his first witch to experience such gratification from his bite. This woman was quite the enigma.

Between the pain from their touch and her moans, Rori's stomach rolled. It wasn't right. Something deep inside him told him it wasn't right. However, the taste of her blood made fireworks burst before his eyes. He couldn't stop drinking. Not yet.

When Rori could no longer handle the intensity of their touch, he broke free of her. He stumbled back panting with his hand going to his heart. The beating, a lazy thrum normally, became a violent rap in his chest.

What had she done to him? Questions swirled in his mind about the meaning of it and his connection to her. Could there be more to the prophecy that he had not yet been told?

Eyes wide, he looked at her. Had she just caused his heart to beat? No, that couldn't be right. Divina brought the rhythm back to his heart. Rori licked his lips to get the last bit of the woman's blood into his system.

Selene kept her body flat against the wall. She too breathed heavily as she looked at him. Despite her relative paleness from the feeding, her entire body was flushed, which surprised him, considering how much blood he had taken from her. He had taken enough to make her dizzy but not enough to cause her any serious medical concern.

"You are remarkable." Her eyes sparkled as she worked to catch her breath.

Rori's heart slowed slightly, and he lifted his chin. He told himself not to worry about the pace of his heart as it slowed. He wrote it off as the excitement of tasting a witch's blood. Plus, a witch's blood could sustain a vampire much longer than a pure human, something Rori had learned from Divina.

Rori swallowed the last of her flavor from his mouth. "How exactly are our fates entwined?"

She smirked. "I'm the witch of the prophecy."

"Bullshit," he scoffed.

"I brought a dead heart to life," she said smugly.

"How charming to think you had such an effect on me, but alas, someone beat you to that," Rori smirked confidently.

Her face fell. The amusement she found in him gone. "How self-absorbed to think you are the only one, Roricus Fromm."

At the sound of his full name, Rori straightened. Narrowing his eyes, which had the supernatural ability to see deftly in the low light of the moon, he fixated on the marks on her neck. Yes, she was familiar to someone, and perhaps that someone was the one who also possessed a beating heart in his or her chest.

"The prophecy is vague for a reason. But I assure you, I am the witch. We have found the wolf. We will take our seats on the council," she said before she stepped away.

Rori's eyes narrowed. "Perci," he whispered. Rori took a step to follow her.

Mischief danced along her features as she walked backward away from him. "The Ember Witches are playing against fate."

"What do you know——" Rori stopped himself. Any witch worth her salt would know the Ember Witches. Wrong question. "Are you an Ember Witch?"

"I will take my place at the table in time." Her fingers trailed along the dirty bricks of one of the walls in the alley.

Rori took another step in her direction.

She canted her head. "I wonder what they offered that you chose it over your destined mate."

Rori stopped dead in his tracks. "She was never meant to be mine," he said.

The witches had attempted to convince him of that. Though he seemed less and less sure of it the more he thought about it.

Selene looked up at the sky as though to consider what he said.

He hissed.

She scoffed. "Mmmm. Or was she?" she said slyly.

Rori didn't like her tone. He didn't like the way her brow arched. He didn't like the look on her face. He wasn't sure how much more of these witch games he could play. He wanted straight answers. The manipulation had to end.

Selene tapped the bricks before turning away from him. Rori took four steps to the end of the alley only to see that the sexy blond witch with all the secrets had mingled into the crowd.

Rori stood on the periphery of the New Orleans crowd with a sated hunger and a mind full of questions. The Ember Witches weren't truthful. He wasn't the only one with the beating heart. He wasn't the only one with a witch. The prophecy might not be about him after all.

His eyes scanned every human, desperate to find her. She was gone.

CHAPTER 14

The distant dripping sound exacerbated the heavy silence of the room. Even with Divina's mortal hearing, it sounded as if it thundered in the room. Not one of the Ember Witches spoke after Divina's demand of them.

Divina shifted on her feet. Had she made the wrong decision in confronting them? The longer they took to respond, the tighter her muscles became. Her teeth clenched in irritation.

They interfered with her life, her livelihood; the least they could do was be direct. Divina didn't have to stand there in a staring contest with a group of witches. With her jaw set, Divina stepped away from the chair to leave.

The scrape of a chair on the cement floor drew Divina's attention back to the center of the table, to the head witches of the Ember Witch Coven. Finally, Florence stood.

"Please." She gestured toward the chair beside Divina. "Sit. We have so much to share with you."

Divina looked at the chair with cynicism. A mere wooden chair, with a worn red velvet seat, seemed benign. She stretched a finger over the armrest. Nothing radiated from it.

There were no enchantments in the chair that Divina could to feel. However, she remained reluctant to sit in it. Distrust flittered through the air.

With a glance around the room to the many witches seated at the table, Divina found no reassurance from them. When she glanced behind her to the opening in the table, she sucked in a deep breath.

He had left her.

Her hand fell from the chair. She backed away from it. She walked toward the end of the horseshoe.

"Please, don't leave." The voice of one of the witches, one Divina hadn't been introduced to, seemed distant when it spoke.

Divina stopped at the opening of the table. She looked over her shoulder at the center witch, Esmine.

"Where did Rori go?" she asked.

A small voice within Divina whispered that the witches knew where he was. Darting her eyes around she pondered the cause of his departure. The witches could have sent him away; they could have wanted to get her alone for some reason. Distrust in the witches ticked higher than before, causing the tension in her body to increase.

Something about the lack of Rori's presence caused Divina's stomach to churn with unease. In a matter of twenty-four hours, he had gone from being her ex-boyfriend, whom she never wished to see again, to her security blanket. She felt vulnerable, exposed, and unsure of the women surrounding her.

Esmine sat forward in her chair. She clasped her hands before her on the table and looked past Divina to the spot where Rori had once stood. She frowned. Perhaps she hadn't realized he had left either.

A throat cleared. It drew Divina's attention. It drew all

the witches' attention. A young, red-headed witch, at the last seat of the table, stood.

"He was famished. I suggested he go feed," she said.

She held her chin high and used a bold voice. She announced this to the group with an air of superiority.

Divina turned to Esmine as if to get confirmation of the truth in the young witch's words.

With tight lips and narrowed eyes, Esmine looked rather threatening. Her cold expression triggered a red alert within Divina. Something wasn't right with this coven. Something wasn't right with all of this.

"No harm will come to you, Divina," Esmine said. "Please, have a seat."

The lack of politeness in Esmine's voice indicated a lack of hospitality in the gesture. The offer of a seat wasn't a suggestion. Esmine had ordered Divina to sit, and the expectation was clear that Divina would obey.

Divina surveyed the room one more time before she took the offered seat. The most powerful witches in her country surrounded Divina. If they had wanted to do anything to her, they would have done it by now.

"The Ember Witches never invite one of their own to the table," Esmine explained. "An Ember Witch finds her way to the table."

"You don't count sending Rori to me multiple times inviting me to the table?" Divina said in defiance

Divina sat back, folded her arms, and crossed her legs. Just because the witches intimidated her, it didn't mean she had to show it.

"Roricus is following his path, which led him to you," Jessa replied with a flat expression. Her vacant eyes stared ahead as if the woman had no emotion to her at all.

"We didn't send him to you. We merely initiated his journey," she added.

"I'm the beginning of his journey?" Divina repeated skeptically.

"Yes," Jessa responded quickly.

"What does that even mean?" Divina shifted her gaze, and thus her question, to any witch within her eye line. "What journey? To where?"

Florence answered when it seemed no one else would step up to the plate. "Fate is a funny thing." Florence glanced at Esmine when she paused. Esmine nodded as if permitting Florence to proceed. Licking her lips, Florence continued, "It's not always what it appears to be, and it's not that seers get things wrong so much as the visions aren't interpreted the right way."

Divina lifted a brow. She had a hard time following, but she figured if she kept silent, they'd keep talking. She'd eventually figure it out.

"You're the witch meant to quicken Roricus' heart once more," Florence responded hopefully.

"But, you aren't meant to remain his mate throughout his life, as is a common belief," Esmine chimed in informatively.

Divina furrowed her brow. "Quicken his heart?"

"Once Roricus drank from you, his heart resumed its rhythm," Jessa explained. "It's a phenomenon that only occurs when a vampire meets his mate. It's extremely rare. It's required for a vampire seat on the council."

Falling back, as if slapped in the face, Divina slumped in her chair. She brought a dead heart to life, Rori's dead heart. That made her Rori's... mate? She couldn't wrap her brain around what all that meant. If it meant anything at all, it was moot. Rori had left her and told her she needed to find a wolf all because of some stupid prophecy and the vampire council thing. Everything boiled down to vampire politics.

Divina shook her head. She looked at the floor and sucked

her lips in so that she could bite down on them. Trying to process what they had said, she sighed.

"So this is all about the council?" she asked in resignation.

"No," Esmine answered. "It's much deeper than that. The prophecy begins with the vampire whose heart beats for the witch." She smiled. "You gave that to Roricus. He is the chosen vampire for the council."

"So I'm just some tool for vampire politics? For the council?" Divina probed.

Her eye twitched as the picture became clear to her. She dug her nails into the arms of the chair. Manipulation and deception were the trademarks of vampires. No other species mattered, unless they could benefit the vampire agenda. Divina's jaw tightened as the thoughts paraded through her mind.

"No," Florence's empathetic response radiated from her. "When you gave Roricus back the beat of his heart, you initiated your own future." The smile on her face lit up the room. She seemed delighted to inform Divina of this hopeful news. "You get to find the one who belongs to you. You will find the wolf your heart chose. You will find your place at the table," Florence said.

A loud groan came from behind Divina. Florence's face fell. It twisted into a mask of annoyance.

Divina stood and turned to see who made the sound.

The redhead was on her feet. "She is one of our own. We need to be honest with her," she said.

"Silence!" Esmine bellowed. "This is not your place, Ines."

"She is a sister," Ines, implored. "We shouldn't be manipulating our own."

"That is not your place to say. The coven agreed." Esmine's firm tone matched the tightness in her face.

"I won't sit idly by while you deceive this woman." Ines

came around the table and entered the center. She turned her attention toward Divina.

Divina regarded her with wariness. Ines reached for Divina's hands, but Divina pulled away. She didn't trust the woman. She had convinced Rori to abandon Divina and leave her unprotected with the witches.

"What they aren't telling you is that you and Roricus are not the only ones." She spoke quickly as the murmurs around them grew loud. "The prophecy is vague. The visions aren't clear."

Out of the corner of Divina's eye, she caught movement. Esmine's wrist flicked, and her lips moved as she spoke a silent incantation. The chair Divina had once sat upon shook before it lifted; floating as if hung on strings.

With a gasp, Divina stepped back in shock. Ines caught her attention and mirrored Divina's expression.

"The only constant is the wolf," Ines shouted. She turned toward Esmine. "You are tampering with fate! You can't do that!" She pointed an accusatory finger toward Esmine.

"Silence!" Esmine boomed in a thunderous tone that echoed off the walls of the subbasement.

Divina shook, and she stepped back.

Ines quieted, yet kept narrowed eyes on the leader of the Ember Witches.

Esmine stood with fire in her eyes, glaring daggers at Ines.

A part of Divina wanted to protect her from the wrath of the head witch. However, Divina felt frozen in place by fear. She couldn't lift her feet, as much as she wanted to at that moment.

"You speak out against your sisters. You speak against your coven," Esmine declared as she stepped up onto her chair. "You have broken your oath." She rose to stand on the table. "There will be consequences, Ines." The malice in Esmine's expression matched her voice.

Divina had heard and seen enough. With one last sympathetic look toward Ines, who was focused on Esmine glowering at her from atop the table, Divina turned and ran.

She didn't look back. She needed to get out of there. She needed to find Rori.

No one followed her. No one chased her. Yet, she continued to run. She pumped her legs with all her strength. The sound of her sneakers thudding on the marble floor thundered in her ears as she traveled through the dark museum.

Divina looked back one final time before she slowed down. She'd made it to the lobby. The exit was in sight. Escape was imminent, and no one chased her.

Maintaining a slight jog, Divina wasn't prepared for the convent's front door to swing open. She gasped. Without thinking, her arm cocked back. Her fingers curled into a fist.

Whoever was beyond that door stood between her and escape. Fight or flight took hold, and apparently, Divina chose fight.

The thud and slight squish of a fist hitting a face weren't as satisfying or dramatic as they made it sound on TV. The pain that radiated up Divina's wrist into her arm was unexpected. She shook her hand to alleviate the sting.

"Owww!" Divina's victim cried out.

Her eyes adjusted to the darkness until she could see the man in the shadows.

"Rori!" she gasped in relief.

Divina shot toward the man holding his cheek. She took his free hand and tried to yank him out of the convent.

"We have to go," she said in a panic.

"Go?" Rori repeated, allowing her to drag him away. "Where?"

"I don't know, not here." Divina marched through the

hedged maze still glancing over her shoulder, expecting to see someone chase her.

Rori's confused expression and reddened cheek filled Divina's vision. He too looked back, as though the answers were behind them. No one was there; nothing was there.

Divina shoved Rori into the cab of her tuck. She ran around to the driver's side trying to think of where to go. The witches would look for her vardo. It wasn't exactly inconspicuous.

Jumping into the cab, she jammed the key into the ignition. With the purr of the engine, she threw it into gear and barreled down the road. She had no clear destination but needed to get away from the witches and clear her mind.

R ori's cheek throbbed. She punched him. He went to check on her, to bring her back to her vardo, to make sure she was safe, and she fucking punched him in the face.

The sharp turn she took flung him against the side of the truck. She also drove like a mad woman.

"What's going on?" he asked clinging to the handle above the door for dear life.

He looked back. Nothing chased them. What had gotten into her?

"We can't trust them," Divina said.

Her frenzied eyes darted back and forth over the dark, and thankfully empty, road.

Rori studied her. He didn't think he'd ever seen her spooked. What had happened in there?

"The Ember Witches?" he asked regarding the "them" she had mentioned. "They're to be your coven. It may not seem like it now, but they're the only ones we can trust."

She shook her head.

"No," she countered, "they're manipulating you. They want to manipulate me."

Of course, they were, Rori thought. That's what the Ember Witches did. He wouldn't verbalize those thoughts. She didn't seem to be in a place where she'd understand them. Divina needed to use them to grow into her power as much as they needed to use her.

As she took another hard turn, Rori reached for the dashboard. The first hints of sunrays felt like lasers pointed directly at him. Clenching his teeth as his exposed skin turned to bubbled blisters he tried to cover his flesh as best he could, tugging down his rolled up sleeves.

"It's dawn," he hissed.

Rori already felt the deep coma-like vampiric sleep creeping into his senses.

"I just need time to think. I just need—" Divina cut herself off as she slammed on the breaks for a stop light.

Rori jerked forward, almost hitting his forehead into the windshield.

"Jesus!" Rori hissed before taking a deep breath. "There's a vampire-run hotel three blocks away."

Rori pointed in a direction, but his arm wobbled as blisters oozed under his shirt, forming wet spots. He hoped it was the direction of the hotel. He blinked a few times trying to force his eyes open, but his vision blurred.

He switched tactics, not trusting his abilities with the sun cresting. Trying to focus on his phone, Rori punched in the address. It took about four tries before he got it right. When the vampire sleep wanted to take over, there was little he could do to fight it. Even on witch blood, his body was about to shut down for the day.

Divina glanced at him, and concern lines wrinkled her face. She snatched the phone.

"Okay." She nodded.

Rori drifted in and out of awareness as they drove. Pain waking him repeatedly as he curled himself into a ball trying to protect himself. Divina had to hold him up while they checked in. Thankfully, the vampire night-shift was still on. They understood what Rori needed. The last thing Rori remembered was the flop of his head onto a pillow. He was out.

CHAPTER 15

The unanswered voicemail left for Bruce weighed heavy on Aric's mind. He wanted to discuss the discord between his wolf and his human before he went out. In his fifty-four years, a blip in the extended lifespan of a shifter, he had never been at such odds with his inner beast. He wanted to understand how one half of him could be so against something while the other half was so eager.

However, for the sake of research—or so Aric told himself—he went to the address Selene had texted to him. He needed more data to present a clearer picture to Bruce. He needed to understand his wolf's response to Selene fully. The only way to do that was to see her again.

Aric arrived early; the tavern bustled with business. The blond had selected a local bar not frequented by many tourists. Street signs adorned the walls alongside taxidermy animals. The dark-stained oak bar was older than Aric. The whole place had a relaxed vibe, despite its popularity with locals. Possibly due to the cheap drink specials, the access to locally brewed beers, and the fact that it lacked the over-the-top fanfare typical of the other bars in the area.

He found a seat at the bar and ordered a local craft beer. No whiskey. He figured he could nurse one beer through the night and be social. He didn't want a repeat of the Jameson evening. A clear mind when conducting research was a must.

It still perplexed him. Aric had drunk Jameson for much of his adult life. He couldn't remember the last time he blacked out because of it. He couldn't remember the last time he forgot his limit. It didn't fit. The explanation of the previous night didn't sit right with him. It didn't make sense. Besides, who went on a date without at least one drink anyway? Wait. Was it a date? Had he agreed to meet up with the female as a date? Hmm. He hadn't thought of it. He snorted at his backward nature. The woman was in his trailer, naked in his bed with his cock balls deep in her before he even bought her dinner. It wasn't how Aric typically did things. He wasn't sure if he was the luckiest wolf on the planet or if something was wrong. His instincts told him something was fishy. Not to mention his wolf's reaction. It wasn't the socially acceptable order of things. Perhaps that's what got his wolf all twisted. His wolf preferred routine as a creature of habit. Aric was as much human as he was wolf after all.

He sipped the beer watching the door. Maybe he put too much stock in his wolf and needed to live a little, be human.

At exactly the time she said, Selene entered the bar. The scent of jasmine tickled his nose over the smell of alcohol and bad cologne. Aric's back straightened as he watched her scan the patrons with disinterest.

When their eyes met, her lips grew into a smile. Warmth spread into her features and his as well before his wolf swiped at him, letting his disapproval of the female be known.

Selene's approach appeared well practiced. She moved smoothly through the crowd. Somehow, she managed to keep her eyes on Aric while navigating the scene of drunks. Not once did she appear off-balance. Rather she strode through the room as if she owned the place, as though the sea of people parted just for her.

Aric nodded in approval while placing his beer down on the bar. The woman was something else. What was his wolf's problem with her? Aric slid from the stool and offered it to her. She lowered her gaze submissively before stepping up to the seat.

That subtle gesture stoked Aric's desire. His wolf should have been right there with him. Females who demonstrated hints of submission were what his wolf craved. The nonverbal acknowledgments of his dominance were what caught his wolf's attention every time with every other female. Not this one. Something about this one was different. She had his wolf tied up in knots. The beast within Aric snapped when she got close to him.

Another piece of data to discuss with Bruce.

Aric lowered his face to meet hers. He pressed his lips against her soft, silken mouth. Shock waves shot through him via their joined lips.

He yelped and sprung back holding a hand to his mouth eying her questioningly. That was different, yet familiar at the same time. Déjà vu swept over Aric.

"Dammit," she muttered.

If he were human, he would never have heard that.

"Ursitoare, Îți cer orbirea," she whispered hurriedly with a quick wave of her hand and a speedy wiggle of her fingers.

He lifted his brow. A witch. She cast a spell. His wolf was right. There was something different about this female. More data for Bruce and something to investigate. Why was she casting spells? Regarding her curiously, he got the suspicion she knew he was wolf and that she had wanted him to hear the spell. The sly smile on her face pointed to hidden motive which unsettled Aric and his wolf.

She swallowed meeting his gaze. "I must have some sort of static thing; I'm so sorry," she lied, and her fingers grazed her lips. "Can we try again?" she asked tilting her head.

The wolf within in him bristled at the idea of another kiss.

Though Aric had to hand it to her, the female was good. Selene laid the innocence on real thick.

He agreed with his wolf now. The female was shady. There was a reason he didn't remember how she came to be naked in his bed. Aric knew it had nothing to do with Jameson.

He did, however, bend down to offer her a quick peck on the lips. He did his best not to break the façade of her fooling him. To find out exactly what game this little witch played, he'd need to play along.

Aric took a long pull from the craft beer. No need to drink light tonight. It wasn't his alcohol tolerance that had failed him. No, it was some witchiness that had tampered with his memory.

Selene arched a perfectly shaped brow. "Thought you were abstaining?" She pointed toward his pint glass.

Aric turned his attention toward the glass and grinned.

"We're in a bar. It would be socially unacceptable to drink water. I think I can handle one." He winked playfully.

She laughed. "It was only *one* bottle of Jameson that did you in."

Aric closed the distance between them. He pressed his legs to hers, forcing them open, to accommodate his left thigh. He towered over her, even seated on the bar stool. Looking down at her, as a wolf would his prey, he sniffed her hair. Rot intertwined with jasmine. Why did she smell of rot?

"Is that a challenge?" His voice rumbled with the offensive growl of his wolf.

He hoped she would miss the aggressive and agitated nature of his voice masked by the music and the conversation around them. Hell, she was pretty much a human. Surely, she wouldn't be able to pick up the different nuances of a wolf growl.

Selene licked her bottom lip seductively. Aric lowered his head and nipped at the glossy, plump flesh. She tasted like sweetened chemicals.

"I'd never challenge you," she shuddered.

Had the words been said by any other female, it would have driven his wolf into a frenzy. However, this witch played games. Aric could play games too.

The faint scent of her arousal drifted up to his nose.

His human response was to enjoy it, and his pants tightened slightly around the crotch.

His wolf paced restlessly within him. This time, the seductress wouldn't sway Aric so easily.

"Good," he whispered in a feral timber in her ear.

His smug grin and lifted brows were meant to play into her seductive game. He could be seductive too. Aric remained over her for longer than would be comfortable for most humans.

She squirmed at his dominant posture. She even leaned into him slightly. Her hardened nipples were visible through her tight crop top.

He smiled down at her, breaking the bubble of dominance over her.

He turned to drink the beer and stepped back from her. His body shifted, faced the bar, but he kept her in his peripheral. Aric lifted his hand and summoned the bartender. When the human came toward Aric, he ordered.

"Jameson, for the lady," he said, giving her a sideways glance.

She bit her lower lip, attempting to hide a grin. However, it escaped, and a blush accompanied it. The pink hue crept up her chest and filled her cheeks.

Aric returned the sentiment with a devilish smile of his own. He may not have any magical powers, but Aric knew that witches were the closest thing to humans in the supernatural world. It was safe to bet that if he got a witch drunk enough, she might get a little less inhibited. It wasn't that Aric wanted to take advantage of her in that way. Hell, he was pretty sure Selene would get down with him in the bathroom if he offered. However, he just wanted to lower that filter of hers. He'd ask her some leading questions about how she found him and what she wanted from him. Most of all, Aric wanted to know what the fuck happened the night before and why he couldn't remember.

When the shot arrived, Aric took it and handed it to Selene. He held up one finger to signal she should wait before drinking it. Laying a fifty on the bar, he winked at the man behind it.

"Keep 'em coming," he said.

The man nodded after Selene chuckled.

Aric then raised his pint of wheat beer. She nodded and did in kind with the small shot of Jameson.

"What are we toasting?" she asked rather jovially.

"To John Jameson!" Aric declared. "May the Irish bastard bless us tonight."

She laughed. Aric drank from his pint. Selene threw back her head, and the brown liquid disappeared.

Aric's wolf settled. He was by no means calm. The animal understood the human's plan. So the wolf watched and paced. The wolf studied. The wolf would be patient.

The predator had his prey in his sights. Now all he had to do was pick his moment. He was in no rush. He'd play the game. He'd allow the witch to think she was in charge.

CHAPTER 16

F ive shots later, the stumbling blond wrapped her arm around Aric's waist. He walked slowly, holding her up, while she laughed and persisted in the claims that she was fine. He led her out of the bar and toward his truck.

They entered the night and the not-so-full parking lot arm-in-arm. The smell of autumn leaves filled Aric's nose. The cool fall air tickled his skin.

Had he gone overboard? Perhaps he should have slowed her down. Pangs of guilt hit him. His wolf balked at the idea he would feel remorseful. However, Aric's human half wasn't in agreement. It seemed to be a recurring theme with him and his wolf when the female witch was around.

Aric helped Selene into the cab of his truck while she sang a song he had never heard. She talked about some bar she went to over the summer and how they made organic alcohol. He only half paid attention.

She'd dropped her filter all right. However, what came from her was useless to Aric. She talked so much; he couldn't even ask her a question because of the nonsense that spilled from her lips. Instead, she droned on and on about drivel he couldn't even follow half the time.

He closed her door and walked around the front of his truck. His wolf's hackles went up, and Aric turned. With his enhanced vision, he scanned the parking lot. With the bar nearing closing time, cars dotted the spaces, leaving intermittent vacancies.

A shoe scuffed the pavement. Arc turned toward the sound. Fabric rustled to his right. Aric shifted his gaze in that direction. He sniffed.

Rot, more potent than the lingering scent of rot that hung on Selene. Without a doubt, it was the source of the scent on Selene, and it was a vampire.

The figure strolled into the light of a street lamp. The rotting stench belonged to a man who wore a dark suit and matching vest, with black hair combed in a deep part. He approached them with a calm and even stride. The odd déjà vu feeling returned as more of the man's scent wafted toward Aric. He'd smelled him before but couldn't place where.

When the vampire stopped, he kept himself out of Aric's reach.

Aric squared his shoulders. He ran his tongue along his bottom teeth; he bent his knees slightly. His arms assumed a position indicating he was ready to pounce if needed.

He wasn't a fan of the bloodsuckers. They were slimy, manipulative bastards. And what this one had to do with the witch in Aric's truck cab didn't sit right with Aric or his wolf.

"I believe you have something of mine," the vampire said with aristocratic undertones. "Now, be a good boy, and fetch it for me." Condescension dripped from the words.

Aric's eye twitched, and he snarled. His teeth clenched and his wolf pushed against his inner core in an attempt to burst through Aric's skin. His nostrils flared. The vampire scent only further agitated his wolf.

"Come now." The vampire remained back, never advancing.

His words continued to taunt and belittle Aric.

"I let you play with my pet once, I thought that was quite generous." The smirk on the vampire's face irritated Aric.

Briefly, Aric looked over his shoulder at the cab of his truck. Only the top of Selene's blond head was visible. It rested on the dashboard of his truck, she must have slumped forward once he propped her inside. Definitely too much whiskey. Aric's gaze flicked back at the vampire. The rumbled growl from within his chest was his only response.

The vampire's eyebrows lifted. "Intriguing." The smile grew on the vampire's smug face. "Is that a hint of possessiveness I see?" he asked hopefully.

"Fuck off," Aric barked.

The vampire chuckled, a bit too gleefully for Aric's liking.

Aric thrust himself forward half a step. His arms jerked toward the vampire in a faux attempt to strike. The vampire hissed and took a step back.

Vampires were inherently weaker than wolves, regardless of age. A wolf bite was a death sentence for a vampire. Something in the wolf saliva reacted horribly with the blood in a vampire's body. So, the instinct of a vampire was to avoid an attacking wolf.

"Whoah." The vampire jumped back. He held up his hands, palms toward Aric.

Careful not to meet the vampire's gaze, Aric focused on his chest. Vampires could hypnotize their victims. Aric wasn't clear on how effective it was on wolves as opposed to humans, but he also didn't feel this was the time to find out.

"I only ask because the prophecy is set in motion," the vampire offered rather smugly.

"Fuck you and your prophecy," Aric spat.

"It's not just my prophecy. It's your prophecy. It's her prophecy." He gestured to the sleeping Selene in the truck.

The arrogance with which the vampire spoke made Aric's jaw tighten. He threw his head back and let out a deep, roar-like growl. Aric's wolf was desperate to spring forward and pounce the vampire.

"Rein it in," the vampire hissed as he stepped closer to Aric.

Aric's teeth clenched. He tilted his head. He tried to keep his canines from extending. His breaths came in shallow quick bursts. He vibrated with the restraint it took to keep his wolf within himself.

"There are humans all over the bloody place," the vampire chastised in a whisper.

The golden flicker in Aric's eyes signaled the wolf's closeness to the surface.

"Perci!" The delighted squeal caught Aric off guard.

He spun, seeing Selene had woken. With the swing of the door, as if made of liquid, Selene spilled out of the truck cab.

With two men possessing preternatural speed, it turned into a foot race as to who would save her from colliding with the pavement. Though Aric, a hair faster than Perci, arrived first, as he crouched to catch Selene midfall, he was knocked off balance by Perci. Having been shoved out of the way, it was Perci who caught the drunken witch.

The witch landed in Perci's arms. He cradled her against his chest. The vampire murmured something while his fingers stroked her hair. Whatever it was, even Aric's preternatural hearing couldn't pick it up.

Aric straightened himself.

Selene snuggled up to the vampire.

Aric's cheek twitched, and his hand thrust forward. His fingers clamped onto Perci's shoulder. He squeezed. Aric tugged back and spun the vampire to face him.

Selene effectively dropped out of his lap. With wide eyes, she gaped at him from the ground. In her drunken state, delayed reaction time, and Aric's enhanced speed, she wouldn't have the ability to react effectively.

Aric used his other hand to press his palm into Perci's throat. Curling his fingers around the jugular, he pressed his thumb on one side and squeezed with the rest of his hand. The delightful gurgle of the vampire choking caused Aric to grin.

He lifted Perci up to his feet and a little bit beyond. The vampire's cool hands pulled at Aric's much thicker and wider one. Perci's legs danced slightly, trying to keep contact with the ground. Aric and his wolf reveled in the display of dominance over Perci.

"Stop!" Selene scrambled to her feet, and tried to get between the two males. "Put him down! Let him go!"

Aric shifted his attention to Selene and snarled.

She continued to pull his arm.

Aric turned his gaze to Perci's forehead. He would not make direct eye contact.

"What the fuck did you two do to me?" he demanded.

"Nothing," Selene whined.

She turned her wide, pleading eyes to Aric. Her bottom lip protruded and quivered in a pout.

Aric growled closer to Perci to make it clear she wouldn't manipulate him. Aric brought his face within inches. He released his grip slightly if only to allow the vampire full use of his vocal chords.

"Try again," Aric rumbled.

Perci coughed. "I took your memory," he admitted in a rasp.

Aric tightened his hold again.

Perci choked. His throat crunched beneath Aric's fingers. Perci's eyes widened. He resumed clawing at Aric's hand.

"Our first meeting didn't go so well," Selene wailed and kicked Aric's legs; she hung from his bicep—none of which phased Aric in his state of complete fury.

"So you took it away?" Aric asked through clenched teeth.

"He had to." Selene resumed her plea.

Aric once more loosened his grip enough for the vampire to speak.

"I can't plant suggestions on you like I can with humans. Wolf's brains heal too quickly. I can only take small memories away," Perci choked out in a gravel voice

The damage to Perci's vocal chords impacted his voice. Aric took satisfaction in that. His wolf howled within him for more.

Aric released Perci who crumpled like a cheap suit. Perci held his throat while coughing. Selene bent to his side, rubbing his back and intermittently glared up at Aric.

Aric stepped back and folded his arms over his chest.

"Why?" he demanded.

"The prophecy," Perci said between breaths. "You're the key." His voice lost some of its rasp, indicating recovery of the damage Aric had caused.

"I don't give a flying rat's ass about any vampire prophecy," Aric barked.

He turned to walk toward his truck. He had gotten his answers.

"It's not *just* a vampire prophecy," Selene's voice called to him.

Aric yanked the door of his truck open. He stepped up to get into the cab. Before he ducked in, Aric addressed the two on the ground.

"You two come on my territory again, I'll rip both your throats out," he threatened with narrowed golden wolf eyes.

He had enough data. The night had thoroughly pissed him off. The two were on some asinine quest and foolishly tried to include Aric in it. Well, they had better find another wolf. As far as Aric was concerned, he'd rather die than help a vampire.

CHAPTER 17

Warmth. Delightful heat radiated from beside Rori. He didn't want to open his eyes and end the dream. Happiness flowed through him in a wave.

As he crept closer to consciousness, the source became clear. The warmth came from a body pressed against his. The soft body had familiar feminine curves.

He curled his leg over the shapely hip. Squeezing her in his arms, he pulled her against him and buried his nose in her neck.

"Divina," he whispered, before pressing his lips to the soft skin of her neck.

She rewarded him with a groan and thrust her rear into his crotch. She remained asleep as they embraced in the soft, comfortable hotel bed.

Rori took another deep inhale of her before increasing the pressure of his kisses. His hand slid up from her waist, under the thin shirt she wore, and found the swell of her beautiful breast. A sleepy, yet erotic sigh escaped her lips as he palmed her bare flesh.

Having her against him with her scent surrounding him,

took Rori back to happier times. The memories elicited his body's response to her touch, to her presence. His erection swelled the more she pressed back into him. It felt incredibly right. She had always felt right. His tongue trailed against the thick cord of vein in her neck, which pulsed and tempted him.

The memory of her blood on his tongue had him salivating. He fell deeper into lustful desire for his Divina.

Rori couldn't risk it. He hadn't had her in such a long time; if he drank from her, he wouldn't stop. Instead, he turned his attention to her ear. He exhaled slowly and flicked his tongue along the bottom lobe. He sucked the flesh into his mouth.

"Rori," she gasped groggily.

"Good evening," he whispered in her ear in his best Dracula impression.

"What are you doing?" she asked breathlessly.

Rori's fingers found her tight, erect nipple. He brought his digits together around it offering a gentle tug.

"Do you want me to stop?" he asked.

Divina groaned and attempted to roll into him. Rori allowed it. His eyesight was uncanny at night; a true hunter's night vision. She looked radiant in the moonlight, practically glowing beside him.

He couldn't resist. His hand squeezed Divina's breast while he brought his mouth down over hers. His tongue swirled around, seeking its old dance partner. He covered her with his body.

She welcomed his kiss and responded with a moan.

With further urging, Rori positioned himself between her thighs. Using his legs to part hers, he nestled his pelvis against her sex. Panties and his jeans were the only barriers between them.

Her hands slid up and down his back, and tugged at the

hem of his shirt. He broke the kiss long enough for the two of them to take a lungful of air and for her to remove his shirt. Even that short reprieve left Rori hungry and desperate for more.

Rori devoured Divina's mouth like a starving man. He nipped at her bottom lip. His extended canines grazed along the soft, plump, flesh. She shuddered beneath him.

He pulled her shirt up and used both his hands to massage her breasts. He teased her nipples with plucks and pinches. Each gesture rewarded him with either a muffled moan or an upward thrust of her hips.

Divina's nails raked down his back causing him to arch. Once more their kiss was broken, both of them panting with need. He tugged the shirt Divina wore over her head and threw it aside. He took a single moment to drink in her beauty.

His cognac-colored gaze raked over her flawless, tanned skin. The swell of her full breasts peaked with tight nipples, begging for his mouth. She was a goddess laid out for him to enjoy.

Rori shimmied down her body so he could lave affections over her chest. He kissed his way across her collarbone and down over one breast and then the other. How he had missed the saltiness of her skin. She had a musky flavor all her own. No one tasted the way Divina did, and it was all he could do not to bite and taste her truly.

His tongue flicked against one nipple while a hand grazed the other. Divina ran her fingers through his hair. She curled her leg, and he felt her heel in his back. The smell of Divina's need for him wafted up her body, enough of a distraction to get his mind off her blood.

Previously, he had marked every inch of her skin with bites. He claimed her each time he fed from her. Anyone who had seen her body knew she was his.

Time had passed. His bites had healed. Not a mark graced her perfect skin. The urge to mark her again, to bite her, to feed from her burned within him.

Rori resisted and trailed his tongue down her belly. He twirled it in her belly button only to hear the impatient, forced, laugh of a tickled, aroused woman. Divina reached back above her head and grabbed for the headboard.

Pushing her legs wider still, Rori positioned his face at the apex of her thighs. He looked up from this position to see her flush. Her dilated pupils accentuated the wanton expression on her face.

He grinned, there was his Divina. The raw, feral Divina he had made love to more times than he could count.

He lowered his mouth and ran his tongue slowly from the bottom of her slit toward the top. With his palms under her thighs, he felt her muscles tighten. Rori resumed stroking her outer lips with his tongue. She whined and rolled her hips. He smiled while he teased her hot sex with his tongue a bit longer.

Eventually, he gave in to her urgings; her moans were persuasive, and Rori pushed his tongue deeper into her sex. The exotic tang, specific to Divina, was his reward while he lapped at her satiny slick, and delightfully-ready-for-anything-he-wanted pussy.

All Rori wanted was to savor her. So, he took his time. He slowly explored the sensitive folds. He paid attention to each little twitch and squirm his tongue elicited from her. When the nubbin of nerves slipped from its hood, Rori gave it his full attention.

He pressed his lips against her clit offering sweet kisses before using his tongue for pressure. Divina cried out, and her legs shook. Good, he had remembered what pleased her. To tease, he flattened his tongue and gave her soft strokes, and she whimpered. He wanted to prolong her pleasure and his ability to give it to her.

Divina's arousal saturated Rori's chin. He slid two of his fingers into her waiting opening. Divina gasped and arched her back. Rori pulled his mouth away. He sat back on his heels between her legs and watched her in all her splendor.

With her feet planted on the bed, her knees spread wide on either side of Rori, she bucked into his hand. Her breasts bounced. Her head twisted left and right. The sounds she made were feral. Her muscles tightened, and she squealed with his fingers buried deep inside her. She took his breath away.

She was a glorious sight when she embraced her hedonistic desires. Using his thumb, Rori circled her clit and thrust his fingers in and out of her slowly. He debated the idea of pushing her to the edge and pulling back.

Divina fisted at the sheets and writhed when Rori curled his fingers within her. There it was; the other sensitive spot that drove her mad. Her pussy clamped around his fingers while he slowly worked them in and out.

Rori's free hand massaged her thigh. He briefly glanced down at his stiff, aching erection trapped behind his pants and pressing against his belly. The smell of her arousal, the moans she gave him, and the way her body reacted to him was enough to have his cock swollen and purple.

Releasing her thigh, Rori used one hand to undo the button of his jeans and drag the zipper down. Trying to focus on two tasks at once, be attentive to his lover, and free himself of his pants, was difficult, but he had a mission. Pushing down his pants and wiggling his hips it took some doing, but soon this pelvis was free, with his jeans just below the crease of his ass, it was all he needed.

Divina's legs stiffened and her walls clenched.

Rori withdrew his fingers and slid his body over hers. He

plunged his cock into the hot opening of her sex. Her walls rippled around his shaft when he entered her, and he let out a gasp of pleasure.

Rori placed his hands on either side of her shoulders and thrust hard into Divina. He watched her bounce back onto the bed. He pulled out slowly before thrusting deeper. Each time he did, her pussy trembled around him.

She whined and clawed at his chest.

"More, more, more," she begged.

More indeed. Rori intended to give her a lot more. Though, he didn't want to rush it. He wasn't sure if he would ever have the opportunity again. He needed to relish the feel of her around him.

He picked up the pace slightly. He lowered his head and took her mouth.

He took possession of the kiss with the passion of a dying man. His tongue swept over her lips, coaxing her to open for him. When she did, he rewarded her with a succession of quick, deep, pumps into her. It was all she needed.

Divina exploded around him. Her walls gripped him as a vice, and Rori could barely move. He buried his cock up against her womb and lowered his full weight on her.

She shook beneath him while her walls pulsed around him in an attempt to milk his climax from him. He held her tight and moved his hips deliberately slow. The angle that he entered her was one to stimulate her G-spot.

She clung to him for life. He waited for her to resume breathing before he pulled back and drove into her.

Rori pulled his body upward, resting on his knees, and reached for one of her legs. He tucked her leg over his shoulder. It changed the angle once more. The friction of her soaked pussy against his cock almost had him there.

With gritted teeth, Rori let out a feral roar. His cock pistoned in and out.

Divina shook her head left and right. Her cries were a toss between painful whimpers and moans of ecstasy.

He needed her. Rori needed to have her. His vision tinted red. The savage need to have her blood took over.

Rori's fangs distended. His balls tightened. Just as his body tensed, he dropped her leg and lowered his head. Divina turned her face away once more, and Rori saw it. He saw her vein.

He couldn't stop himself. As his orgasm rocked through him, Rori sank his teeth into Divina. Rori plunged against the opening of her womb and came. He sucked, and her blood spilled onto his lips while his seed spilled into her body.

Jolt after jolt. Rori closed his eyes and euphoria hit him. Pure joy. Pure pleasure. All of it rolled over his body until he collapsed, gasping for breath atop Divina. He was vaguely aware of her ragged breathing. He tucked his head beside hers. The blood dripping from the bite smeared along his cheek but he didn't care.

He wrapped his arms around her and pulled her against him. He ran his tongue over the sharp receding fang enough to split it. Rori licked at the puncture wounds on Divina's neck. Blood pulsed from the wound, a good sign he hadn't taken too much. Slowly, with his licking, and mixing his blood with hers, the wound closed. Rori nuzzled against her and held her against him. His Divina; his. Even if he couldn't have her forever, he could have this moment with her. Nothing could take this moment from him, not even the prophecy.

CHAPTER 18

As her breathing returned to normal, Divina smiled and snuggled against Rori. Her eyes closed as she enjoyed the moment of pure sexual satisfaction. Tucked against him, she let out a contented sigh and relaxed.

Rori's front was to her back. With one arm under her neck and the other wrapped around her waist, she felt sated in his embrace. His mouth on her neck brought warmth to her. While familiar, something felt amiss.

While his tongue laved against her skin, she let out another moan. He had bitten her. She knew the sensation well. He had drunk from her more times than she cared to remember. Par for the course when one took a vampire lover.

The initial slice of his teeth past her skin had always jarred her. Even the throes of passion couldn't mask the pain of his bite. However, the pleasure that followed mirrored an orgasm.

At times, his bite intensified an orgasm. Not that time, however. Her neck felt sore where his teeth had punctured her. Instead of feeling happiness after their joining and his feeding, remorse blossomed in her chest. She likened it to the sense of mourning a loved one. She wasn't basking in the knowledge that she had nourished him. She wasn't bathing in the afterglow of their coupling. She just felt sore.

While she did enjoy the feeling of his newly warmed body against hers, the emotional connection she once felt after sex with him was absent. Their post-sex cuddling felt more like a forced intimacy after an anonymous sex encounter than that of old lovers. Rori had satisfied Divina. There was no doubt. He had learned to play her body like an expert fiddler. There just seemed to be something missing. Something more spiritual than the carnal pleasure of sex. The connection they had once shared wasn't there. She felt empty where she should have felt a sense of love.

Rori altered licks and kisses before focusing on nuzzling, Divina tried to break away. The intimacy of his gesture felt misplaced.

Rori didn't fight her. He allowed his arm to flop to the bed in her absence.

She slipped from under the sheets and reached for her pants. Once she had her privates tucked away, albeit without the luxury of panties, Divina turned toward him.

Rori lay on his back, his arms behind his head with his elbows out. He stared up at the ceiling with tight lips and hard eyes.

"Something's changed," she said, seating herself on the desk chair.

"Yes," he agreed to the idea of the change in emotional connection without looking at her. "What did they tell you?"

She furrowed her brow. "The witches?" she asked rhetorically before answering. "It was all convoluted."

She didn't understand the suggested connection between their lack of emotional bond and the witches. Did he suspect they had done something to them, to their bond? The spell.

Had Florence's hand movement when they arrived at the convent been a spell to separate them?

"It usually is with witches." He groaned rolling over onto his side.

He bent his elbow so he could hold his head. Using his index finger, he traced circles into their sex sheets as if in an attempt not to meet her eyes.

She sighed trying to make sense of what the witches had said. Pulling her knees up to her chest, she wrapped her arms around them and rested her chin upon them while she thought it over.

"Something about journeys and paths." She pursed her lips. "That I made your heart beat again and that I am some, like, tool for vampire politics or the council or something. Mates, something about mates. Then this one girl, she was young, she interrupted them. She said they were manipulative and not telling the truth."

That seemed to get Rori's attention. He stopped drawing circles. "Mates." He repeated the word.

"I don't understand that," she admitted.

With a far off look in his eye Rori didn't respond. His lips tightened and he resumed drawing circles. Waiting for him to comment on it, for him to explain, Divina held her breath.

"What did the young girl look like?" he asked dismissing the mate comment.

Divina regarded Rori curiously. "Red haired. I think her name was Ines?"

He nodded.

"Did they tell you what it means to make a vampire's heartbeat?" he asked.

She nodded her head, "the mate thing."

"It happens very rarely and only to vampires who meet the one they are meant to be with for all eternity. It makes the vampire feel things he hasn't felt since his human death,"

Rori explained in a rather bored tone. "Emotions are felt more deeply. The whole experience of life after death takes on a different meaning." He raised his gaze to her. "They say it's why only a vampire whose heart beats is thought to be fit to sit on the council. It's believed with deeper emotions come more tempered choices. I'm not sure I believe this. To be at the mercy of your emotions just seems weak to me."

Divina swallowed and looked at the floor. She tried to process all that Rori explained to her.

"So someone you are meant to be with for all eternity, like, jump-starts your heart?" she asked.

"Jump-start is a very strong way to look at it," Rori said. "My heart has beaten since the first time I took your blood. You awakened me, in a sense. However, my heartbeat is subtle. It's not enough to sustain human life. So, I'm still pretty dead. It also doesn't impact my immortality."

Divina nodded.

"If I'm supposed to be with you for all eternity, then why did they tell me about my heart choosing a wolf?" she asked.

Rori pursed his lips and looked away with a groan. He rolled onto his stomach and hid his face in a pillow.

"According to the Ember Witches, I'm not meant to keep you," he made a muffled reply.

"But you want to?" she pressed.

As she asked it, she wasn't sure if she wanted him to want to keep her. She had spent a lot of the past three years hating Rori. She never wanted to see him again. Here she was, asking him if he wanted to be with her for the rest of time. Not the rest of her natural life, nothing that short. She had just asked him if he wanted her for eternity. Did she want that?

"It doesn't matter," Rori said.

"What does that mean?" she demanded.

He turned his head from the pillow.

"They said I'm not meant to have you!" he growled back.

Divina narrowed her eyes at him. She tightened her jaw and stared.

He stared back.

Lowering her legs to the floor, she leaned forward, resting her elbows on her legs while she replayed her meeting with the witches through her head. She reheard all they had said. Like a movie in her mind; she got to watch it from the sidelines this time, instead of being in the thick of it. In her mind's eye, she watched Ines protest.

"Do you believe in fate?" she asked him, as if he were in her head watching the same memory she had been.

Rori sat up on the bed. The heated expression fell from his face. He tilted his head and eyed her with compassion.

"I don't know," he said.

The way he twitched when he spoke signaled that he withheld something. Rori never outright lied to her. However, he had withheld from her before.

"They said I was a stop on your journey but not your future," she said and shook her head as if trying to clear the confusion. "But then Ines said they were trying to change things. She said they weren't truthful."

Rori pursed his lips again. He nodded. "The redhead seems to be full of information."

"She also said we weren't the only ones," Divina recalled.

That caught Rori's attention. "What do you mean?"

"I don't know." Divina shrugged. "She didn't get to say much. Esmine got all mad, told her to stop talking, said she would be punished for going against the coven. That's when I hightailed it out of there." Divina's words sped up. She nearly tripped over them to get them out.

Rori swallowed and looked away.

"Curious," he muttered.

"What is?" she asked.

"Perci is in line for the vampire seat at the council," Rori explained. "But you can't take the seat unless your heart beats." He spoke as though to a far-off person, as though he still had to sort things out. He tapped a finger against his lip. "If there are two vampires and one is meant to expose us and one might not...." Rori trailed off. He climbed out of bed and turned in circles. His eyes scanned the floor.

Was he looking for his clothes? Divina wasn't about to help him. She wanted him to finish his train of thought. When it seemed he wasn't about to share, she cleared her throat.

"What does all of this have to do with the witches and me and some wolf?" she asked impatiently.

"A vampire whose heart beats for a witch... The witch who belongs to a wolf... He will save all kinds. He gets the throne," Rori murmured as he found his pants and stuffed his leg into them.

"What are you talking about?" Divina asked with a hiss. His answer sparked an ire in her chest, the heat of it spread through her body, causing a prickle of tiny electric shocks spreading through her limbs. She balled her fists, slamming them on the armrests of the chair.

"The vampire who belongs to the witch will end all kinds," Rori said with a far-off stare.

"Rori!" Divina screeched standing from the chair, flinging it backward.

The air in the hotel room shifted, charged with the energy now radiating off Divina. With her eyes narrowed on Rori, she lifted her arms and the curtains blew away from the windows as if a windstorm rolled through the room. Pens, plastic cups, and the ice bucket on the desk behind Divina vibrated as she snarled at him. Her rage would not be ignored. She would not be ignored.

The time when she was a helpless pawn in his games was

over. She'd stand up for herself now. As a powerful witch, she'd not allow him to manipulate her any longer. She'd show him exactly what she'd been studying in the years they'd been apart.

Swinging her arms so they went from out at her sides to straight before her, she flicked her palms upward. With that motion, a gust of wind barreled into Rori sending him flying back against the wall.

The thud of his body hammered against the wall, and he preceded his slide down to his butt. Blinking a few times, Rori peered up at her with a puzzled wonderment. He lingered on the floor a moment before scrambling to his feet. As he did so, he tugged his pants up over his hips. "They have the wolf," he said as if this would mean something to her. He hurriedly did up his fly. His belt buckle clinked as he struggled to secure it.

"Who?" Divina pressed. Another flick of her wrist, pushed Rori against the wall once more.

His arms flailed out as he once more collided with the wall. "I don't know which one I am." Rori looked panicked. "The witches seem to think they know which one I am, but I don't know which one I am."

Lowering her arms, the wind in the room stopped. Stepping around the bed she approached him. He'd answered her the best way he could, and she still didn't understand. When she raised her hands again he flinched, and her heart pinched.

Unaccustomed to that response in him, Divina softened her features. Cupping her hands against his cheeks, she tilted her head and studied him. "Rori," she whispered in an attempt to soothe him, to ground him, to get him to focus on her, and to explain clearly.

〜

Rori recoiled in the face of the shooting shocks from her palms upon his skin. He pulled her hands from his face and then thrust them at her. Gaping in confusion, he stared at her hands as if some sort of answer would spring forth from them.

They'd just had sex. They'd just touched quite a bit. Skin on skin, skin in skin, yet there hadn't been that pain, that shock that he now felt. It didn't make sense. Florence, Florence's spell had taken it away before perhaps it wore off?

Lifting his gaze to meet hers, he frowned at the implication. Selene had explained it to him and now, now it made sense. With an ache in his chest, he explained it the way Selene had explained it to him.

"That was against fate," he whispered.

"What?" Her face flushed red.

What had Selene said about that burn? She said it meant that two fates were crossing in a way that wasn't meant to be.

He hadn't felt it when he and Divina made love—that was meant to be. He felt it when she comforted him—that wasn't meant to be. It made no sense.

"Rori!" Divina shouted.

He blinked at her. "The only way to know which vampire of the prophecy I am is to find you the wolf."

"What if I don't want the wolf?" Divina asked. Ever the defiant one, Divina folded her arms over her bare chest. "Don't I get a say in all this?" she said.

Rori frowned. "If you don't want the wolf, then I'm the one that will end all kinds."

Divina peered at him in disbelief. She shook her head.

"No," she said softly. "That can't be. You don't want to end anything."

Rori sighed. "Doesn't mean it won't happen. We have to see the witches again."

"No!" She held up her hands to him. "No," she repeated with less drama. "I can't go back there. They scare me."

Rori approached her. He reached his hands out. He wanted to comfort her, but he hesitated. The thrum of electricity in the air prickled his skin. That zing, that sharp electric jolt of touching her in any caring manner, it fucking hurt. Could he bear it to help her? Part of him wanted to. Part of him screamed to comfort her. The female voice in his head reminded him of the prophecy. If he comforted her, it would only further cement their bond together. If he fought through the pain to do what was best for her, then he would be the vampire who belongs to the witch.

He stepped back from her.

She regarded him with wide eyes.

He looked away. The pain there; he caused it again. He hugged himself and turned his full body from her.

"We have to see the witches," he said softly, "just to find the wolf. Just to find out if I will end us all or save us all."

"I'm not going."

She turned on her heel and disappeared into the bathroom.

CHAPTER 19

A ric sat in the red vinyl booth of the diner peeling the
label off his pony neck beer. His wolf curled up within
him lazily, completely content at being surrounded by his own
kind. Owned by shifters, run by shifters, and just outside the
touristy area, the diner was a spot Aric frequented.

Since Aric had memorized the menu, he scrolled through
his phone, reading the text message returned from his pack
elder, Bruce. He'd agreed to meet with Aric after work to
discuss Aric's concerns. Despite the previous night's revela-
tions, Aric kept the meeting.

Bruce was an advisor to the pack alpha. He had done his
time as an enforcer and even as a beta. He was a valuable
resource to the pack. Aric hoped he would be able to shed
some light on why anyone would come to him regarding some
prophecy.

The booth cushion wheezed under the weight of a two
hundred-plus pound wolf. It awoke Aric from his thoughts.
Opposite him sat a stocky man with salt and pepper hair. A
human would assume he was in his fifties. The exaggerated
creases in his face were a telltale sign of a man who'd seen a

century or more. Bruce's pale grey eyes confirmed he'd seen his fair share of life and history. They pierced their target in an inquisitive and scrutinizing manner, which left the most resilient of wolves showing submission. His eyes had a way of putting a guilty conscience on edge.

Yet, they were bright when he smiled and greeted Aric. Aric had known Bruce his whole life. He considered him family and trusted Bruce with his life. That was what it meant to be in a pack.

"How's it going old timer?" Aric said, placing his phone beside the unread menu.

Bruce thumbed through his, though Aric suspected he knew it as well, if not better than he did himself.

"Oh, same ole, same ole." He sighed. "So what's this I hear about you and your wolf not getting along?"

Aric snorted and took a sip of his beer. Bruce didn't waste time with pleasantries and polite conversation. He cut right to it.

"Ehh, that worked itself out. It seems I should trust my wolf more," Aric admitted, placing the bottle down.

"Our inner beasts tend to know more than we give them credit for," Bruce replied.

The waitress came and took their orders. Once the menus were gone, Bruce folded his hands together and studied Aric. The air filled with the heavy silence between the two, despite the bustle of the other customers getting their food and drink beyond them.

Aric shifted under the scrutiny.

"You ever hear about a prophecy?" Aric asked.

Bruce grunted. "Vampires and witches have been spouting off about prophecies for as far back as time goes." Bruce waved a hand and dismissed the words and their implications.

"Yeah." Aric nodded. He had believed the same thing. "What about one that involved a wolf?" he asked.

Bruce lifted his brow. "A wolf prophecy?" he repeated.

Aric nodded.

Bruce shook his head. "They ain't never included us in their prophecies before."

Aric frowned and slumped a bit in his seat. He fingerd the lip of his beer bottle. It wasn't that he wanted the prophecy to be true or anything. He wasn't some white knight. He had no delusions of having some great importance in the world. He just hoped to make sense of the last two evenings.

Bruce narrowed his gaze at Aric.

The cute waitress returned, carrying their food. She went unacknowledged by Bruce as she placed their two beers down and took away Aric's empty. Instead, Bruce's old and penetrating gaze remained on Aric while he tilted his beer into his mouth.

The weight of the look caused Aric to lower his gaze in recognition of Bruce's place in the pack and out of respect. He took a hearty swig from his new beer, filling his mouth with the hoppy flavor, trying to swallow down his unease.

"You been to a seer or something?" Bruce asked.

Aric shook his head. Internally he debated how best to explain things succinctly. "Let's say a witch came to me claiming I'm some prophecy wolf," Aric said as he lifted his gaze toward the pack elder.

Bruce paused with his beer halfway to his lips. He blinked. His full body shook, and his face turned red when he laughed. He brought his beer down with a slam and shook his head.

Heat crept up Aric's chest and spread across his reddening cheeks. The response, though familiar, wasn't what he expected. He wasn't sure what to expect, really, but laughter? That wasn't it. He picked at the label on his new beer.

"Sorry," Bruce said trying to stifle his chuckles with a hand over his mouth. "I didn't mean...." He took a deep breath. "And what exactly did this witch say you were supposed to do in this prophecy?" Bruce asked once he settled himself.

Aric focused on getting the label off his beer in one piece. He wouldn't lift his eyes to the other shifter. He couldn't face him after being laughed at just yet. How could he even think of troubling an elder with such absurdity?

"That's the thing. I don't know. They never really said. Or well, if they did, they didn't let me remember. All I know is they said I was the key," Aric said.

"They?" Bruce pressed. "They didn't let you remember?"

"It's a witch and a vampire," Aric clarified.

Bruce's face dropped. His jovial laughter had ceased completely. He put his beer down and leaned back in the booth.

Aric raised his gaze and furrowed his brow, sensing the shift in his pack mate. The older wolf regarded him with an intensity he'd never seen before in the man. Had he done something wrong? Had he spoken too loud about their kind? Were there human's around?

Aric looked over his shoulder but saw nothing other than dining wolves. He faced Bruce's assessing gaze.

Aric rolled his shoulders back, which thrust his chest forward. His wolf, fully awake stood on guard, prepared to pounce if needed.

Who was he kidding? Bruce's age and training would have Aric dead in moments if it came to it.

Aric slumped back into bad posture on his side of the booth.

"A witch and a vampire came to you about a prophecy," Bruce said.

Bruce's inquisitive and skeptical tone sparked something within Aric. He sat upright again. His wolf paced alertly within him. Aric studied the elder shifter. The sharp contrast from the laughter indicated something was very off.

Aric nodded unsure where this conversation would lead.

Bruce pulled out his phone. He tapped at the screen quickly. Aric tried to peer over the edge and get a glimpse at the screen.

"What?" Aric asked when Bruce tilted his phone so that Aric couldn't see.

Bruce didn't answer. Instead, he swiped his finger over the screen. His cheek twitched when his jaw tightened.

Aric's wolf nipped at his insides urging Aric to press for answers.

Two grass-fed Angus burgers were plopped in front of each of them by the cheery waitress. Aric forced a smile to the waitress in thanks so that she would go away.

Bruce concentrated on his phone screen. Consumed with whatever it displayed, he ignored the waitress and the meal she had brought them. She left without a word from Bruce.

"Klaus met the sun," Bruce muttered eventually.

Aric waited for more. Nothing came. Bruce still stared at his phone.

"What does that mean for wolves?" Aric asked.

Bruce lifted a dead-eyed gaze. "On the new moon, the council will have a new member," he said. "The vampires have to decide which one of them will take his seat on the council of others."

Aric had expected more of an explanation. However, the two just stared at one another. He regarded Bruce with curiosity. "Still not seeing how that has anything to do with wolves," he said.

Bruce put his phone down. He leaned in. "It's complicated. And with witches, it's always riddles," Bruce said, exasperated. "But suffice it to say, that the wolf who's mated to a witch will have a lot to do with the vampire who takes that seat."

Aric furrowed his brow. "She's not my mate."

Bruce sighed. "By the new moon, she might be."

Aric's wolf's hackles went up. The rumble in his throat accentuated the snarl of the human. The wolf snapped within him in displeasure.

Bruce regarded him with a lifted brow.

"Then we might have to have that talk about my wolf and I not agreeing," Aric said.

Bruce sat back and folded his arms over his chest. His hard features glared at Aric. "Then you just might not be the prophetic wolf," he said.

Aric's inner beast balked at the statement. Aric sat back and stared off at nothing, his eyes looked ahead without focus. He wasn't an alpha wolf. He wasn't even an enforcer. He was just a run-of-the-mill average wolf in a pack. He wasn't meant for any prophecy.

"You and your wolf disagreeing again?" Bruce asked and broke through Aric's thoughts.

Aric blinked, and the world came back into focus. Bruce chewed on his burger. Aric glanced down at his own untouched meal. He had lost his appetite.

"I need to run," Aric said. He placed his palms on the table and pushed himself up out of the booth.

Bruce nodded. "Best thing to do." He shoved three French fries into his mouth. "Let the beast roam, give him control. Your human is fucking it all up," Bruce said.

Aric looked down at the old wolf enjoying his meal. The man had gone from laughing at him for the idea of him being the wolf of some prophecy, to pretty much confirming he *was* the wolf. Aric shook his head. He had sought the elder for answers and only left with more questions.

CHAPTER 20

W ith the warm water cascading over her, Divina
followed the directions on the shampoo bottle for
the first time in her life. She actually rinsed and repeated,
until the tiny hotel bottle was empty. She allowed the warm
water to run over her skin in an attempt to wash away the
betrayal she felt once again by Rori.

The white-tiled tub and shower combination served as a
sanctuary away from Rori, his prophecy, and the witches. As
the air around her steamed, she cursed herself. She should
have known. She should have anticipated his disregard for her
needs. How foolish of her to believe he'd changed. Then she
slept with the manipulating bastard! What was she thinking?

When she'd run out of soaps and hot water, she wrapped
herself in fluffy towels and a plush hotel-supplied robe. She
sat upon the toilet and generously slathered lotion on her
skin. She blow dried her hair with extra care. By the time she
exited the bathroom, she smelled of a floral mixture and had
perfectly styled hair.

Divina glanced around the small hotel room and noted
there was not one single sign of Rori. She chewed her bottom

lip as conflicting emotions battled within her. Her body lost the tension with his absence, but her shoulders slumped in disappointment at his persistent lack of loyalty toward her.

With a sigh, she collected the few belongings that had made it to the hotel room in their rush. She left the keycard on the end table and closed the door. Closing her eyes, she flopped back against the wall.

"Everything all right ma'am?" The male voice awoke her from wallowing in discontent.

Turning toward the voice, Divina saw a young man, who couldn't have been more than sixteen, in a polo shirt and khakis.

"Not really, but I knew that going into this," she said.

The young man quirked a brow. "Are you locked out of your room?" He gestured toward the door. "I can help you get another key made."

A half smile crossed her lips. "No." She looked back at the door. "I think I might have finally shut that door for the last time."

Turning back toward the young hotel employee, Divina was met with a perplexed expression. She offered him a weak smile and pushed off the wall.

The man shrugged. "Okay, well"—he rubbed the back of his neck—"if you need anything, just call the front desk."

She nodded. "Of course."

With her head high, Divina sauntered past the young man. How many times did Rori have to leave her before she got the point? He wasn't on her side. He'd never be. His only concern would be about the prophecy and doing the witches' bidding. He'd never put her first. She *had* to do this alone. Most importantly, she *could* do it alone.

She didn't need him. She didn't need the Ember Witches. She didn't care about vampire politics or thrones. She could be a powerful witch without a meddling coven. She'd do it on her own.

Divina made a plan for herself: get to the vardo, change her clothes, and then pack up her shit, and move on out. She had no further business in New Orleans. She had no further business with Rori or the Ember Witches.

The prophecy bullshit was on him. Divina did her part, according to him and the witches. She made his heart beat again. There wasn't anything left for her to do. Why did they keep dragging her into his shit? She had things to do, and none of it had anything to do with blood-sucking or their spells or even wolves.

Wolves. Divina snorted as she stepped off the elevator. She wasn't even a dog lover. She wasn't an anything lover. She only wanted to take care of herself. Everyone else and everything else could mind their own business. Divina's only problems were her own.

Once at her wagon, Divina stood back from it a moment. The restoration of the piece had been an arduous process. She ran her finger over the brightly-painted, hand-carved wooden swirls and filigree. When Rori had told her about what she was and her heritage, she felt the urge to connect to it. So she bought the one thing she felt was a giant symbol of Romani culture: the vardo.

It gave her something to do to take her mind off Rori. She threw herself into returning the wagon to its prime. It also helped her parley her newfound skills as a witch into a profession. Who didn't love seeing a fortune teller?

"Are you open for business?" The male voice startled her.

Divina spun on her heel. Her heart skipped. She scanned the lot searching for the source of the voice.

A man stalked toward her with his hands in the pockets of his well-tailored suit. The smug grin on his face gave Divina pause. He jutted his chin high, projecting an air of confidence.

Divina eyed him warily. Her sign wasn't out. She wasn't dressed as her character. She wore old jeans and a hooded sweatshirt. How could he possibly know she owned the vardo? How could he know she practiced fortune telling? She could just be admiring the craftsmanship of the wagon.

"What do you want?" she asked.

With palms up, the international sign of surrender, of "I mean you no harm," he closed the distance between them until they were a few feet apart.

"Just a little glimpse into my future. I heard you are one of the best," he said with a smug grin.

She backed away from him as a chill of unease trickled up her spine. Her body thumped against the outer wall of her wagon.

"Who are you?" she asked.

"Just a man with a bit of curiosity," he teased with a hint of sparkle in his eye.

"How do you know—"

"You have a gypsy wagon," he interrupted. "Are you not a fortune teller?"

Divina swallowed and looked back toward her vardo.

"I'm...," she began.

Her attention returned to the man, only to find him inches from her. Having not heard him move, she gasped not expecting him so close. With nowhere to go, she tried to flatten herself against the wagon.

The man stroked her cheek, and his eye twitched.

"Rori has found himself a lovely witch," he whispered.

Divina raised her arms with the intention to push him back from her. With the preternatural speed of a vampire, he gripped her wrists and slammed them back against the wagon and on either side of her head.

"Fuck!" she cried out, wincing at the slight pain.

He canted his head to the side. His cheek twitched with the clenching of his jaw. The man's green eyes roved over her making her skin crawl. "What a delightful suggestion, but alas I am not in the mood," he said in a pained voice. His eyes twitched again. He sucked in a breath that sounded like a hiss. His hands tightened around Divina's wrists. The muscles in his neck bulged.

In an attempt to take advantage of his distraction, Divina lifted her leg, hoping to knee him in the groin. However, he wedged himself between her legs effectively taking away her ability to do so.

"What the fuck do you want? Who are you?" she all but spat in his face.

Amusement decorated his features. "I wanted to know what I'm up against," he purred, lowering his face toward hers.

Divina turned away.

The man's cool cheek brushed hers. She shivered on contact.

He grunted in what Divina almost believed to be a pain.

"I don't know who you are, so it's not me you're up against," she said in an attempt to use logic to get her out of a possible raping.

He tsked. "Come now." His warm breath slithered along Divina's skin and made it prickle. "You expect me to believe that no one has told you about the prophecy?"

"I don't give a shit about your fucking vampire politics," she shouted.

She wriggled attempting to slip from his hold. She squealed when pain wrapped around her wrists. The tiny bones threatened to crack from the tightening of his grip. She should have known better. There was no way Divina would get out unless the vampire allowed her to get out.

At first, the silken lips touched her neck. Her eyes widened. Then sharp teeth scratch her delicate skin. Divina froze. Her heart thundered in her ears. She wasn't sure which was worse, the idea of being raped by this guy or being bitten without permission.

"Ahhh," he whispered into her ear. "I have your attention now, do I?"

Divina instinctually tugged her arms in an attempt to free herself. He responded with an iron grip.

"Let me go," she growled.

"Feisty," he mused and pulled back.

When he released her, he took a full step back from her.

She rubbed her wrists in an attempt to get the blood flow back to her hands. She glared up at him and flexed her fingers testing the dexterity.

"I'm not involved with this prophecy shit," she said, thankful for the distance between them.

He regarded her with a curious expression.

She met his gaze and refused to leave it.

One thing Rori had taught her about vampires was that they had this ability to do some mind trick on humans. They could not only manipulate them into accepting a bite, seducing them essentially with some mind control, but they could also wipe memories. Divina wasn't a true human; she was a witch. He couldn't do that to her, and a small sense of safety blossomed within her.

"You're Percival," she said connecting his words with what Rori had told her and the witches' claims.

He gave her a slight nod. "I prefer Perci in this era," he said with a bow.

"You're the one who is going to end it all," she said.

Echoing the words Rori used in the hotel room, Divina made the connection. This guy, this was the asshat that Rori was up against. This was the guy who wanted to take the throne to ruin everything for all supernatural beings, according to the prophecy.

Perci wrinkled his nose. "Pffft." He waved a hand dismissively. "None of that interests me. I never understood that part of the prophecy."

Divina furrowed her brow. That didn't make sense. Had Rori lied to her? He had never outright lied to her before. She eyed the man she didn't know. Was she about to take the word of this guy over Rori?

"What *does* interest you?" she asked.

His eyes sparkled, and he grinned in amusement. "A beautiful witch and a darling chair."

She blinked at him. Perci stepped into her personal space again, crowding her. Nonetheless she needed to appear confident.

"I'm not interested," Divina declared.

He arched a brow. Then his eyes widened in recognition. His smile grew wider than before. His body shook slightly. He snorted. The laugh erupted from him eventually. Perci covered his mouth as if to stop it. He couldn't.

She cowered at first but then lifted her chin. The laugh mocked her. Who was this guy anyway? Divina scowled at him.

"While I have no interest in the prophecy, my role in it is done. I already did the heart thing," she said with her chin high.

He laughed harder. Perci backed away from her a few steps, if only to give him more room to laugh.

"You're truly clueless," he finally wheezed out between fits.

Divina's cheeks heated. Her fists balled at her sides. "The witches—"

Perci's laughter stopped dead. His eyes grew cold and

Divina couldn't finish her statement. His fist slammed against the vardo causing Divina to jump.

"Those meddling bitches seek to take what is mine," he growled. "They are using you and Rori to do it, and I will not have it. My witch will take her seat at their table and rule the witches the way they were meant to be ruled, and I will take my seat to do the same with the vampires."

Divina gulped. Once more, she flattened against the wagon. Her pale blue gaze darted beyond Perci. She had no way out. He had backed away a little bit, but when it came to her speed and that of a vampire, yeah, she had no shot of outrunning him.

"You two are too weak for the task!" he elaborated. "You, a baby witch yet to come into her power, cannot be trusted with such things." Perci sneered. "And Rori crumbles at the first pussy that crosses his path. He knows nothing of loyalty." He regarded her with complete contempt. "It's good you want nothing to do with the prophecy and believe your part in it is done. It should make taking my rightful place all the easier." He turned his back on her and sauntered off.

CHAPTER 21

Hearing the shower start, Rori let out a cry of exasperation. He fisted his hair. He lingered, pacing the hotel room.

The water kept running.

He approached the door and knocked gently. "Divina?"

No response.

He fought the urge to pound on the door. As much as he wanted to, he didn't rip the door from its hinges. Instead, he paced a few more times.

Fine.

He'd go himself. He'd make them tell him the truth. He wouldn't fall victim to their riddles and their backward speak. Rori would bite every one of them if he had to.

He didn't have to continue on this path of hurt for Divina, this path of giving her up to some wolf, if he wasn't the vampire of the prophecy. He could have Divina. Screw the wolf. Perci had the wolf. Selene said so. Rori could have Divina; he just needed to get those meddling witches off their damn backs.

As he sat in the back of the cab, his mind raced. What did

an elder witch taste like? What sort of high could he get on super witch blood? Rori grinned at the thought of dark, thick elder witch blood spilling into his mouth until he was stoned off his ass.

Rori stormed up to the Convent prepared to tackle a locked gate with ease. He had the power of Divina's blood coursing through his veins. He could take on the world.

However, the moment he approached the gate, it opened. He stopped, then gaped and blinked in disbelief. He stood ill-prepared for the lack of challenge.

Rori hadn't expected them to be prepared for him. Hell, the majority of his half thought-out plan was based on the element of surprise. He paused in an attempt to reconnect with his purpose.

He'd demand answers. The witches deceived him and Divina. They'd have to answer for that. With renewed resolve, Rori marched through the trimmed hedges toward the door of the convent.

At the door, Esmine stood and waited for him. Her head high, her hair pulled back into a loose braid and her arms folded in front of her.

"He has the wolf!" Rori shouted.

Esmine's firm gaze set on him. Her jaw tightened. She didn't respond immediately.

"You said I was the vampire with the witch and the wolf thing," he said.

Rori couldn't get the puzzle phrase right in his current state. It didn't matter; what mattered was what repeated in his mind.

"Perci has the wolf," he told her.

Esmine pursed her lips. "We believed and still do believe you to be the vampire who will save us all," she said.

"But he has the wolf!" Rori repeated.

"He doesn't have the right witch," Esmine explained. "Where is Divina?" Esmine looked past him.

"How do you know who is the right one and who is the wrong one?" Rori demanded.

He shifted so that he would be in her field of vision. He desperately needed her attention.

"How do you know that this wolf will pick Divina?" he asked.

Impatiently, Esmine met his gaze. "It's not about picking. It's about fate. You can't change fate."

"You made me change mine!" Rori shouted. He wouldn't allow her to dismiss him. "You made me leave Divina. You made me sacri—"

Ire filled the witch's eyes when she glared up at him. Rori's words stopped mid-sentence.

"You were never forced, Roricus Fromm. You made choices. We merely laid them out for you. You chose to leave Divina after she gave you a heartbeat because we told you to. Recently, you chose the promise of power over eternal love. You cannot blame the Ember Witches for that. It is because you chose the allure of the council seat over that of your mate that we believe you to be the vampire of the prophecy who will save us and not the one who will end us," she said.

Rori's lip quivered. Choice? Did they call that a choice?

"You said I was never meant to have her," he said in a low growl.

Esmine smirked. "I said you couldn't come here without an invitation." She waved her hand. "Yet here you are." She arched a brow. "Has telling you that you couldn't have anything ever stopped you from having it before?"

Rori's nostrils flared as he balled his fists. He wouldn't take responsibility for this. It was the witches. The witches denied him Divina. The witches put the idea in his head that he could be on the council. This wasn't his choice.

"You were told that the vampire who sat on the council would be the one who abandoned his love, freeing her to find the wolf, her true partner," Esmine added salt to his wounds. "You were never instructed to do so."

Rori looked away. How power hungry had he been? He scanned the ground, his hands, anything for an answer.

Esmine sighed and tilted her head, observing him.

"Know that Divina will be happy. The pain will be dulled for her. She will find love. It will be magical. The love of a wolf and his mate is far purer than that of a vampire and his. It will rival what you two shared, if not surpass it. I'm sorry to say that, but it will. And you know as well as I do that one day she will get old," she said with empathy.

Tears filled Rori's eyes when he lifted his gaze toward her.

Esmine nodded, and with a voice filled with compassion, she continued. "You were going to have to give her up eventually. You would never turn her, Rori. You love her too much. That is why you are meant for the council. You turned your back on your mate for power, yes. On the surface that seems cruel, but you did it as an act of mercy." She licked her lips. "Even if you cannot see it now, you will. You know a witch cannot be a vampire. She cannot be turned and maintain that part of her that connects to the vrăji. Once she dies the mortal death, that would go away. She would have been an empty vampire. She would never know happiness again. You set her free, Roricus."

Esmine's hand came out to cup his face. He closed his eyes and found that he nuzzled into it. He needed the comfort of the old witch. He needed her counsel.

"She will be happy again. She will find love. Divina will grow into the witch she is meant to be. She will find her seat at the table. She will eventually take my seat on the consiliu," Esmine explained further.

Rori opened his eyes again. He turned his gaze to Esmine.

Hope bloomed within him. He wanted what she said to be true. He sacrificed a lot based on what she told him.

Sure, initially the power of it all had seduced him; the emperorship had lured him. With the full explanation, he knew there was so much more. He'd do it all, if it meant Divina would find happiness. He'd sacrifice alone, so she wouldn't have to share in the pain forever.

"You are the vampire of the prophecy. You are the vampire whose heart beats for the witch—the witch who belongs to the wolf," she repeated the prophecy. "You are the one who will save us all."

Rori felt like a husk of himself. All he had known felt stripped from him. Along with it, went his anger and skepticism of the witches. He felt like a child at the feet of a wise scholar, being schooled on life.

"But he still has the wolf," Rori whispered.

Esmine took her hand away and smiled in amusement.

"He cannot have the wolf. The wolf is not something that can be possessed. That is where Percival fails, and you shine. You love Divina. He possesses his witch. He believes if he possesses the wolf, he can control all things as well. This wolf is not one who will be owned." She shook his head. "The wolf is wild and free. The wolf will make a choice; none can make it for him."

Rori nodded in acknowledgment. He allowed Esmine's words to fill him, to rebuild him. Her words became his gospel. They became his law.

He had little experience with wolves. He found them to be rather crude. Rori was much more aristocratic, preferring the finer things and luxury. Wolves were more common in their tastes. They were closer to a feral beast. Rori found he had little in common with them. Plus, there was the whole nasty bit about their bite being quite painful and probably deadly for vampires. Yes, Rori kept his distance from wolves.

"How do I get the wolf to Divina?" he asked.

"Were you not paying attention?" Esmine asked rather indignant.

"I-I was," Rori stammered though, confused. "But you didn't—"

Esmine placed a finger over Rori's lips. "Go find her, Rori-cus. Bring Divina back where she belongs. The rest will work itself out."

CHAPTER 22

The metallic and salty taste of fresh rabbit blood lingered in Aric's mouth, now that he was back in human form. While the beast within Aric had been free, the wolf ran to vent the frustration from disagreeing with the human version of Aric.

The wolf hunted down some small game. Squirrels, rabbits, anything he could take down alone. The triumph over the prey and devouring it had aided the wolf in tempering his emotions. By extension, it calmed Aric, as well. Two beings shared a body and emotions.

Giving the reins to his wolf was the opposite of an out-of-body experience. Aric could see through the wolf's eyes, smell through the wolf's snout, and taste what the wolf tasted. All senses were fully functional, but he couldn't actively do anything else. He had no control over the actions of the beast. Aric could only watch, listen, and experience.

However, when the time came, the human dominated the beast. Aric pushed forth from wolf form, releasing control, and withdrawing within Aric. A tired wolf had little energy to resist the shift.

The slow burn spread over his skin as the fur of the wolf receded into Aric's pores. Joints popped to realign into a humanoid form. Pain jolted through him as each ligament found its new place, the excruciating crack of bones morphed into human position.

Sweating, gasping, and drained, the human Aric slumped where a wolf once stood. The amount of energy involved to regain control from the wolf was massive. Aric remained on all fours panting afterward. He needed a moment to collect his humanness.

Typically, Aric's wolf returned to the original shift spot as soon as Aric initiated the process of regaining control. This time, however, human Aric found himself among unfamiliar scents and on unfamiliar land. A survey of the area led Aric to believe the wolf had taken him to a narrow strip of woods behind a parking lot.

He shook his head. He assumed the wolf had distracted himself with a rabbit or something. Of course the beast hadn't meant to get this far out of territory. The thrill of the hunt took him farther than normal.

With his back against a tree, Aric pressed his hand over his heart, trying to catch his breath. He looked over his shoulder, relying on the superior vision of a supernatural predator to watch the man in the suit walk away from what looked like a gypsy wagon. The breeze allowed Aric to sample the air with an inhale.

The wolf in him growled. Aric snarled himself. His legs wobbled in protest as he attempted to lift himself. He flopped back to the ground with a groan.

The suit-clad vampire stormed past him muttering, "Interfering witches need to get dealt with."

The rotting scent turned Aric's stomach, causing the rabbit not to sit well. Perhaps rodents of different kinds weren't a wise meal when vampires were around. He didn't want to taste them a second time.

The wolf preferred fresh, raw animal meat. The human liked a little spice and seasoning with his cooked meal.

He knew that scent; the vampire, Perci. Aric's lip curled with the recognition of the undead man. Why was he there? Why did Aric's wolf bring him there? Was he chasing Perci?

Aric turned when Perci had left his sight. A completely different aroma delighted his nose. It wafted toward him, carried on the slight breeze of the night. His wolf perked with interest at the earthy tones of moss and the forest after rain. The smells seemed displaced so close to a parking lot and with there not having been rain recently.

With a furrowed brow he crawled closer to the scent and it got stronger. This further perplexed him as the direction of the scent was closer to the asphalt and father from the trees. The scent called to him. At the edge of the lot, the potency of the smell made absolutely no sense. What was the smell if not the woods his wolf had hunted? The wolf pushed him further to investigate, all thoughts of Perci forgotten as his nose and his wolf delighted in the new scent.

As if to remind him of his own condition, Aric's cock twitched as the smell awakened it. He looked left and then right, he needed something to cover himself. He cursed under his breath at his wolf. The filthy mongrel within him must have lured Aric out there out of spite.

Out in the middle of nowhere, with no clothes, and smelling the equivalent of filet mignon, his wolf had set him up well. Torn between the desire to investigate the fragrance, and maintaining human societal norms of modesty, Aric lingered under the cover of bushes and trees.

CRACK!

Metaphorical thunderbolts splintered before his eyes. Pain shot through his skull as he flew forward bracing himself on all fours. Aric's hand reached to the back of his head protectively and to check for bleeding.

"What the fuck!?" he rumbled in confusion.

"Who are you?" a feminine voice demanded.

Lifting his chest, getting to his knees, Aric turned toward the sound of crunching leaves beneath shuffling feet. Blinking a few times did nothing to cure his double vision. He assumed he had a concussion. If he had been human, he'd be unconscious. The pain in his head throbbed while Aric struggled to see properly.

"W-wh-why are you naked?" the female voice questioned him.

Rising to his feet, Aric shifted his position, in an attempt to both hide the chubby semi-erection and to offer some modesty. It must have been interpreted as a sign of aggression.

Aric heard the whoosh and put his arm up to block the giant branch the female wielded as a weapon. The vibration of pain ricocheted up his forearm when it collided with the impromptu weapon. Aric howled and his eyes watered.

Aric twisted his wrist, wrapped his fingers around the branch, and yanked. It came loose from her hands quickly. He tossed the stick away and thanked his supernatural genes and the strength given to him by his wolf, who, oddly, pranced about within him with elation rather than recognizing the aggression the woman showed toward them.

"Wha—" she gasped.

Still unable to see her clearly, the blurry female form stepped back from him. Aric wobbled slightly and fell to his knees again for stability.

Once his vision slowly returned to normal, and in the glow of the moon, he gasped when he finally laid focused eyes on her visage. Her high cheekbones, plump lips, golden skin tone stunned him. His mouth fell open. The mass of dark waves pulled into a messy pony shimmered in the moonlight giving her a halo effect. Aric felt as if he knelt at the feet of a goddess.

She wore an extremely large, faded, hooded sweatshirt and tight jeans. Aric lifted himself to a standing position on shaky knees. He stood several inches over her at his full height. His wolf howled within him while he fought the wolf's urge to grab the woman. It did nothing to ease the pounding pain in his head from her attack.

"You're magnificent," he murmured.

The unknown female took another step away from him.

"Uh, thanks?" she said.

Her pale blue eyes darted left and right, as though she searched for an escape route.

The throbbing pain in the back of his head dulled as he studied her. He absentmindedly raised a hand and rubbed at the place where she had struck him. The semi was now a full-on raging erection and proudly protruded from his pelvis as if to salute her.

Aric's face heated when her eyes dipped to it. Her cheeks reddened. She held a hand over her mouth.

"Oh my God!" she gasped.

Her expression reflected panic. She bent her knees prepared to run. Her eyes sought the best escape route.

"No. Don't," Aric protested, surprising himself.

She paused. The female stared at him, bewildered.

He brought both his hands over his crotch. "Sorry."

"Why are you naked?" she demanded a second time.

"Uh," Aric stalled. For some reason, he didn't think telling her he had just shifted from wolf to human form would be a good idea. Humans tended to freak out when confronted with creatures they thought were mythical. Plus, there was the whole death thing, if the council found out about a super-natural being outing himself to humans. They took that shit super serious. Aric liked his life. He liked it even more, having met this female.

While the woman was wary of him, she didn't seem particularly freaked out. Sure, she hit him with a stick but that was self-defense. She must not encounter naked men in the woods often.

A grin grew on Aric's face at the thought. That would be good for Aric. No wolves sniffing around her. She'd be all his. Aric stiffened at the possessive idea. Where had that come from?

Lost in his own thoughts, he didn't realize she had done it until he heard the tones. She pushed buttons. Those were phone buttons. He sprung toward her, fast as lightning and snatched the phone, sure to keep one hand covering his crotch.

Again, she flew back, on guard against him. With her arms raised, the leaves around them swirled and the bushes shook with a sudden strong breeze. "Give it back." She growled at him.

His wolf swiped at his insides to indicate his displeasure with her reaction to human Aric's movements. The wolf growled in warning, sending the message that Aric shouldn't scare the female again.

"I'll give it back if you don't call anyone," he said.

He extended his arm, holding the phone out to her, then snapped it back when she reached for it. The gusts around them intensified, and Aric fought the sudden wind as it seemed to be pushing him back from the woman.

"Or text. Or snappy gram, whatever," he added with an arched brow.

She groaned and rolled her eyes. The female's hand shot forward, and she took the phone from his fingers with a huff. She stuffed the phone back in her pocket.

Aric chortled in amusement at the fire within the female.

He agreed with his wolf in that they both enjoyed the passion the female displayed. Glancing about, he realized the wind had stopped just as suddenly as it had started. When his attention turned back to the female, he found she narrowed her eyes at him.

Aric puffed his chest and couldn't stop himself from flexing. Was he posturing? What was he doing? He moved his hands back to cover his genitals.

"I'm a nudist?" he said unconvincingly, in a weak attempt to explain his current state.

"Are you asking me or telling me?" she asked.

Her gaze swept over him again. The warmth of her attention on him sent a shiver up his spine. His wolf panted within him.

"Telling you?"

Her brow rose. "You don't seem so sure."

He sighed. "Do you have something I can cover myself with?"

CHAPTER 23

Divina cursed silently. Standing in the woods with a predator, unarmed, wasn't her idea of a good time. Especially with one who could not only out run her, overpower her, and pretty much do whatever he wanted. She assumed Perci left some sort of vampire guard to intimidate her or whatever, and it was a dick move.

If only she had studied some sort of war magic, she would have a better defense than harnessing the wind. Sure, it was better than nothing, but shooting electric bolts out of her fingers or palm, could do a lot more damage. She had no defenses against a naked vampire.

"What do you want?" she asked the naked man, while trying to keep her eyes north of his erection.

"You mean, aside from not having my dick out in public?" he asked with an arched brow.

In the light of the moon she noted a scar split his eyebrow. The only flaw in his perfect features Divina could see in such poor lighting. The street lights from the parking lot and the glow of the moon didn't offer much where he hid in the trees and bushes.

"I don't really have an agenda," he said interrupting her attempt to ogle at him in the dark.

Divina chewed her bottom lip, debating her response.

He shifted his position, entering into the cone of light casted from the streetlamp behind her.

She gasped. Scars littered his broad body. They weaved a tapestry of near misses. Eagerness weaved with desire to know the origin of the line across his chest that wasn't meant to be there. An unexplained urge to trace the pale puckered flesh zig zagging over his skin confused her. Her fingers twitched and lifted of their own accord to touch him.

He snorted and brought her attention back to his face and away from his body.

She cleared her throat and stepped back.

"Okay," she said.

She didn't really indicate what she had okayed, but she felt the need to say something.

She turned away from him, hoping it would hide her reddening cheeks. Internally berating herself for the urge to touch and ogle him as she led him out of the woods and into the parking lot. *He's a naked vampire in the woods beside a parking lot!*

Facing her vardo, she remembered he'd asked for a covering. She could do that; she had to have something in his size. Maybe not a piece of clothing, but something he could wrap around him. A sock perhaps.

Climbing up the stairs of her wagon, she couldn't fight the urge to look over her shoulder. His amused grin spread on his face. The man could have been sculpted from marble. He had muscles bulging where Divina didn't even know there were muscles. To add insult to injury, his pectorals danced. Divina's throat went dry.

She turned back. Caught gawking at him, her entire body felt ablaze. Parts of her tingled with sensual heat unfamiliar to her. Never had just the vision of someone sparked such a visceral response in her.

Once inside, she took a moment to regroup. She took deep breaths trying to calm herself, then closed her eyes and engaged in a self pep talk.

Yes, the man was gorgeous.

Yes, he knew it.

Yes, he was a vampire.

Divina had enough vampire problems. She didn't need another.

"Vampires are bad, Divina," she whispered to herself, "no matter how hot they are."

Opening a trunk, she sifted through its contents. Exactly how many sheer scarves with tassels did one woman need?

Holding one up, she dismissed it, too short. Tossing it over her shoulder, she continued. She held up another, too narrow. That one, she flung over her head.

Peering down at the crochet nap blanket she cocked her head to the side contemplating it. It held no sentimental value. She couldn't even remember where she had gotten it, so it seemed the best option to offer to the naked man.

"I think that's just my color," his voice came from behind her.

Divina startled, using the blanket to cover herself. She whirled around seeing the naked man leaning in her door-frame. The familiar heat bloomed in her chest and spread up her neck to fill her cheeks. It wasn't like she was the naked one. Yet, there she was, clutching a blanket to her neck.

He covered himself with two hands.

Divina's mouth watered at the idea he required two hands to keep himself hidden. As the warmth spread downward, it pooled between her thighs.

She never in a million years would have thought her type

would be vampires. *Vampires are bad, Divina,* she scolded herself internally.

Divina tossed him the blanket. "Here."

She tried to sound mad, but wasn't sure she pulled it off. Hard to do when her entire body was the color of a tomato and she couldn't stop drooling.

He caught the blanket and wrapped it around his waist.

"Thank you." He bowed slightly.

Lifting herself from a crouched position, Divina crossed her arms over her chest. The heat in her face dissipated with the application of the blanket. Though, the disappointment that replaced it surprised Divina. She pushed that thought out of her mind.

"Are you here to threaten me too?" she asked.

His head snapped up from tucking the blanket.

"Who threatened you?" he demanded in a husky baritone which almost sounded like a growl.

She stepped back, eyeing him unsurely. "Peeeeeerci?" She drew it out wondering if she had said too much.

"Fucking leech." Another rumble came from his chest as if it disconnected from his voice.

Divina's heart quickened at the sound, though she couldn't be sure if it was in fear or in arousal. She licked her bottom lip with her eyes intently trained on the assumed vampire wrapped in an afghan. Somehow, he had her tied in knots.

Pacing in the small space of her home, he mumbled to himself.

Divina took another step back watching as he clenched and unclenched his fists repeatedly.

"Did he bite you?" he asked coming toward her with his large calloused hands out.

Divina's eyes widened, and she stepped back. Completely unaware of the length of her wagon, the back of her legs hit the couch which doubled as a bed. She flew back and flopped onto the pillowed seat.

He stalked toward her. His body found its way between her splayed legs. His hands cupped her face and turned her head one way and then the other.

She couldn't bring herself to speak. The warmth running through her was like nothing she had ever experienced before. Warmth was an understatement. It was pure, unadulterated heat. Heat transferred from his rough hands and billowed out until her whole body caught fire.

The hazel eyes with a flash of gold narrowed as he studied her neck. He ran a thumb over the vein.

"It's fresh," he commented.

She fought the urge to moan under his tender touch. She placed her hands on his wrist and found her voice.

"It's fine." It didn't sound as assertive as she intended. Surely he had left similar marks on his victims before. Divina cringed internally at the idea of being a victim. She wasn't Rori's victim, and she had no intention of being the naked vampire's victim. "Perci didn't bite me, now let me go," she added without conviction. She didn't want him to let her go. She wanted to touch him too. She wanted to kiss him, to straddle him, to ride him into the dawn. The erotic thoughts jarred her, and she shook her head slightly as if to shake them loose from her brain.

He furrowed his brows at her and canted his head. Her gaze shifted to his hands and his brows lifted.

"Oh!" he gasped, removing his hands from her face. He stepped back, and she caught the flash of pink on his cheeks. She couldn't help but grin. He awkwardly dangled his arms at his sides. As if rethinking it, he shifted them to his hips. He must have thought better of it because he crossed them over his chest. He cleared his throat. "Sorry about that," he mumbled.

Surprised at how her skin cooled when he let her go, Divina pushed herself upward.

"He didn't bite me," she said again.

"But someone did."

His eyes did that flashy gold thing again when they landed on her neck.

Divina covered the spot Rori preferred when he drank from her. She looked away from the stranger in her home. The man who had been naked, she reminded herself. The man who just showed up in the woods, she further clarified.

The man she wanted to drop the blanket and strip her down, throw her on the bed and... She couldn't finish the thought. Divina had clearly lost her mind.

"Why are you here?" She tried to change the subject.

She needed to focus on vampires being bad for her. Maybe he wasn't sent by Perci, his obvious distaste for the guy sent that message loud and clear. With his intentions unknown her mind wandered. Perhaps, he wanted her to start his heart too. She didn't just do that for everyone. She didn't even know how she did it for Rori!

His hand came up and wiped his face, then clung to his chin.

"I was hunting," he said.

Divina peered at him perplexed. "Naked?"

"You've never hunted until you do it naked." His chin lifted, and he preened.

"Well, I guess when you can do that memory wipe thing on people—"

"Wait. What?" he interrupted.

She waved her hand a bit, trying to pantomime the hypnotic trick vampires did. "You know, where you make the people you feed on forget and replace their memories."

He stared at her with hands on his hips.

Divina continued. "What I mean is, if you are going to

hunt naked." She paused. He continued to look at her oddly. "The people, they wouldn't be all that caught off guard because they won't even remember you."

"I don't hunt *people*," he said.

"Oh." She bit her lower lip once more, giving him the once over. "I just assumed. You're so warm."

"Why wouldn't I be warm?" he asked.

She stared at him.

He stared back, as though expecting her to continue speaking.

Divina looked away. Puzzled, she stroked her hair contemplating just how to tactfully ask what he apparently needed her to come right out and say. Giving up, she sighed. "You are a vampire, right?" She put it out there.

The growl from his chest caught her off guard. He curled his lip and his adorable face transformed into something akin to menacing yet, not.

"I. Am. Not. A. Vampire," he stated through gritted teeth.

She swallowed. She should've been scared. She should've told the man to get the fuck out of her wagon.

She wasn't.

She didn't.

Instead, she felt bad for assuming him to be a vampire.

Divina cleared her throat. "So you're just some guy, hunting in the woods, behind a parking lot." She paused. "Naked?"

The man stood proudly in her wagon. He regarded her with hungry eyes that flashed gold. He stroked his five o'clock shadow, and with a grin he replied, "That about sums it up nicely," he said.

The smile fell from his face instantly. The gold flashed again. He stepped toward Divina and sniffed. She pulled back with a bit of a whine.

"Now tell me," he began in a deep nearly inhuman baritone. "Who bit you?" His hands once more cupped her face.

Divina's breath caught. She should've pushed him off. She should've moved away from him. There were so many things she should've done or felt, but she didn't.

A sense of need for the naked man in her home washed over her. A wanton desire she had never felt before consumed her. If she'd let it, it could cloud her judgment. *If* she let it, she told herself.

CHAPTER 24

Aric's wolf howled like crazy within him. The distraction of it in his head made talking to the female quite difficult. That smell—oh, her smell. It wrapped around his body, coiling around his cock keeping him rock solid. It stroked every fiber of his being. He couldn't inhale enough of it.

Touching her, when he laid his hand upon her cheek, he blasted off to another planet. Starting in his fingers, slowing through his hand, and covering his heart in a warmth he'd never imagined possible. The implications of the euphoria he felt just from touching her wasn't lost on him.

His erection pressed against his stomach, and thankfully, was hidden by the thick crocheted blanket he had fashioned into a kilt. The blanket scratched at the sensitive skin and made his ache much more painful. What the hell kind of yarn was this thing made of?

The unpleasantness of the blanket did nothing to quell his desire for the female. His wolf needed her and that feral need contributed to the human ache. The primal urge to have her almost took over his common sense.

However, the idea that someone, some vampire, had fed off her, pushed him to levels of anger he had never imagined existed. He cupped her face, her beautiful, enchanting face, and gazed into her light blue eyes, waiting for a reply. His thumb stroked her cheek while his jaw ticked and he fought his wolf for dominance.

Kiss her. Mark her. Claim her. He had to shove all that down. Even though she mentioned vampires and Perci, she gave him no indication she was anything but human. He had to control himself and his wolf.

Touching her seemed to be the only way to silence his wolf. Touching her, in any manner, let alone as intimately as he was, drove his desire for her that much higher. He needed to get ahold of himself. His erection twitched and he gritted his teeth.

Searching her face for a sign that she felt the pull as he did, caused his features to soften. Wondering if humans possessed the ability to feel the mating pull did nothing to distract him or his wolf from the desire for her. He studied her reactions to him, desperately wanting to see something, anything indicating she felt it too.

For her part, the woman looked up at him wide-eyed and innocent. "I-I-I." She paused on her stumbled words. "It doesn't matter," she whispered.

He frowned at her. Leaning down over her, pressing his bare chest against her clothed one sent a shiver up his spine. Oh, what he wouldn't give to rip the oversized hoodie off her and touch her skin, her breasts, her nipples.

The zing, the heat, caused him to clench his jaw upon contact. He thought his teeth would crack from the pressure. Even with a clothing barrier, the intensity rocked him. His cock pulsed.

The need within Aric to have this female tested his

control. His wolf pressed against him to force his release. Aric tightened every muscle he had to fight to keep the wolf within. In his current state, he didn't trust the animal to be civil. Who knew what the beast would do if let out of his human cage?

"It matters to me," he replied.

The hedonistic desire dripped from his voice. He barely recognized his own words. Closing his eyes, he prayed to all that was holy she couldn't hear his struggle with humanness. The feral beast within didn't understand humans, all he wanted, all he needed, was to claim what was his. Aric knew better, and Aric needed to be in control.

He towered over the female, his female, as she sat. He released her face and stroked her hair.

She leaned into his hand at first, but pulled back after a moment.

His wolf snapped. He didn't appreciate that one bit. Neither did Aric. He studied her as conflicted emotions flashed across her face.

"I don't usually concern myself with the opinions of naked hunters." Her voice shook.

Aric grinned while she tried to sound convincing and cutely failed. How fucked up was he to think an unsteady voice was adorable?

Aric's hand dropped, he didn't want to invade her space more than he already had. Well, he did, but he didn't want her any more uncomfortable than he'd made her.

"So, if I had clothes on you would be more concerned about my opinion?" he teased.

The female's cheeks turned a beautiful shade of red.

Aric decided he would spend his life seeking to trigger that response from her.

"No" she said.

Once again, Aric reached for her hair.

She allowed him to run his fingers through the strands that had escaped her ponytail.

"I'm Aric Braun," he said realizing they had yet to exchange names. "Thank you for the use of your blanket. I'll wash it before I return it to you."

"You can keep it. Consider it an apology for cracking you over the head with the branch," the female announced dismissively. "I don't plan on sticking around that long."

She pulled away from him, stood, and scooted past him. The female made her way to the opposite end of the wagon.

Confused, Aric turned toward her. Was the female leaving?

No.

That can't be right. His wolf balked at the idea.

Studying him a moment, the female turned and checked on a few of the cords and such she had wrapped around various items within the wagon. She tugged on one, testing its tension. The cabinet near her smelled, almost nauseatingly, of herbs and dried spices.

"Where are you going?" Aric asked.

She busied herself with moving items, testing cords, and kept her features hidden from him. Was she purposely not looking at him?

"I have a carnival thing I need to catch up to," she replied.

He arched a brow. "You're a carnie?"

Aric wasn't sure if that was still a thing. Did people who worked carnivals still call themselves that? He didn't want to offend her.

She turned her head sharply and frowned. "No."

Had he insulted her? Shit. Apparently, "carnie" wasn't the right word.

The female pointed to a sandwich board. "I'm a fortune teller," she said.

Aric's gaze drifted to where she pointed. There it was, a

board proclaiming prices for such things as tarot cards and palm readings.

Aric snorted in amusement. "You're a seer?"

"Sure," she agreed half-heartedly.

That got Aric's attention. He eyed the female skeptically. Aric hadn't met many seers that he knew of anyway. However, if they were anything like other supernatural beings, they were proud. When faced with another kind, other than human, they announced themselves.

She didn't.

"Sure?" he repeated.

She sighed impatiently. "I read fortunes," she explained. "It's the same thing."

Aric blinked. He tilted his head unsure what to make of the little spitfire who had captivated his wolf.

"Listen," her tone softened. "I've had a long night. I really need to get some sleep."

She stepped toward him.

Aric's wolf panted in excitement at her proximity.

"You're welcome for the blanket. I'm happy to help a man in need." She offered him a weak smile.

Was he being dismissed? Aric wouldn't have that. No. No. No. He returned her smile.

"I insist on returning the blanket," he said firmly.

She groaned. "I really won't be here. You'll be wasting your time."

"You're tired," he reminded her. The female narrowed her eyes at him. "So, if I understand correctly, you're rushing me off so you can get some sleep?"

She didn't answer.

Aric grinned smugly. He had her.

"So, I propose you let me wash the blanket and return it to you tomorrow," he said. "And, in repayment, let me take you to dinner."

The female eyed Aric warily.

"I'll even be dressed." He waggled his brows in an attempt to sweeten the deal. Though, if the shoe were on the other foot, clothing would not sweeten the deal for Aric. He and his wolf agreed the less clothing on this female the better. His cock agreed, showing his interest with rush of blood causing a twitch. Aric groaned.

The female smiled in amusement. "That isn't necessary."

He shook his head. "I insist. Clothes are very socially acceptable."

She snickered and shook her head. He considered the crack in her stern façade a victory.

Confidence sprouted within Aric. He had won her over, or so he thought.

Her smile faded. "I really have to catch up—"

"I'll even pay you to read my fortune," Aric offered and extended his hand palm up in a cheap ploy to get her to touch him again.

His wolf missed the feeling of warmth she gave him. His wolf missed the zing of their joined skin. His wolf wanted to touch her again and wouldn't shut up until it happened.

Her gaze flicked from his palm to his face and back again.

For a moment, Aric thought he saw fear in her eyes. Was she afraid to touch him? Why would she fear him? What had he done?

Surely, she couldn't smell the rodent blood on him. If she had seen the golden eye flashes, she hadn't mentioned it nor reacted to it. Then again, she had thought him a vampire. Were his eyes gold? How else could he prove to her that he wasn't a vampire than to have a meal together?

"We can meet for lunch," he haggled. There, perhaps suggesting a daytime meal would end her believing him to be a night crawler. "That way you won't be too held up," he added.

The inner debate played across her face. Aric waited with baited breath. He had never wanted to take a woman to lunch as badly as he wanted to take this woman to lunch. He shook his wrist as if to tempt her with his fortune.

She bit her lower lip. "Fine," she agreed. "Lunch." She looked at his hand. "Put that away."

He chuckled. "There's a diner," he explained. "It has the best hamburgers; we can go there."

She nodded and reached for a bit of paper to take the address.

Aric gave it to her before he asked, "So what name should I put the reservation under?"

She eyed him with a puzzled expression.

Aric smiled waiting for her to realize he had asked for her name without actually asking. He gave himself a mental pat on the back for his creativity.

It took only a few seconds for it to dawn on her. Her eyes widened in recognition before she frowned.

Aric and his wolf agreed they would work very hard to keep that expression from her features in the future.

"Divina," she said. "My name is Divina."

Aric reached for her hand.

She flinched at first, then took his hand and relaxed.

He took her hand to his lips and kissed the back gently. The taste of her skin gave him goosebumps. Beyond the chemical floral hint of soaps and lotions, he picked up her pure flavor. Like her scent, Divina tasted of earthy notes that sung to him. Aric's mouth watered for more. When he pulled up, he licked his lips hoping for one more sample.

She blushed.

Aric grinned and said his good nights. He strolled rather proudly for a man wrapped in a crocheted blanket kilt with a purple erection sure to transition into blue balls in the next hour or so.

Pretty sure he had just met his mate, Aric strutted through New Orleans without a care in the world. It would take more than the scratchy wool of the blanket against his nut sack to bring him down.

CHAPTER 25

L eaving the convent, the world felt a bit clearer. Everything appeared in sharper focus than before. Rori had the whole picture. Esmine had shared the full prophecy with him. The blinders had been lifted for the first time and confidence pulsed through Rori's veins.

Sure, there'd be sacrifice. What hero didn't sacrifice something for the greater good?

Rori paused at the gate of the convent. Hero. Thinking of himself as a hero didn't feel right. It didn't fit him, but it fit the situation, it fit the prophecy. The vampire meant to save all supernatural kind from the wrath of humans, if they found out about their existence, that would make him a hero.

He blinked. Yes. *Yes, he's that vampire. Of course he's a hero!*

He couldn't let that go to his head, though. He'd lose focus if he fixated on the grandeur of it all. Besides, saying he'd sacrifice his love for Divina and understanding the need to sacrifice his love for Divina were all well and good, but the actual act of doing it would impact him forever. He'd be a fool to believe he could do it easily, no matter what the promised glory.

The idea of never having Divina again the way Rori had that evening stabbed him in the gut. He tried to find solace in the bigger picture, the idea of being a hero to all.

It didn't help that Divina's blood coursed through his veins. With Divina's blood giving him warmth, pumping in his heart, he had to remind himself of not only his own fate, but his duty to save all kinds. Their love was minuscule when compared to the fate of all kinds.

However, his mind drifted to the possibility of eternity with Divina. He'd never thought further than being in the moment with her. The witches had planted his purpose in her life in his mind since before he met her. He had never allowed himself to think of their future, because there was no future with Divina. He sought only to cherish the few precious moments he had with her before they were gone forever.

When Esmine brought up the idea of Rori changing Divina into a vampire, he'd dismissed it. He'd never ask Divina to sacrifice so much of herself for him. She talked him out of it as if to affirm his previous decision. At least, in that moment she had. Being away from her, and having time with his own thoughts, brought him back to the possibility.

With hands shoved in his pockets, Rori stopped under the light of a street lamp a block from the hotel. Contemplating his conversation with Esmine, Rori pondered the idea of being a hero and weighed it against the possibility of being with Divina for eternity. Both required Rori to be a lot more human than he had been in centuries and he wasn't sure he had it in him.

His shoulders slumped with the weight of the questions. He sighed and shook his head to clear them from his mind.

He'd talk to Divina. He'd get a feel for what she wanted before he decided on his hero-ness. Truthfully, if she wasn't on board with eternity with him, it wasn't bad having hero-ship to fall back on as a plan B.

He approached the hotel where he had left Divina. He clung to the long shot that she would still be in the shower. If not, Rori hoped she had at least stayed in the room. Worst case, he'd get a cab and meet her at the wagon. She loved that thing. It was her safe haven.

The man working the desk didn't stop him. He took it as a good sign she hadn't checked them out.

Rori fingered the key card in his hand as he stood at the elevator bank. The lazy beat of his heart picked up into double the speed, though still not enough to be considered a normal heart rhythm.

"Roricus." A familiar female voice called to him.

Rori turned looking for the source. His gaze landed on a crouching woman, wrapped in a brown wool blanket. He couldn't immediately place her. The visual did nothing to jog his memory. He narrowed his eyes at the woman. She seemed out of place in the posh establishment. Her stringy red hair and the waxy pale skin caused Rori to frown. He regarded the way she clutched the blanket, as if she were freezing to the bone, with a wrinkled nose. Had he given a homeless woman the address of the hotel? Had she followed him after he drank from her? He couldn't remember all the human's he had sampled since being in New Orleans. Her familiarity irked him.

Rori stepped closer. Maybe she wasn't human, perhaps another vampire he had met in his years. There was a small chance she could be starving for some reason or another and sought him for help of some kind. Seemed unlikely, but not completely absurd. Rori mentally ran through the catalog of vampires he had met over the centuries.

"Don't let them fool you," she whispered when he got closer.

Within two feet of the woman, Rori froze in recognition of her. The red-headed witch, the one Divina called Ines, was a ghost of the youthful witch she had been but a few days ago.

He gaped at her. The shock of her current appearance, of the weakness he saw in a once powerful witch, shook him.

"They are trying to change fate. Don't let them." Ines coughed and resumed cowering between the two planters near the elevators.

Rori crouched beside her and got a better look at her greying face. The witch, who had once appeared youthful, had aged several decades overnight.

"What happened to you?" he asked in a concerned whisper.

She shook her head. "There's no time," she insisted. "Just know that you can have her, Roricus. You can go forth with your true fate and have Divina. You don't need to give her to the wolf."

The exact wrong words to hear as a hero waffled with his decision to sacrifice love for the good of all kinds. Though, it didn't fit with what the youthful version of this witch had said just days before.

Rori eyed the witch in disbelief.

"Did they do this to you?" he pressed.

He knew the Ember Witches were extremely powerful. Without a doubt, they would be capable of reducing the woman to the shriveled heap before him. If she meant to punish them all, the witches, himself, and Divina, for what was done to her, sabotaging the prophecy would be the way to do it. The intent behind her current words had Rori cautious.

"Pay attention," she snapped. "You don't need power, just Divina," she spoke simply. "You don't need the council seat, just your witch."

Tightening his mouth into a firm line, Rori considered her words. The witches could be testing him. Through this manipulation, this appearance of Ines, they could be testing his resolve to sacrifice love for the throne, for the good of all kinds.

"If I do that then I will be the one to end us all," he said, wary of Ines' intentions.

Ines shook her head. "You have no desire to do such a thing," she pointed out. "How could you end us if you don't want to?"

She coughed again harder and longer this time. She looked at her hand and cursed before wiping it on the woolen blanket she held close around her.

"They are forcing you into a place you're not meant to be, Roricus. You have to follow your heart, now that it beats. Don't let the witches make you a puppet," she said urgently.

He regarded her with a sideways glance. Her sickly form shivered under the blanket.

"What did they do to you?" he asked again.

With words in direct conflict with not only Esmine's but Ines' own words, Rori questioned her motive. Add her withering appearance, and it felt wrong.

With a tight-lipped frown Rori pondered his previous idea of her presence being a test by the Ember Witches; a test to his commitment to the throne. The more she talked, the more Rori felt the witches were pushing him toward the sacrifice.

She turned away from him. She tried to get up, but the witch lacked the strength and fell back down.

"Love, Roricus. Love is what you need to fight the prophecy," she rasped.

Rori clenched his teeth. The manipulations needed to stop. His nostrils flared as his frustrations grew. The incessant games of the Ember Witches, of this witch, was enough to drive a lesser man crazy.

"They cast you out," he surmised. "Did they strip you as well?" he asked.

She said nothing.

However, her trembling increased and the blanket slipped from her shoulder revealing her state of emaciation. She bowed her head and displayed just how thin her once lush red hair had become. She refused to lift it to him or, perhaps, she lacked the strength.

"Divina is to take your seat isn't she?" Rori further concluded.

Silence.

"You went against the witches knowing that it was your seat up for grabs," Rori said.

He breathed in sharply with the belief he knew Ines' true intentions. He closed his eyes, trying to push down the bloom of rage growing and spreading in his chest. When he opened them again, the world was tinged red.

"You are here to sabotage—"

Ines sprang up interrupting his words. The blanket fell to her feet and exposed her skeletal body with clothing dangling from her. Sores covered her gray skin. Her eyes lacked the shine and youth they had the first time she promised him power.

Cold radiated off her and crept over Rori's skin.

"I went against my coven for what is right!" she hissed. "I went against my coven for love," she declared. "For your love, for Percival's love! For Divina and Selene!"

Her bony fingers gripped his forearms. The sharp digits dug into the muscular flesh of Rori's arms, threatening to pierce through with a strength he didn't realize she possessed. She shook as all her energy appeared concentrated on her hold on him.

"You are not fit for the council, Roricus," she seethed.

"You lack the age and the commitment. It is meant for Percival. The coven fears Selene's devotion to her vampire."

"You were the one who said I could have power," Rori said through gritted teeth.

The chill forced its way through his body stemming from her hands wrapped around his arms.

"I lied," she said. Releasing Rori's arms she hung her head and shrunk back into her blanket. "I'm not proud of it. I did it for my coven. But, my coven is wrong." She peered up at him with wide eyes. The fury gone from them, sadness took its place. "They can't tamper with what is meant to be. And what is meant to be is you and Divina, your love," she said as her voice cracked.

She took a deep breath, obviously tired from the energy it took to speak of such things in her weakened state.

"You can have love. You will, if you chose Divina. The throne is meant for Percival. The seat is meant for Selene. The coven wants to change that but they shouldn't." As she spoke, she collapsed into a heap between the two planters.

Crouching, Rori reached out for the arms of the witch. When he gripped her, she howled in pain. Rori held her frail limbs and shook her. The tortured woman wailed as the skin on her arms ripped in his hands.

He pulled back, letting her go. His eyes widened and his mouth fell open in horror seeing the bits of flesh stuck to his fingers and palms.

Rori flicked his attention to the pained witch. She crumbled flat to the floor.

"Go to your witch, Roricus. Chase your love. Don't let them strip you too," she sobbed.

Rori's mouth hung slack-jawed. He held his hands away from himself disbelieving the grotesque sight.

It occurred to him, the blood didn't smell right. He closed his mouth and brought his hands closer to his nose. The putrid and nearly black blood held no odor. He peered down at the witch pleading with him. He could see her, hear her words, feel her touch, but not smell her. As a vampire, Rori's possessed a keen sense of smell. A scent that a vampire could detect from hundreds of miles was blood, no matter how black and vile.

Ines sprawled on the ground, atop her woolen blanket. Her arms bled black blood from the sores he had created. It pooled around her, darkening her blanket and inching toward Rori. It dripped from her nose and the corners of her eye sockets. Her hair dropped from her head in clumps.

Rori gawked in disbelief at the vision before him. However, it nagged him that the rotting witch with black blood held no scent.

A hotel worker approached Rori from behind. "Sir?"

Startled, Rori turned to the man, the shock clear on his face.

The hotel worker's youthful face morphed into concern. "Are you okay?"

Rori looked back to the spot between the two planters.

Nothing.

The red-headed witch, Ines, no longer lay dying on the tile. Her woolen blanket and the pool of black blood absent as well.

Rori held up his hands again.

Nothing.

Wide-eyed, Rori regarded the young man in his collared shirt and khakis.

"Should I call someone, sir?" the hotel employee asked.

Rori's disbelieving gaze went back to the spot where the witch had been and looked back to the man.

"Did you—" Rori stopped himself.

Silence in hung heavy in the air while Rori attempted to put it all together. Questioning whether she had been there at all had Rori questioning his own sanity. If the Ember Witches planned on pushing him over the edge to insanity, they were pretty damn close to succeeding.

"Did I what?" The boy tried to coax something from Rori, awakening him from his thoughts.

Rori made a final sweep of the spot where Ines had been.

"I think. I think I need blood." Rori swallowed.

He didn't need blood. He still had Divina's in his system but he felt cold from what Ines had done.

What he needed was to get the hell out of New Orleans.

"The bar, sir." The young man pointed. "They have plenty. Shall I help you?" He leaned down and offered his arm.

Rori shook his head. He stared, not seeing, in the direction of the bar. "I can get there," he said pushing himself back to his feet. While waving him away dismissively, the young man reluctantly stood and regarded Rori with suspicion.

He would go to the bar. He'd collect himself. Maybe, he would drink from someone, for pretenses or just to feel warm again. He just needed a minute.

He needed to figure out what had happened. The possibilities rattled around Rori's mind. The witches could be testing him, Ines could be lying to him, he could have Divina, he could ruin Divina's life. Scrubbing his face with his hand as he walked, did nothing to alleviate the questions. Though he had many, the one question that seemed to dominate all others was whether or not he had passed the test the witches may have laid out for him.

Rori sipped from a waitress who never served a drink. She was hired by the hotel to serve herself. They had several human blood donors available for such a thing. Rori never knew if they were willing donors or if they were merely mind tricked into being there. He assumed it to be some combination of the two.

As he drank from the brunette's wrist, he tried to shake

off the imagined encounter with Ines. The nagging feeling that he had imagined it, that it hadn't occurred at all haunted him. If he hallucinated the encounter, he might be slipping into madness. He wasn't young or that old.

He dismissed the woman with a generous tip. He barely drank from her at all. Rori sat there, in the hotel bar, staring into space. He had no idea what any of it meant. He didn't know who to believe; Esmine or the imagined Ines.

Rori fingered his key card. He didn't need to sort this all out tonight. He had time before the new moon. Not much, but there was still time.

He would rest this night. He'd have a peaceful slumber without anyone to distract him, then figure it all out at the next night. Right now he needed to remove himself from the situation and think about it.

CHAPTER 26

C hirping birds and the sun shining through Divina's window awoke her from a deep, dreamless slumber. She couldn't remember the last time she had slept that soundly. She awoke with the energy of a toddler ready to discover the world.

Divina rolled over and cocooned herself in the duvet. The blanket couldn't match the warmth that danced across her skin when Aric had touched her. The memory of his touch from the previous night sent a tingle through her belly, fanning out over her intimate core. She fought the giggle of a teenage girl with a crush.

Divina smiled, picturing his face: the lopsided, cocky grin he used when he had joked with her. She sighed and whispered his name. Heat spread across her cheeks at the immature behavior.

She had liked guys before. Though, none had left her feeling as content and hopeful as the naked possible, not yet disproven, though probably unlikely, vampire hunting in the woods. Chortling at herself, convinced she'd lost her damn mind, she shook her head.

Having only met the man hours ago, naked mind you, and hunting, her head spun with the insanity of it all. At least when he left, he'd been covered. Really, how much crazier could it get? Not to mention, she had just slept with Rori.

Covering her face with both her hands, Divina buried herself into her bedding. Guilt washed over her at the thought of Rori. The man who tried to enlist her in some supernatural war for the vampire throne and a council seat had just shared a bed with her not twenty-four hours ago. Yet, there she was, lusting after some naked guy who just showed up outside her wagon.

Speaking of which, Perci had shown up outside her wagon as well. As much as Divina wanted to shut out the whole supernatural council prophecy thing, it seemed to know exactly where she was at all times. The only way to get any peace from it, was to deal with it.

Sitting up in her bed, she scrubbed her eyes. She had to go to the witches herself and tell them she wasn't interested. As a powerful witch, she could handle this and not hide behind Rori. They'd said so, as had Rori. She even felt it... sometimes.

Divina would tell those witches where they could stick their seat at the table. She didn't need a damn coven. She had gotten by just fine up until that point without one. So, the prophecy said she had to get Rori's heart going again. She did that. Now, Divina would take back her life.

Fuck the Ember Witches.

The memory of Ines crept into Divina's mind. She wondered what had happened to Ines after Divina took off and left her to her fate. She'd left her to the Ember Witches without a second thought. Ines had stood up to them on Divina's behalf. They didn't like it. And Divina had done nothing for the poor young witch. Instead, she ran like a coward.

Divina pulled her knees up and wrapped her arms around them. She hugged them to her chest and sucked in her bottom lip. They said they were going to punish Ines for going against them. What would they do to Divina for denying them?

Divina mulled it over. Ines had already agreed to join their coven. Divina hadn't.

She swung her legs over the edge of her bed and reached for her clothes. As she tugged on some jeans, she lied to herself. That was the difference between her and Ines. Ines had joined, Divina hadn't, she affirmed while tugging off her nightshirt.

They couldn't punish her. Divina didn't belong to them. They didn't hold the same power over Divina as they did Ines. Divina slipped her arms into her bra while giving herself a mental pep talk.

Divina wondered how badly they hurt Ines. Whatever the punishment, she assumed it involved pain. Would she have the same painful fate for going against the Ember Witches?

She imagined not many did. It couldn't be good not to give some thousands of years old coven what they wanted. Did many live to tell the tale?

Shoving her head into a white linen shirt, Divina stood up. She buttoned her jeans, pulled her shirt down, and looked in the mirror while brushing her teeth. Her wavy hair was an absolute rat's nest. She frowned and tried to finger-comb it. There were too many knots.

She reached for a hair tie and braided her hair loosely. Once satisfied with her look, she left her wagon.

Divina would face the Ember Witches and tell them she wasn't interested.

"Thank you, but no thanks," she said out loud as she climbed into her truck. "You can do this."

~

Goosebumps rose along Aric's skin, following the trail her tongue left behind. He moaned running his fingers through the dark, tangled mane on her head. He threw his head back when her warm mouth made contact with his cock.

She sealed her lips around him and took his full length into silken heaven. Aric's toes curled as he tightened his grip on her hair. He wouldn't guide her, he would hold.

Slowly Divina teased him with her swirling tongue. She bobbed up and down. Aric's hips rose to meet her thrusts. Her mouth encased him in moist satin ecstasy.

Beep. Beep. Beep.

Aric grit his teeth. Her tongue flattened against the underside of his cock.

Beep. Beep. Beep.

Aric tapped her head. The noise stopped.

Strange.

It didn't matter.

He wrapped his arms around Divina. He held her soft naked body against his. He kissed her neck.

Wait. Wasn't he just getting a blowjob?

Beep. Beep. Beep.

Fucking hell! What was that noise? He tapped her head again.

It stopped.

He buried his nose into the crook of her neck and inhaled.

Sawdust.

Aric pulled back.

Sawdust?

He opened his eyes to find that he hugged his pillow. He

turned in his bed, tangled in his sheet, frantically searching for her.

"Divina?" he called out.

She wasn't there. The sawdust scent on the pillow was Aric's. He groaned and fell back against his bed. Maybe if he fell asleep quick enough, he could get right back into the dream.

Beep. Beep. Beep.

Aric's eyes shot open. His phone. He reached over and turned the noise off. He sat up on his bed with it.

He'd be lying if he wasn't half hoping to find a good morning text from her.

No such luck.

He frowned. Not sure what he expected since they didn't exchange numbers the night before. Hell, they barely exchanged names. But, they had made plans and everyone knew plans were better than no plans. He'd see her in a few hours.

Focusing on his phone begrudgingly, he found a series of texts from Bruce. Apparently, the elder wolf was concerned about Aric. Aric lifted his brow at the string of texts he had missed.

The elders had summoned him to breakfast.

Aric climbed out of bed with a groan directed at his erection.

"Sorry, big guy, we have some breakfast business," he said to his cock with a smile.

He threw on some jeans and went to the bathroom without buttoning them.

After doing his business, brushing his teeth, and finding a shirt that didn't smell too offensive, he left his trailer. He had never been summoned by the elders before, and he wasn't too sure how he felt about it.

At the Alpha cabin, located at the center of their pack

territory, the elders gathered for meals. Other pack members could join them at any time, and some did. However, when summoned by the elders for a meal, no one else would be there but the elders and the pack alphas.

Reasons for a summoning varied from an offer to a higher position within the pack, to a demotion, to outright exile. Scrubbing his face with both hands, Aric pondered the reason he could be summoned.

The only thing that came to mind was Selene and her damn prophecy. With a sigh, he climbed out of his truck and headed to breakfast. He wasn't quite sure how Bruce would take the news of Aric dismissing Selene and her prophecy.

Aric approached the giant log cabin the size of a hunting lodge with numerous bedrooms and a sprawling living space. Before he could reach for the knob, the door opened. The petite blond alpha female, Kerry, greeted him with a warm grin. She showed him to the table of elders.

Aric eyed each of the six men with respect. He nodded to each and did a half kneel toward his alpha who sat at the head of the table. Kerry took her spot at the foot. Aric quietly sat in the only open chair, opposite the elders, with no one beside him.

Nothing intimidating about that at all, Aric thought to himself sarcastically.

"Bruce has told us about your conversation with him," the Alpha, Thomas, addressed the group with the authority a king would have spoken to his court.

Aric reached for bacon and scooped some onto his plate. He respected his alpha and he didn't fear the man; speaking with him felt natural.

"About the witch and the prophecy," Aric said.

"Yes," Thomas agreed as he speared some biscuits and gravy with a fork. "You can imagine my surprise at finding out one of my wolves is the key to the fate of the council."

Aric kept his eyes on the plate. His tongue poked at the inside of his cheek. To anyone watching it would look as if he were contemplating what else to sample. However, he was stalled. He wasn't sure about being the wolf of the prophecy. Especially after meeting the human, Divina.

Eventually, Aric regarded Bruce. "I think the witch was wrong," he said.

"Letting your wolf run hasn't cleared your head at all?" Bruce asked with a hint of annoyance in his tone.

Aric tucked some bacon in his mouth. He surveyed the elders and the alphas while he chewed.

"No." He swallowed. "I gained a lot of clarity on the run. I found my mate."

Bruce canted his head. "Your wolf agrees?"

Aric grinned. "If he had his way, we would have claimed her last night."

He shoved another slice of bacon in his mouth in triumph unable to hide his smugness. He wasn't the damned wolf of the fucked-up prophecy.

"I'm sorry to have wasted your time," he said to the group as a whole but his gaze lingered on Bruce a bit longer than the rest since he had been out to the diner to counsel Aric on the whole thing.

"And she's not the witch you met before?" Thomas asked after swallowing some of his biscuits.

Aric turned his attention to his alpha.

"No, thankfully," Aric said.

His loose posture and comfort at the idea of Divina being his mate eased all tension within Aric. The trouble Selene had brought with Perci didn't matter. The prophecy didn't matter. His mate, Divina, she mattered. Getting her to mate with him, that mattered.

Bruce murmured between the elders that sat near him. Worry lined his face. Aric sipped some milk, rather content to not be involved in this prophecy nonsense. However, he did feel a bit guilty having caused the hoopla.

Bruce cleared his throat. "Is she a witch?"

Aric considered the question.

Was she a witch? Good question.

She said she wasn't a seer. Or did she? She said fortune teller. That sounded like human speak for someone who cons other humans out of money. Surely, no self-respecting witch would use that language.

"A fortune teller," he repeated Divina's explanation.

The elders exchanged glances with one another.

Their silence roused the wolf within Aric. The wolf snorted with impatience. Aric shifted uncomfortably.

"Have you ever met a witch before, Aric?" Kerry asked while she moved some eggs around on her plate without looking up.

Aric turned toward her, not quite putting his back to the men.

"Not before the one who came to my trailer," he said.

She smiled and lifted her chestnut gaze toward him. "They don't like to be known," she explained. "Their kind is often exploited for the gains of others. Humans are known to come to them for enchantments and then persecute them. Vampires feed on them for the long-lasting effects of their blood. Not to mention, the allure of magic being a potential way for them to walk in the sun."

The alpha female regarded her mate from across the table before she placed her fork down. She put her hands on her lap and continued.

"Then there is our own kind. We have not been fair to witches historically, either," she said solemnly.

Aric considered her words. He glanced at his plate of bacon for answers. His eyes drifted upward toward the elders.

Bruce nodded in his direction.

Once more, Aric glanced around the table. Just as he had assumed, all attention directed at him. No one ate anything. A buffet of breakfast, everything you could want displayed out in front of them, but they all watched him. As he met each of their intent gazes he wondered if they wanted him to mate a witch. Did they want him to be the wolf of the prophecy?

Aric cleared his throat. "How do I know if she is a witch?"

It wasn't like they wore signs or anything.

CHAPTER 27

With the morning sun at her back, Divina took a double take at the open gate of the Ursuline Convent. Taking it as a sign they knew she'd come made her linger at the gate a bit longer, hesitating whether or not to go through with her plan. If they expected her, she wouldn't have the upper hand.

A middle-aged couple, with cameras around their necks, passed through the gate beside Divina. Their wide smiles matched the excitement in their eyes. They headed toward the small hedge maze near the door.

Perplexed, Divina blinked at them. They couldn't be witches. Then it dawned on her: it was an active museum open to the public. People loved the history of New Orleans. Of course, humans would be there touring the convent in the daylight hours.

Taking a deep breath, steeling herself for the confrontation, Divina headed toward the maze. Two older people passed her on their way out, raving about the beauty of the museum and the rich Catholic history. Divina hesitated as she watched them pass.

Doubt creeped in and hacked at her confidence in her decision to confront the witches. Question swirled in her mind regarding whether or not the witches would even be there during the day, it seemed risky to convene with so many humans about. Surely, the access to the subbasement, where they met, would be off-limits to Divina. She couldn't just waltz in, give a wink and nod to a guard, and have access to the full place. With a sigh, she leaned against the post trying to formulate a new plan.

For all she knew, the witches only met under the cover of night. They'd call to the moon to summon its pull on the earth to add potency to their vrăji. She snorted as the thought crept into her mind. Perhaps the witches were vampires after all. They only did their witchiness at night. It seemed plausible.

"Hello, Divina," a warm voice greeted her as a woman approached.

The greeting pulled Divina from her thoughts. She shifted her attention to the woman, Josephine.

Dressed in a loose-fitting, cotton smock-like dress, Josephine looked like a tourist. If the witch was trying to look nonthreatening, she nailed it.

Despite this, Divina regarded her with apprehension. She wasn't Esmine but she still belonged to the manipulative coven. This made her trustworthiness questionable at best.

Josephine reached out her arms for Divina.

Divina pulled back slightly, cautious of the woman and her extended limbs. Divina eyed Josephine as though she might come at her with a net, meant to ensnare and trap her, rather than welcoming arms meant to greet her. Josephine took Divina's hands into her own patting them in a tender gesture.

"I'm so glad you came back," Josephine said.

"I have questions," Divina retorted, not wanting to fall for the warm, welcoming act.

Josephine nodded. "I expected nothing less."

"First, what happened to Ines?" Divina asked.

Josephine's friendly expression faltered ever so slightly. The sparkle in her eyes lapsed. The smile lines weren't as deep. She looked away a moment, and her gaze surveyed all who were around.

Her attention returned to Divina. With it, came the 100 watt, friendly, non-threatening smile.

"Covens are very strong, dear," she whispered as she released Divina's hand and gestured for her to walk. "And ours is renowned for its strength."

Divina followed, staying silent. She wanted an answer. What she got wasn't an answer.

"The only way for covens to remain strong is for the witches within them to work together," Josephine said. Her voice didn't rise above a whisper as they made their way out of the hedges and into the convent museum. "When a witch joins a coven, she agrees to work with the other witches. No one witch's agenda should take precedence over the good of the coven," Josephine continued.

She stopped to smile and wave toward a guard. The young man nodded and stepped away from a stairwell door. Josephine progressed through it with Divina in tow. "The Ember Witches have the added pressure of Esmine serving on the Council of Others. So our group agenda far exceeds that of any individual. It extends to all covens in the territory." She paused as the door closed. "We do not take our responsibility lightly."

Divina studied Josephine. While her words were heavy and serious in nature, they were delivered in a kind and loving tone, filled with patience. Josephine looked upon Divina as a grandmother would when she passed advice about the world onto her granddaughter.

"Ines knew this." Josephine's voice soured slightly. "She was a young witch. She had a lot of potential." Josephine shook her head, and her voice cracked. "Ines chose her own agenda over that of the coven and over all other witches."

"I know what she did," Divina pressed. "I want to know what the coven did to her."

Josephine lifted her chin, her arms folded across her chest. She regarded Divina with a downward glance.

Divina straightened her spine. She intended to give the illusion of confidence.

"The coven protected itself, and in doing so protected all of the others," Josephine declared vaguely.

Divina glared. "How does the coven protect itself from its own?"

Josephine's throat bobbed as she swallowed. "Her offense was very grave, Divina."

The way Josephine justified the actions rather than coming out with them led Divina to believe that Ines's punishment must have been something awful. Divina needed to know. She didn't want to lose her resolve.

"I'm supposed to join your coven," Divina said. Josephine nodded, and the two descended a stairwell. "I'm supposedly this very powerful witch," Divina reminded.

"It's not supposed. You are very potent."

"So then tell me the punishment for-for-for...." Divina struggled with the right words.

"Betraying your coven?" Josephine suggested.

Divina hadn't thought of it that way. Ines had betrayed her coven. Ines had done something strictly prohibited. Divina took in a deep breath. "Yes," she said unsure she was fully prepared for the answer.

At the bottom of the stairs, they stood before a large door. Beyond it, after a storage closet, was the great room with the horseshoe-shaped table.

While the convent itself thrummed with the energy, Divina couldn't tell the difference if the static in the air was due to the table of witches she'd seen the last time or from the witches of years passed who had come to this place. Running a hand up her own arm, she doubted her ability to face all the witches again, especially Esmine.

"A coven can strip a witch of her power," Josephine said with a hint of pain in her voice. "It's very hard to do and can be detrimental for the witch being stripped."

Wide eyed, Divina's mouth fell open. "You killed her?"

Josephine twitched. "We stripped her. Ines had friends who could have given her more time if she so desired."

Unable to reconcile the cold action with the soothing nature of the woman before her, Divina shook her head. She turned away from Josephine.

A witch without her power was a husk of a human. She would continue to exist, hollow, never feeling complete. They had sentenced her to a death of sorts. If she lived through the act of stripping, the emptiness could drive her to suicide. From what Divina had read, a stripped witch led a painful existence of pure hell.

Divina met Josephine's gaze, searching for some sort of remorse or regret.

With her hand on the door, she turned away from Divina.

"Ines knew it was coming," Josephine said.

Unease and disappointment flowed through Divina. Rori had painted a picture of an understanding coven where she would be taught the ways of the witch. She'd learn from Bătrânii, spells passed down through generations. She expected a sense of belonging, of love, and family.

Yet, she stood with the elder witch, speaking of sentencing another witch to an empty existence with detachment. The justification of Ines knowing the consequences, of Ines knowing it would come, left Divina wondering if the punishment fit the crime and furthermore, whether it mattered.

The motherly presence of Josephine, her soft tone of voice, and large eyes gave Divina the idea that the explanation of Ines's knowledge of what would happen would somehow comfort Divina. Though, she felt anything but comforted with the thought, and Ines's knowledge of it didn't make it better.

"She knew she would be stripped?" Divina asked.

Josephine nodded. "It was foretold in her youth. She would have the opportunity to be an Ember Witch, but it would have a price for her. Ines paid the price for the honor of being in the coven."

Once again, Divina's features reflected her disbelief. She blinked, trying to comprehend the information given to her.

"She chose it?" Divina whispered.

"Ines chose to join the coven knowing what it would cost her," Josephine clarified. "She could have joined any other coven, but she chose this one because she understood the greater picture."

Divina's gaze fell to the ground, as though she couldn't face the words, the situation, or the information coming at her. She brought her hands to her temples and tried to massage understanding into her head.

In that short period of time, Divina had been given an encyclopedia of information to process. She placed a hand to her throat to stave off the drowning sensation taking over.

Josephine's hand rested on her back. The soothing gesture sent a calm wave through Divina. She looked upon Josephine the way a child looked upon her mother after a nightmare. She desperately needed the comfort in the face of all that overwhelmed her.

"When we are born into this life, as witches, we are born into a life of self-sacrifice. It is our burden as Ember Witches." Josephine sighed and added, "It is now your turn. Her seat is meant for you."

"But," Divina started to protest.

Josephine rubbed circles into her back gently. "You quickened the vampire's heart. You found the wolf. Now, all that is left is for you to join your coven and become the strong witch you are fated to be."

Divina gasped as breath was stolen from her lungs. Wide-eyed Divina opened her mouth and closed it while words failed her. The weight of Josephine's statement crushed Divina.

They had told her she would have a seat at the table. Surely, that had meant after some training or something. Wanting her to take the seat now, felt immature. The table was for proficient witches, Divina could do simple spells, summon the wind, but nothing like she thought would be expected for one to be seated at the table.

"The wolf?" Divina said.

Josephine smiled. "All in time, Divina," she said. Pushing the door open, she revealed the storage area of the museum. "We have a lot to teach you before the new moon."

Divina numbly followed Josephine through the basement. In a state of overload, Divina wasn't sure she could process any more information. She tried to sort through it all in her mind as they walked through the storage shelves.

Days; it had been mere days. She was a fortune teller at a carnival. Then her vampire ex-boyfriend showed up and turned her whole world upside down.

Now she followed a powerful witch telling her she's supposed to be a leader of the most prevailing coven in all the country. If that wasn't enough, she was also some prophetic witch about to change the world. Oh! And she forgot to mention this mysterious wolf she was supposed mate with. The world responded by spinning, making Divina light-headed. The ground fell out from under her feet. Her knees threatened to give out. Divina couldn't do it.

She reached out for Josephine. Making contact with her arm, Divina gripped it tightly. Josephine came to Divina's side and supported her with large worried eyes. "Are you okay?" she asked.

Divina shook her head. "No. This is all too much. Rori, the Ember Witches, joining a coven, the council, and a wolf! A wolf!"

Josephine's gaze swept over Divina with understanding in her eyes. She rubbed Divina's arms sending a soothing wave from her touch through Divina.

"Our fate often comes to us when we feel we are least prepared," Josephine whispered close to Divina's ear.

"I don't want any of this!" Divina shouted. "I don't want to be at the table. I don't care about the council and vampires. I'm not even a dog person. I don't know a wolf." She turned to Josephine pleading. She gripped the smock dress Josephine wore in her fists, desperate to get her message through. "I just want to go back to my wagon and tell fortunes and be left alone," Divina said with eyes filled with tears. Her body trembled as she reached the breaking point.

Josephine's brows knitted together. She stood in silence while her hand stroked Divina's hair.

Tears streamed down Divina's cheeks. Sobs erupted from deep within her. She fell to her knees holding onto Josephine to keep from crumbling into a pathetic heap.

Crouching down, Josephine wrapped her arms around Divina.

Divina fell into Josephine's embrace and rested her cheek against Josephine's chest. Allowing Josephine to envelop her in patience and understanding, Divina cried.

Josephine stroked her cheek and placed her chin on

Divina's head. "Shhh." Josephine soothed. "It's a lot, I know." She pulled back so that she could look into Divina's eyes. "You can do this. You are a strong witch. We can teach you. We can help you through this. You just have to let us," she said with Divina's face cupped in her gentle hands.

Divina sniffled as she scanned Josephine's features desperately seeking some sort of sign of trustworthiness. She felt like a child cradled in her mother's arms, having just seen the boogeyman under her bed. She cleared her throat and did one final swipe at each cheek. She swallowed down future sobs and willed her tears away. Taking a deep breath, she tried to center herself. She was a grown woman, a witch—a powerful witch. She needed to get a hold of herself.

Josephine beamed. "Here."

Still holding Divina with one arm around her shoulders, Josephine reached up to the shelves. She tugged out a large, leather-bound tome. Enchantments pulsed from it and tendrils of power reached for Divina. The leather, though old, had been well oiled and maintained and held no title. It smelled of old papers and dust.

"This is the first book of the Ember Witches. It is meant to introduce you to us. Read it." Josephine licked her bottom lip. "Seers can foretell times when we are fated for big decisions. They see a point when we are going to face major choices; that is fate. Fate is making important choices that will have a lasting impact beyond our years." Josephine patted the top of the book. "You always have a choice. Come back at midnight," she said.

Divina ran her hand over the soft leather of the cover. She nodded to Josephine's instructions, unable to muster any words.

The book held Divina's focus. Hope sprang up within her, feeling unfamiliar. This book held the answers. This book would explain it all.

CHAPTER 28

Witches are humans with a little extra. Aric rolled his eyes as he drove to the diner. Wasn't every supernatural creature a human with a little extra? The elders were of no help whatsoever.

Witches, much more on the human end of the spectrum compared to wolves or vampires, were almost indistinguishable from humans.

They had no silver allergy. They could walk in the sunlight. They didn't melt when in contact with water. Hell, they even smelled like humans.

Movies had not prepared Aric well for witch determination.

Their only weakness: their humanity. This, for supernatural beings, was a major disadvantage. With a human level of endurance and lifespan, a witch was vulnerable. Casting spells and enchantments took energy. If the witch wasn't practiced enough for a spell, she either wouldn't be able to perform it or couldn't hold it for very long.

So, what was Aric supposed to do, trick Divina into

casting a spell? Aric snorted as the thought passed through his mind. He could ask her outright. That wouldn't make things awkward in the least bit. Plus, hadn't he already done that when he asked her if she was a seer? She sure as shit dodged that.

He pondered that idea for a moment. Divina did know about supernatural creatures. She had assumed he was a vampire. The wolf within Aric bristled at the memory. Aric most certainly wasn't a vampire. How could she mistake him for one? She mustn't know much about wolves. Maybe she only knew about vampires. She did have the scarring that suggested having been bitten before.

The thought triggered a rumble from Aric's inner wolf.

"Quiet you," he chastised his inner beast. "We can't change her past."

The wolf within him settled, albeit begrudgingly, and flopped down within Aric.

He refocused his thought process. Perhaps she was just a human blood donor. Well, a reformed donor.

Aric wouldn't allow his mate to give blood to any vampires. Nope. The only mouth touching her from now on would be his. He and his wolf nodded in internal affirmation. They agreed on that point. With their agreements seeming rarer and rarer as of late, it relieved Aric to find some common ground with his inner animal. Perhaps things were looking up.

Aric climbed out of his truck, grabbing the freshly washed and folded blanket. He arrived early at the diner but sauntered in any way. He wanted a good booth and didn't want to make her wait.

Plus, she was a flight risk. He didn't want to give her any more excuses to leave without seeing him. The early wolf gets the mate, he mused.

Selecting a booth against the window, toward the back of the diner seemed the best for a hint of privacy and intimacy. Sure, the brightly lit diner was a stark contrast to a romantically lit steak house, but Aric made do for what he thought would be the first of many dates.

Next time he'd do better. Next time he'd woo her with elegant food and ambiance. There would be a next time. He wouldn't let his mate get away so easily. He'd chase her to the ends of the earth and back again if he had to.

He hadn't been sitting long before the smell of moss and forest rain wafted over burgers and fried diner foods. The wolf within Aric snapped to attention.

Aric looked up from his memorized menu to see Divina escorted to the table.

The male shifter showing Divina to their table stood too close, offering Aric a quizzical look. Aric's wolf didn't take too kindly to other wolves being that close or the insulation that Divina didn't belong there. Aric's inner beast snapped territorially. Yes, she was a human in a wolf den, get over it. Outwardly, Aric glared toward the young diner employee.

Making eye contact, the young male shifter bowed his head toward Aric in a submissive gesture to Aric's glowering. He dashed off, leaving Divina's menu on the table without further explanation.

Divina furrowed her brow watching the fleeing worker.

Yep. No doubt about it. That female was his. Aric's possessive instinct was almost overwhelming.

Shaking her head, Divina turned and grinned at Aric.

Aric's stomach flipped, and his pants got tight in the crotch. Another sign she was his mate, his body's uncontrollable reactions to her scent, to her presence, to everything about her. He couldn't remember a time when he had responded as viscerally to any female.

Sure, females had inspired erections before, but not like this. The steel in his pants pressed painfully against his thigh.

He wanted, more than anything, to have her in his bed. He wanted all of her, in every way imaginable. He wanted to be near her, to touch her, to hold her, to protect her, to mark her for all to see.

His inner animal panted in eager agreement with these ideas. The impulsive beast could get him in trouble if Aric released him anywhere near Divina. Without a doubt, the wolf would pounce on her to stake a claim before the human Aric could ease her into it.

Divina scooted into the red, squeaky vinyl booth across from him. "Well, you clean up nice," she said while her ice-colored eyes scanned him. Her gaze landed on the blanket. She chuckled placing a hand over her smile.

"I told you I would get it back to you before you left." Aric's smugness persisted.

She lifted the menu off the table a few inches. Aric appreciated that she didn't hide her face with it. He enjoyed the view in the sunshine. The afternoon rays accented her tawny complexion. Her eyes glittered in the brightness in a way they hadn't when they'd met in the dark. Her entire demeanor radiated a sense of energy he hadn't seen in her the night before.

"I told you I wasn't a vampire," Aric said in a low whisper.

Divina peered at him. "Hmm?"

Aric gestured to the window as the sun's rays warmed his skin. He'd purposely sat in a window with a lot of sunlight coming through it. Though, the position of the sun sent beams right into his eyes making him squint to see her fully.

It didn't matter, though. He wanted to make a point.

"I'm not burning," he half teased, half clarified.

She furrowed her brow for a moment before realization set in. "Oh!" She laughed.

She admired him for a bit longer, and Aric puffed out his chest.

With a snicker, she shook her head and brought her attention back to the menu. With a pink hue flushing her cheeks, she blushed. Oh, Aric liked that look on her a hell of a lot. His wolf howled in agreement.

Without looking at him, she responded, "I'm not sure if I'm leaving."

Well, that didn't take long. One lunch date in the sun and she agreed to stay. That couldn't be right. As confident as he was in himself, even he had to admit something else was at play. Aric lifted his brows in surprise. His wolf sat up to attention.

"Did a handsome nonvampire convince you to stay?" Aric suggested hopefully, but jokingly.

She raised her ice blue eyes to him. "Someone thinks highly of himself."

Aric postured and flexed his muscles. "Being humble is overrated."

She laughed. Her body shook as a subtle tension visibly left her. When she completed her laugh with a sigh, she took a second to look upon him.

Aric swore he saw a fondness in her gaze. He waggled his brows in an exaggeratedly suggestive move.

Divina raised her menu higher and hid her face.

Aric frowned. He fought the urge to pull the menu down. His mate should feel free to show her emotions, especially to him. He wanted to witness them all.

"It seems fortune tellers could make a good profit here," she said casually.

Fortune teller; the evasive answer to his seer question. Her dodge of his subtle attempt to find out if she was a witch. He regarded her with pursed lips.

"It is New Orleans. I imagine you could do well here," he

said unable to shake the feeling the two were dancing around a giant pink elephant in the room that neither acknowledged.

"What do you do?" she asked lowering the menu.

Aric's heart, wolf, and dick swooned at the sight of her eyes again. He tried to push the image of her looking up at him from her knees out of his head. That idea would do nothing to ease the painful stiffness testing the limits of his jeans.

"Construction. Modular homes mostly," he replied.

She placed the menu on the table and folded her hands over it.

"So you're out in the sun a lot." Her gaze went to his hands and then his neck.

He canted his head in curiosity. "Yes. Looking for tan lines?" he asked with a raised brow.

Divina's cheeks turned a shade of red. Aric's wolf howled within him. Aric licked his lower lip and bit down on it as his persistent raging erection strained against the denim around it.

She cleared her throat. "No."

Her eyes shifted left and right as she surveyed the room. She leaned over the table.

"I just, well, I am still a little...," she whispered, trailing off and not completing her thought.

"I'm still not a vampire," he returned her whispered and leaned over the table closer to her.

Their faces were inches apart. Her scent wrapped around Aric causing his skin to tingle. His cock threatened to burst through his jeans. She intoxicated him.

If possible, Divina's cheeks turned a deeper shade of red. The blush extended down her neck and Aric couldn't help but wonder how far down. Unashamedly, his gaze traveled down her chin, her neck, and to the neckline of her shirt.

They followed the trail of adorable embarrassment on his mate until blocked by her clothing.

She sat back and shrunk down a bit.

Aric grinned in amusement.

"It's been an odd few days," she confessed.

Aric narrowed his eyes to study her. Something bothered his mate. His need to make her life easier, to be her partner in all things rushed out of his mouth.

"How can I help?" he asked impulsively.

Divina blinked at him. Help? He'd offered to help her, and for some reason that felt odd to her. Surely someone had offered to help her before at some point in her life. Of course they did, when she was a kid. She got help all the time as a kid.

Not as an adult. She couldn't remember the last time someone offered to help her with much of anything important without an agenda. Sure, to help her carry something or open a door. Yes, people offered to help her all the time in that respect. Cordial politeness couldn't be considered help.

Of course, Rori and the Ember Witches offered help, but only to help themselves. Help with strings attached wasn't truly help. Conditional help didn't count.

With her internal debate regarding help sufficiently explored, she made a decision. Aric offered help because he had no idea the help she needed. She chalked it up to the social politeness offer of help.

"I don't think you can," Divina declined. "I'm not sure anyone else could handle this sort of stuff."

"Try me," he urged.

Persistent little bastard, he was. She admired that. Good-looking and persistent; score two for Aric Braun.

A waitress came by to take their orders. Divina noted the woman's attention lingered on Aric after she took his order. The woman licked her lip as she took in the muscled physique of Divina's date.

Possession surged through Divina. She clenched her fists at her sides and glared at the woman. Divina tightened her jaw to the point she thought her teeth might crack. The gall of the woman, the rudeness, it grated at Divina. She sat right there. Aric was on a date. Yet, the unprofessional waitress mooned over him like Divina didn't exist.

"I'll have a cheeseburger," Divina began her order, in an attempt to interrupt the woman ogling Aric.

The waitress cleared her throat. She turned toward Divina to take the rest of her order with the fakest smile Divina had ever seen. A small sense of victory filled Divina. She needed that. She had a feeling the road ahead of her would be riddled with defeats. So even this tiny victory, over a waitress's eyes on her man—well, that she would take.

Sitting back in the seat, Divina's own thought stunned her. She'd just met the guy. Jealousy wasn't common for Divina. Especially, when it came to a guy she barely knew. Hell, she'd never felt it with Rori.

She pushed the thoughts and emotions aside. She didn't need to worry about any of that. However, the waitress's entrance had awarded her an opportunity to switch topics from her needing help and the witches.

Polite, "get to know you" conversation seemed to be working for them so far. Might as well stick with that course of conversation and forget all about the irrational possessiveness.

"Do you live around here?" Divina asked.

Aric's face fell. He must have picked up on Divina's not-too-subtle topic change.

She smiled back and sipped her water innocently.

"Yes, been here my whole life." He fingered the straw to his water.

Divina squirmed under the intensity of his gaze upon her. She felt like a specimen behind observation glass. She shifted in her seat. Torn between wanting to posture for Aric, to make a good impression, and shrinking away from the inquisitive gaze, she chewed at the inside of her cheek.

He lifted his brows. "And where are you from?"

CHAPTER 29

Time passed as the two not only enjoyed their meals, but Divina found his company delightful. The relaxed, easy-going way Aric joked and carried himself allowed Divina a reprieve from the pressures of the prophecy, the witches, and Rori. It felt like ages since she had been able to be this normal, this human.

Flipping her hair, batting her eyelashes, Divina flirted effortlessly with Aric. Charm and humor came from him and it drew her in. Each moment that passed, Divina felt transported back to the days before Rori; the days when she believed herself to be just a human. Her life had been so simple once.

Dragging out their lunch longer than necessary led Divina to believe Aric didn't want their little date to end, either. Leaving the diner, she suggested they walk around New Orleans. Aric took it upon himself to point out historical sights, acting as her personal tour guide.

The smile never left Divina's face as he excitedly told her both history and lore of the sites they passed. It wasn't long before his hand slid against hers and their fingers entwined as they strolled. The simple act of their joined hands elicited a skip in her heart beat. A pulse of infatuation pumped through Divina as she tumbled into being smitten.

Spending the afternoon with him lacked all the drama to which she had become accustomed. There was no worry about the sun or from whom he had recently fed. Aric was normal. Aric was human, and Divina was practically human. She could pretend.

Not to mention it felt right.

Aric's infectious laugh made Divina's cheeks hurt from joining him and smiling along with him. His smile caused her heart to flutter when she saw the dimple in his one cheek.

With playful storytelling of haunted buildings and supposed brothels, he held Divina's rapt attention. When speaking of ill-fated lovers, Aric pulled Divina close offering gentle squeezes of reassurance. Each time she all but melted in his arms.

Entering New Orleans City Park, Divina couldn't help but get wrapped up in the romantic scenery while they walked past a sea of wildflowers. An enchanting oasis amid the urban development of New Orleans, couldn't have been a more perfect setting for the tail end of their lunch date. Divina marveled at the massive oak trees, whose branches webbed together making a canopy for her and Aric to walk through.

Pausing while walking across a stone bridge, Divina peered over the edge as some ducks swam beneath the bridge. Taking a deep breath, appreciating the reprieve from the craziness of the last two days, she wished time could stand still.

Exploring every inch of the park was a much more preferred option than dealing with a prophecy she had been dragged into. Pausing the day with Aric, just the two of them, enjoying an endless moment in a beautiful setting spurred a longing for him like Divina had never experienced.

Aric approached from behind her taking her out of her whimsical thoughts. The heat of his body against her back gave her goosebumps. His arms came around her sides, effectively caging her against the stone railing. A piney scent, that she assumed to be his cologne, wrapped around her along with his body. With closed eyes, Divina inhaled deeply to fully revel in it. Despite having been held similarly on two occasions, previously by two vampires, Divina didn't bristle at the closeness. There was no fear, no prickle of wrongness; with Aric, it felt delightful and right.

Stubble grazed her shoulder in a tickle as he lowered his chin to nuzzle into the crook of her neck. Shivers ran through her from the sensation. The warmth from his body, the feel of his hard muscled arms around her, and his smell enveloping her left Divina dizzy with desire.

Slowly, Divina turned her back to the water but remained in his arms. Hazel eyes peered down at her with the hunger of a starving man. Aric slouched so that his mouth came down on hers. With his finger crooked under her chin, she tilted her head upward and welcomed his kiss.

Silken soft lips, surrounded by the coarse nubs of his five o'clock shadow, pressed against Divina's lips. Gently, yet enticingly, his tongue swiped along her bottom lip, prompting her to open for him. Aric tilted his head deepening the tender kiss. Callused hands rested on her hips, and she looped her arms around his shoulders.

As he pulled her closer, Divina's soft body pressed against Aric's hardened wall of a chest. Welcoming the closer embrace, she wrapped her arms tighter around his shoulders. Divina's heart pounded rapidly as the kiss grew in passion.

The pressure of his mouth against hers stole her breath. His tongue speared into her mouth seeking to dance with hers. She couldn't tell if the moaning from the kiss came from her or him.

217

Little pinpoints of pain mixed with pleasure, as Aric's fingers dug into the flesh of Divina's hips. Rolling them toward him in response, Divina lifted up onto her toes. Teeth scrapped along her bottom lip, as Aric nibbled into their kiss, causing Divina to groan.

The heat from their joined bodies cascaded down Divina as a wave of pleasure-seeking need pooled in her sex. Tingles radiated up from her pussy through her body, and she returned his kissing nibbles with her own. Each swipe of his tongue and grip on her hips fed the desire for him, which left her needy for just that bit more.

The rough stone of the bridge wall scratched her back as Aric pushed her against it. Pinned between the wall of sex god, Aric, and the literal stone wall of the bridge had Divina swooning into the kiss. She half believed that if he were to step back, she'd crumble into a puddle of wanton lust.

Running her hands over the back of his neck, she entangled her fingers in his hair. A rumbled growl came from him sending a jolt of arousal through her entire body fueling her greedy need for more of him.

Sliding his arms around her waist, Aric's rough hands each gripped a globe of her ass. Kneading her butt sent a flurry through Divina's core. She broke the kiss gasping for breath.

Before she could make eye contact, Aric trailed his lips down her jaw and ran his tongue down her neck. Shuddering, she tugged at his hair again while the warmth of his breath, and tongue, tickled her skin causing goosebumps.

Divina fisted his hair as she threw her head back.

Aric's teeth grazed her shoulder, and Divina hissed loudly.

"I thought you—" She paused licking her lip when he sucked on her neck. "—weren't...." Formulating words was hard under his attentions.

Disctracting her with erotic nips, he didn't give her pain

so much as pressure hinting toward it. Feeling like a single giant exposed nerve, her body thrummed from the senstions.

He growled loudly and took her face in his hands. With his forehead rested against hers, she could finally meet his eyes. Gone was the soft hazel color she had seen most of the afternoon. In their place, blazing golden irises, filled with hedonistic passion.

It should have scared her. She told herself to be scared. She wasn't.

Instead, the desire to have him, to devour him in kisses and feel him buried inside her overwhelmed her. Slipping her hands from his neck, down his sides, she gripped his hips. Crushing her mouth against his, she tugged him hard against her as wanton lust consumed her thoughts.

"I'm not," he breathlessly assured her in between kisses.

Vampires. Vampires, her care for vampires vanished, no longer mattering, when he continued to claim her mouth. His kisses grew hungry and needy. Alternative between rubbing and groping, Aric's hands roved over Divina's ass. He ground his stiff erection against her hip and, once again, Divina lifted up onto her toes, moaning into their kiss.

Divina's sex burned with need for him. Butterflies swarmed her belly fluttering about. The sensation traveled through her, settling into her core. Barely able to contain her desire to strip him down on the bridge and beg him to take her, she broke their kiss and gasped for breath.

"Can we go somewhere?" she asked while panting.

Short of breath himself, with his chest heaving Aric's golden eyes scanned her face.

"Yes," he agreed and kissed her one more time.

Even the brief, chaste kiss had Divina's toes curling. She wasn't sure how much more she could take, or how much longer she could wait before she exploded. The man did things to her she hadn't imagined possible.

CHAPTER 30

A ric's wolf howled loudly. The animal within him pushed
to claim Divina. Tightening every muscle in his body,
he fought to restrain the animal within. Not out in the open.
He needed privacy for such an intimate act.

The suggestion to go somewhere, the idea of getting her
alone, eased Aric's tension. The two of them were on the
same page.

Thankfully, his pack's land was not far from the park.
Taking her hand, he led her in a jog toward to his truck.
Though the distance was short, it felt like an eternity when
done with a raging erection and a howling wolf in his head.

Arriving at the truck, Aric couldn't control it. He gripped
Divina, pushed her against the cab and claimed her mouth
once more. The curves of her soft body begged to be
explored, and Aric's hands were up to the task.

Divina's lips tasted like strawberries. Her earthy scent
coiled around Aric causing his steely erection to strain for
release. Sure it would burst from his jeans at any second, Aric
ground himself against her once more.

He needed his mate. Controlling the desire to have her tested every fiber of his being. If he didn't rein it in, he'd take her in the bed of his truck.

Slipping his hands under her linen shirt, he sought to explore her body without barriers. Disdain for her clothing preventing him from having full access to his mate, tempted him to tear it from her, to expose her to him. His wolf urged him to do just that, to reveal her natural form to them.

They were in public; he couldn't strip her. Doubting she'd want to bare all to the park, he restrained himself. Plus, he'd lose his shit if another male even looked at her naked.

"I need you," he rumbled as he yanked open the truck door.

Divina's hungry blue eyes swept over him, and she nodded. "Me too," she agreed breathlessly.

Inside the car, he had to touch her again, to taste her again. Reaching for her, he pressed her back on the bench seat, settling his larger body over hers. Without a fight, without hesitation, she yielded to him and allowed him to cover her.

Divina pulled her leg up and curled it over his hip. Gods his female was tempting. If he didn't know any better, he swore her hips rolled against him as he caught her earlobe between his teeth.

She gasped.

He smiled and flicked his tongue before pulling back. Too little space, he needed room to fully enjoy his mate.

The two were able to catch their breaths on the short drive to Aric's trailer. Once there, he all but ran around the front of his truck to pull her door open. With his hands on her hips, he lifted her out of the cab.

She laughed, and it was the most wonderful sound he had ever heard.

Throwing her over his shoulder, he gave her a hearty spank to the ass.

Wide eyed, Aric froze in place. Tangled in her earthy scent was another that had his wolf in a frenzy. Her sex, so close to his nose, brought the aroma of her need for him close enough to smell. The thick musky scent invaded his awareness, overwhelming him.

Aric's cock pulsed in his jeans, and the zipper painfully scraped against his erection. With her need for him filling his nostrils, Aric clenched his teeth to the point he thought they'd crack. Kicking open his unlocked door, with disregard for the potential damage, Aric carried her toward his bedroom. His confidence in his own ability to hold back from taking her waned with each inhale of her scent.

Tossing her to the mattress, Divina bounced down laughing. When her legs fell open when she landed, Aric's mouth watered. He nestled himself between them reaching for the button of her jeans.

Tickling his belly, Divina's hands went to the hem of his shirt and yanked it over his head. The cool air on his hot skin sent a chill down his spine.

Not wanting to be the only one missing clothing, Aric tugged down her jeans. Simple turquoise cotton panties covered her. Lips curling in an appreciative smile, Aric drank in the image of his panty-clad mate. His hands jerked when the pants hit a snag.

Apparently, he had forgotten that shoes were a thing.

Laughter erupted from the two of them, while Aric desperately fought to untangle her feet from her jeans. With a few simple kicks, Divina freed her legs, and her shoes fell from her feet, followed by her jeans.

Electricity shot through his fingers, quickening the beat of his heart, as he trailed his hands up the smooth skin of her legs. The jolt of touching his mate in an intimate way had the beast within Aric howling in anticipation.

"You are absolutely marvelous." An unrecognizable gravelly voice came from Aric.

The blush ran through her body, starting in her chest and flourishing at her cheeks. If possible, the intensity of his need for her kicked up another notch.

"You're pretty impressive yourself," she retorted, and her teeth pressed into her swollen bottom lip.

Delicate hands reached for him and pulled him down to her. Once settled with his body over hers, she snaked her hands upward and tugged fistfuls of hair at the base of his neck. Prickles of pleasure danced across his scalp.

Groaning, he pushed her shirt up and tugged her bra cups down. Taking a moment, he marveled at the rounded, tanned flesh of her breasts propped up by the underwire. Lowering his head, Aric mouthed one her breasts. Palming the other, he teased her until her nipples tightened into hard nubs. Plucking one between his fingers, he grazed his teeth along the other until she hissed.

Her body squirmed beneath him and her hips thrust up against his. The pressure from her and his jeans against his erection elicited a painful grunt. They needed to be removed before his cock was too damaged to be useful.

"Gods!" she cried.

Divina's erratic breathing turned into moans. Minor pains trickled down his back and her nails scraped either side of his spine. Sucking her nipple into his mouth, he pulled back until it snapped and she groaned, bucking up against him again. He smirked before his focus switched to the other breast.

"I want to touch you." Laced with decadent desire, her voice mesmerized him.

Each time Aric's teeth, tongue, or fingers made contact

with the tight buds on her breasts, Divina twitched under him. Each movement from her sent a surge of need to his dick. If he wasn't careful, he would explode in his jeans. He wanted her. His wolf needed her.

Two hands on the thin fabric covering her hips, Aric slid her panties down with a good yank. Urgently, Divina kicked out of them. The uninhibited scent of arousal wafted toward Aric like a slap in the face.

Crashing down on her, Aric covered her mouth with claiming kisses. He nipped at her demanding she yield to him, submit to his will. Drunk on her sexual scent, his wolf wanted to send a message that this female was his.

Aric only broke the kiss so that he could drop his own pants.

"Wait!" she gasped.

Stopping every movement, Aric froze in place. He regarded her with wide eyes. The idea he had read the situation wrong, that she might not be a willing sexual partner, had him stuck. He'd never taken a female unwillingly, and he wouldn't start with his mate.

The musk from the apex of her thighs told him her body wanted him. Remaining statue still, his painfully stiff erection bobbing between them, he wouldn't proceed without her permission, despite his feral urges.

"Condom," she rasped.

Her hungry eyes roved his body, locking on his erection. Her pink tongue slid along her bruised lower lip and Aric winced.

Aric tilted his head. Condoms? Did he have condoms? He reached for the drawer of his nightstand.

Aha!

A quick bite of his teeth, the wrapper ripped, and he proudly displayed a disc of protection. It took him a full second to roll the blue latex condom down his stiff erection.

The break in action did nothing to deflate his cock. Pausing, with a blue pole protruding from his pelvis, he awaited her approval.

She reached for him.

He smiled.

Resuming his position between her legs, he shuddered as their bare skin touched. Tingles traveled through every inch of his body, curling his toes, as he felt almost her entire form pressed to his. Nothing was between them save the blue latex.

Resting the bulbous end of his cock at her entrance, he held his breath realizing nothing stood between him and marking her, claiming her, taking her as his own. After he entered her, she'd be his. They'd be mates. There'd be no going back.

The heat coming from their joined skin had Aric's forehead beading with sweat. Using the swollen mushroomed end of his dick, he teased her opening. With her wetness, his cock easily slid between her sensitive folds but he pulled back before entering her.

The slight clench of her sex begged Aric to plunge into her. As if to confirm it, another shot of musky need traveled to his nose, causing his resolve to tease her to melt away.

Thrusting forward, Aric's cock pressed inside his mate. Her vice-like walls spasmed around his erection the further it went in. Pulling back, he studied her face.

Large ice blue eyes stared back at him filled with heat and need. With flushed cheeks, her mouth hung open and she murmured for him to keep going.

He drove deeper into her and stars appeared before his eyes. An animalistic cry came from him and his wolf as the walls of her pussy stretched around him.

Once again, she pulled up her leg and curled it over his

hip. Changing his angle of entry, his cock bottomed out with a deep thrust.

Divina screamed and threw back her head. With her neck exposed to him, Aric buried his face into it, nipping at her throat. Pain striped his back when her nails once more clawed down it.

Aric gave her a few slow deep thrusts to get used to him. Her pussy rippled around him assuring him that she was made for him. No pussy had felt as good as hers. She was his mate.

On another inward drive, Aric claimed her mouth again. Divina's internal and external quiver spurred him on. Sliding his tongue past her lips he found hers. All the while he sped up his movements and pistoned in and out.

Divina's whimpered moans stoked Aric's fire. The way she writhed beneath him coaxed him to go harder and faster. Each twitch of her leg muscles was a pulse of her pussy around his cock. Gritting his teeth, he held back.

Not yet. He wanted to savor the first time he and his mate joined. He showered her face with tender kisses.

Slowly, he dragged his cock back and forth, sliding within her, teasing her. He needed to catch his breath before he exploded. Though, it seemed his mate was not the patient kind.

Digging her nails into his back, the pain shot straight to his balls.

"More," she begged and it was all he could do not to release right then.

Pumping harder, her sex spasmed around him again. Sweat dripped from his forehead as he pulled back, studying his mate's impassioned face through the tangled stands of his hair.

Holding his weight on his arms, drilling into her, she twisted beneath him. Clamping down on his cock, her walls gripped him like a vice as her body went rigid beneath him. Snapping open suddenly, her large blue eyes stared vacantly toward him. Her mouth opened into an O but no sound came from her lips.

"That's it. You're right there." Aric leaned down and kissed her neck.

The tingling at the base of his spine grew in intensity and traveled to his groin. As his balls tightened, his wolf lunged with in him.

Now, his wolf urged.

Now, the animal pushed.

Rearing back a final time before burying himself deep into his mate, Aric's cock slammed home. Tightness gripped him to the point of pain.

Shaking beneath him, Divina shrieked. Fingers coiled around his biceps, and he watched her face twist in pleasure as her orgasm struck.

Aric's jaw distended and his teeth elongated. With his head back, mouth open, he took a deep breath before he swung down clamping onto her shoulder. The sharp wolfen fangs pierced her skin like a hot blade through butter.

She screamed louder trembling beneath him while her walls rippled around him.

As his orgasm rocketed through him the ecstasy of marking and claiming his mate sent Aric to another planet. Warm, thick blood pooled in his mouth and he sucked down her essence, claiming her officially.

Pain. Orgasm. Pain. Heaven. Pain. Euphoria. Emotions overwhelmed Divina as she succumbed to Aric's attention. Tears welled in her eyes and a lump lodged in her throat.

Raking her nails down his back, she quivered beneath him in the aftershocks of her orgasm.

When he pulled his mouth from her shoulder, she saw the blood on his lips.

He'd bitten her.

Gasping for air, his full weight on her, he seemed content.

Divina wanted to be outraged.

"You. Said. You. Weren't. A. Vampire," she said between breaths.

Running his fingers along her cheek, he grinned. His cock twitched inside her, and she moaned involuntarily. Sensitive from the brutal way he had just taken her, her body reacted to the subtlest of touches as if they were electric shocks.

"I'm not," he whispered.

Kissing both her cheeks and then her forehead, he nuzzled into her neck.

"I'm a wolf."

The world came crashing down on Divina. Her escape, her reprieve, her salvation from the prophecy was a lie.

A wolf. The wolf? She blinked at him while the fresh wound throbbed in pain.

The content expression on his face remained. He stroked her hair and went back to nibble and lick at the place he had bitten her seemingly unaware of her internal conflict.

Flinching, she sucked in a sharp breath. However, the pain from the bite faded, replaced by a euphoric tickle in the crook of her neck that sprinkled down her body.

While Aric laved affection onto the bite, Divina couldn't help but compare it to Rori's bites. While Rori's tended to infuse an intensity into the orgasm, afterward she'd still feel sore. The aches lasting days. However, the moment Aric's kisses and licks caressed the punctures on her skin, the pain went away and replaced with a need for more and a need for him. That never happened when Rori bit her.

Heat bloomed within her again and she couldn't believe with Aric still inside her, her body amped up for another round. Surely, she had lost her damn mind.

Human. She'd thought him human. She couldn't have been more wrong.

"A wolf?" she repeated.

Biting back a moan as his tongue laved over the fresh bite mark, she tried to focus. The ache from the bite warmed her still-moist core.

In complete confusion, she couldn't understand how her body craved his touch with him still inside her. Trying to hang on to logic, she felt as though she were losing the battle, as his gentle attentions fogged her brain.

"Mmm hmmm," he hummed. "And you're my mate."

The color drained from Divina's face. Aric's words took over her awareness and a cold feeling splashed over her. She wriggled from under him.

"What?" she asked.

Pushing up on his arms, taking his weight off her, Aric furrowed his brow. Regarding her with confusion, he sat back on his heels. He studied her with hazel eyes tinged with golden flashes.

Scrambling from under him, she scurried to the end of the bed until her back hit a wall. In order to focus, she'd need distance from him. Unable to understand why it happened, she needed to get away from his touch, even if for just a moment, so her mind could clear.

"What did you say?" she asked.

Canting his head, Aric studied her.

"You know about vampires but not about wolves?" he asked with a curious inflection.

Swallowing, she reached a hand up to her shoulder. Landing on Aric's bite which trickled blood on her fingers.

"I don't have much experience with wolves," she admitted.

Her mind swirled. Without her consent, the pieces to the prophecy fell into place. The loss of control in her own fate taunted her. The past few days, perhaps even the past few years, had been a parade of people pushing her toward something without so much as asking her if it was what she wanted. Now, she was the witch who belonged to the wolf.

"Good." The bed dipped with his reply.

Her attention flicked toward him. With the full blue condom dangling from his slightly shrunken dick, he crawled toward her. She froze, only able to watch his advancement.

Torn between fear of what it meant and the desire to have him again, she felt paralyzed.

Gingerly, his hand took hers. With a gentle tug, she allowed him to pull her into his lap.

"You bit me." Her voice cracked.

Anxiety vibrated within her until his rough hand covered hers. Once pulled into his lap, he ran his fingers through her hair. A soothing calm took over, pushing the anxiety away.

"I did." He kissed the crown of her head. "I claimed you. No other wolves will come near you. You are mine."

Subtly, she shook her head, desperate to understand it all. Pressing her cheek to his bare chest she inhaled the scent of sweaty wolf man and her temperature rose; neediness pooled in her belly.

Mates. Claiming. Belonging to. Emperors. Councils. The Ember Witches.

Overwhelmed with it all, she sought solace in his arms. All she wanted was to have a moment, a moment without the intrusive prophecy. She wanted to feel connected to someone without the nagging feeling of being a puppet with her strings pulled by another. The prophecy seemed to steal every semblance of peace from her.

Crushed by the pressure of the prophecy, the meaning of his bite, his claim that they were mates left her wondering if she could she handle it. She had no idea what it meant to be a wolf's mate. On top of that little pickle, according to the prophecy, it meant she'd be an Ember Witch. And not just any old Ember Witch, but a witch who had a seat at their table, and she wasn't sure she was ready for any of it.

Divina trembled in his embrace. Unsure if she shook from her orgasm, or if she had reached her limit, she wanted to not care. The desire to let it all go taunted her.

Aric squeezed her in his large arms and Divina took a deep breath. Drowning in the pressure of the prophecy, the idea of forgetting it all and letting things happen tempted her. Every fiber of her being screamed she was where she belonged. The safety of Aric's arms combatted her inner conflict into submission.

Turning in his lap, she lifted her chin and gazed up at him.

He smiled a crooked smile revealing one dimple.

Ducking to meet her mouth, he kissed her. Soft. Tender. Her heart swooned.

Reaching up to cup his face, she allowed his kiss to melt away her concerns. The uninhibited affection in Aric's kisses was almost enough to sway her into giving into the prophecy. His talented mouth could be her new addiction.

The way his mouth took hers stole her worries. Her mind lost its focus, and all she was aware of was her need for him, her need for more. Anything else took a back seat.

As the pressure increased against her lips, and Aric's passion grew, Divina's matched. He held her tighter, crushing her body against his. The concern about the prophecy slipped out of her mind as his tongue slipped over her lips and tangled with hers.

One more go; one more time. She could worry about what

it all meant later. Now... now she had an itch that only a wolf could scratch.

As if reading her mind, his hardness pressed against her. Overtaken by carnal lust of it all, Divina lost her head and succumbed to the primal urge to be with Aric again if for no other reason than while joining with him, her anxiety about the prophecy evaporated.

CHAPTER 31

Drifting in and out of wakefulness, Divina pressed up against Aric's warm body. Her head fit perfectly in the nook between his shoulder and his neck. Large arms cocooned her and she didn't want to wake. Against his side she felt as though they were adjoining puzzle pieces. Basking in the orgasmic afterglow of their several rounds of sex, she nuzzled against him. If the world could stop on its axis, Divina would be eternally grateful.

The gentle stroking of Aric's fingertips on her arm ceased. The limb around her stiffened and pulled her tighter aginst him. No longer tenderly cradled against Aric, she was crushed to his side, and struggled to get full breaths.

"Get the fuck out." His chest vibrated as he rumbled to someone Divina couldn't see.

"Don't you two make the pretty pair?" A feminine voice crooned.

Attempting to look up toward the voice, Divina pushed off him. Releasing his grip, the bed bounced as Aric rose from it.

Cool air prickled her skin where Aric had once made

contact. She grabbed the sheets to cover herself and fight off the shudder that followed.

"What part of 'get out' do you not understand, Selene?" Aric demanded.

Twitching, startled at his tone, Divina regarded Aric with a wary curiosity. Peering toward the door for the source of his ire, Divina clutched the sheets tighter to her body. She wasn't prepared for what she saw.

"Aric," the woman purred his name with a pout, "you don't mean that."

The blond with the killer body stalked toward him with sensual steps. Wearing several layers of sheer blue fabric, that danced around her as she moved, her entrance into the room was more of an erotic dance than anything else. While the layering made the fabrics opaque, and less risqué, the sensuality of her attire called to mind the image of a genie from a bottle. The scent of jasmine that surrounded her only added to the genie image.

"I have never meant it more in my life." Aric cracked his neck.

Scrambling to her feet, Divina flopped a few times in an attempt to keep her modesty. Trying to keep the sheet around her as she knelt on the bed, Divina studied the interaction between the two.

The woman opposite them was nothing but poise and grace, who owned her sexuality while Divina, in coiled navy sex sheets, felt inadequate and uncoordinated in her presence. If this was Aric's girlfriend, Divina didn't need to be in the middle of whatever was about to happen.

Pangs of envy stabbed Divina as she scanned the floor for her clothes. Of course he wasn't single. Fury heated her chest with the embarrassment at her foolish belief that a charming, funny, sex god would be single or at the very least honest with her about *not* being single.

"My my, Roricus has been busy," Selene said as she leaned against his small dresser.

The mention of Rori awoke Divina from her angry and envious thoughts. Halting her search for clothing, Divina turned her attention back to Aric's girlfriend.

At the foot of the bed, Aric stood, naked as a jaybird without a hint of modesty. Becoming a wall of muscle between Divina and the stranger, who could best be described as a walking wet dream, he blocked her view of the curious woman.

"How do you know Rori?" she asked, peering around Aric.

Not many called Rori by his full name. Hell, Divina hadn't learned it for three years, and that was by accident. To hear the woman use it, sent alarm bells off in Divina's head. The stranger knew more than Divina was comfortable with and Divina wanted to know how. The possibility of a her being an Ember Witch crossed her mind, but Divina couldn't recall seeing her at the table. Not that it mattered, they were clear that Ember Witches were plentiful, she could be one of them but have not risen to the status of being at the table yet.

"Who's Roricus?" Aric turned with a quizzical, yet jealous, expression on his beautiful face. Another distracting pang of jealousy at the idea he had a girlfriend. She needed to focus on what the woman knew, the whole girlfriend thing could be hashed out later.

Offering his open arms, it felt as though he beckoned her to his side.

With feet that had a mind of their own, Divina stepped into his embrace. The heat returned once his arm circled her and pulled her against him. To add to the confusion that swirled in her brain, Divina's tension eased with the over-whelming sense of security and comfort from his touch.

"Yes, Divina," Selene nearly sang, "who is Roricus?"

The smug expression caused Divina's blood to boil. With

clenched fists and narrowed eyes, Divina glared at the intrusive woman.

She had to be an Ember Witch. There was no other explanation for her to have the knowledge she did. Though, if she was, that would make her like Ines in that by showing up, by being with Aric, she went against her coven. Her coven wanted Divina with a wolf. It wasn't Divina's fault the wolf was Selene's wolf.

Acting with a will of its own, her hand went to her neck covering the fresh, what felt like mirrored crescent-moon marks Aric had given Divina. Curiously, Divina scanned Selene's neck for similar markings. Finding markings but, from what Divina could see, they were a different sort. Divina furrowed her brow switching to focusing on the woman's face. Something didn't add up. She peered at Aric as though he'd have the answer.

Flicking his gaze between the two women, Aric settled his hazel eyes, flashing gold, on Divina questioningly. Unprepared for the wounded expression upon Aric's face, Divina shifted her attention back to Selene.

"Who are you?" Divina asked.

"I'm the witch in the prophecy, my dear," Selene announced with a bit too much delight.

The prophecy. It never fucking ended. A new rage heated Divina's skin causing her entire body to tense. Her eye twitched as she clenched her jaw. The wolf. Now another witch. Fuck, this damn prophecy never left Divina alone.

"Enough of the prophecy bullshit Selene," Aric barked.

Nearly stumbling against him with the force of Aric's tug at her to stay behind his back, Divina took a moment to find her feet.

"Go back to your leech," he added with a sneer.

Caught off balance by both his words and actions, Divina gaped at Aric. He knew about the prophecy. She blinked.

The conspiracy that was the prophecy was getting to be a bit much for Divina. The whole fucking world was in on the damn prophecy it seemed. An image of Aric at the center of the Ember Witch table, surrounded by the rest, being informed of his role sickened Divina. A hand went to her stomach as it rolled.

Selene sauntered the few steps further into the room appearing unfazed by Aric's warnings, drawing Divina's attention. Narrowing her gaze at Selene, the burn of possessiveness surged through Divina. The woman's confidence around him, despite his obvious disdain for her, didn't sit right with Divina. None of it did, she was in an alternative universe for sure.

"Have you told Aric who he has to thank for having you?" Selene directed her question to Divina.

"You're threatening my mate," he warned. "My wolf isn't taking too kindly to that."

"I'm having a conversation." The feigned innocence grated on Divina's nerves. "I guess you could say the Ember Witches are to thank. I mean, if it weren't for those meddling fucks, you wouldn't be here. You wouldn't be a concern at all."

It always came down to the damn Ember Witches. At this point, Divina almost believed they orchestrated her entire existence. They were masterful puppeteers pulling strings, choreographing a life, just to get her to this point. Nothing for Divina was real or genuine. Everything was a part of some elaborate scheme cooked up by the Ember Witches. Looking at her hands, Divina half expected to see strings or wires controlling her physical movements as well as her emotions. Opening her eyes wider, as the lightbulb of an assumption lit over her head, Divina considered the Ember Witches might have spelled her. No physical wires needed when one had a spell cast upon them.

Glancing up toward Aric, she frowned. The idea of being

under the manipulation of the witches had her questioning her choice to sleep with him or Rori for that matter. Feeling like a pawn for the coven in an attempt to get some sort of power over all kinds, weighted Divina down with regret, disappointment, and shame. Her heart sunk at the idea.

Aric snarled again distracting Divina from her own thoughts.

"Down boy. Don't you want to know about your 'mate' and her vampire?" Selene used air quotes.

Steel encased Divina, as Aric's arm held her awkwardly against his back.

"You reek of rot," Aric seethed. "I know the smell of vamps. I know the smell of their kin. Your lies have no place here."

Maybe he wasn't working with them. They could have tricked him too; they could have cast a spell on him as well. The thought hurt Divina's heart. None of it was true.

Selene smirked. Her eyebrows rose in amusement. "Of all the things I have done to you Aric, lying is not one of them." She snickered.

Without so much as looking at Divina, Aric responded to Selene. "I'm not blind. I know she knows vampires. If you are trying to get between my mate and me, you are going to be very disappointed, and in a lot of pain," he said.

Definitely bespelled. With his words confirming her suspicion, Divina's body slumped in disappointment.

Selene's eyes sparkled with mischief. "You know it's a funny thing about fate." Selene kicked the articles of clothing out of her path so she could take a seat on his bed. "It's not all that concrete. You are really only fated to get to a point. That point is when you are supposed to make a major, life-changing decision. So, are you sure your decisions have been made? Are you sure nothing is going to change?"

Selene's words were eerily familiar. They were Esmine's

words. Trying to make sense of it all, Divina's head spun. The feel of Aric's arm across her body, protecting her, gave her a sense of footing.

"Mates are not one of the things that change," Aric snarled.

"You see, the road to finding one's mate is rarely as simple as finding one another at a coffee shop or a bar." She looked up at them with that shit-eating-grin. "A lot of things happen between birth and mating."

"I have no expectations of my mate being a virgin, so you can just take that shit—"

"Did she tell you that she gave him a pulse?" Selene smoothed the sheer fabrics over her thighs.

Silence.

"Ah." Selene was amused. "I have your attention. So, I guess you know what that means. Yes?" Selene nodded. "Your mate was meant to start a dead heart."

Putting his back to Selene, Aric turned toward Divina.

The intensity of his gaze forced Divina to look away feeling as though she'd betrayed him. The idea that a spell by the Ember Witches had brought them together shamed Divina. It wasn't real. His feelings for her, his mark on her, nothing that he claimed was real.

His grip loosened and her heart broke. With a whimper, Divina's need for it to be real, for them to be real, crashed into her so hard it nearly knocked her over.

"Originally, the prophecy stated that the vampire who belonged to the witch will take the throne to overthrow all who know." Selene sang it with delight.

Divina, used the sheet as a shield against Selene's words, gripping it tighter around her. That was not the prophecy Rori had told her. What game was this woman playing?

Swinging his head toward Selene, the rumble in Aric's

chest filled the room. "That wasn't what you told me," Aric countered.

Selene's delight left her face. She sighed. "Yes, well, that would be because the Ember Witches got involved. Nosy bitches couldn't leave well enough alone. No, they had to go and mess with a perfectly good vision.

"They got in there, and they dissected the vision," Selene explained. "They chased down every witch, wolf, and vampire they could find at the point in fate that could change the prophecy. They found it in Divina Bihari, Roricus Fromm, and you my dear sweet, Aric Braun."

"I have nothing to do with the vampire throne," Aric declared.

His resolve seemed to steel, as his strength returned to his arm and he yanked Divina behind him again. Knocked off her balance once more, Divina felt like a ragdoll, physically and emotionally.

Selene rolled her eyes. "You're the wolf. You are destined to defeat the vampire not worthy of the throne." Selene groaned. "However, the key to this is you will only do this once you find your mate. And unfortunately, as we have tested, it must be your true mate, not just any witch you fuck." She grumbled that last bit.

Fury burned in Divina once more. A territorial fire lit in her belly and her teeth clenched. She eyed the woman with pure hatred. She wasn't his girlfriend. She was just a manipulative bitch who got into Divina's mate's bed to further her own cause.

The prickle of energy started in her core, spreading out to her limbs as Divina glowered upon Selene. Her fingers spread wide, curling slightly, twitching while the barbs of emotional turmoil took control of her call to power. Outside the trailer the wind howled, shaking the walls slightly. The one thing

Divina had mastered thus far was harnessing the wind, and she'd use the full extent of it upon Selene if she had to.

"The only way for you to meet your mate was for your mate to bond with the vampire, and for him to choose power over her love. Really, if you think about it, Roricus is getting the shit end of the stick." Selene seemed unfazed by Divina's posture and the increased breeze outside and continued in her explanation. "I mean, he is forever tied to Divina here, but he never gets to have her. 'Cause she has to shack up with you"—she pointed to Aric—"so he can win the throne. You two get to go off and live happily ever after while Roricus pines for her forever." She paused. "But then again, he gets to rule over all those who know, so I guess, it's an even trade." She shrugged.

CHAPTER 32

Patience wearing thin and the room tinged red, Aric's wolf clawed within him for release. The inner beast sought to eradicate the unwanted female in their den. Fighting to keep human control, Aric closed the short distance between himself and Selene.

To her credit, she stood her ground with a tightened jaw.

With the repeated disregard for the sanctity of his home, Aric's limits were tested. "Leave. You have entered my den twice without an invitation. That is two times too many. There will not be a third," he said to Selene through clenched teeth.

With a twitch, Selene's eyes lost their confidence. Fear reflected in them as she rose from the bed. Lifting her chin, she took a deep breath. Regarding Aric with an obviously false air of confidence, Selene stepped back.

"I just wanted to make sure you had all the facts," she said with a quiver in her voice.

Eyeing Aric as she spoke, he suspected her words weren't meant for him. She hadn't presented any new facts to him, none that meant anything anyway. That left him to wonder what Selene knew of his mate, and what his mate had known.

Taking the last full step toward Selene, their bodies all but touched. Purposely invading her space, he glared down at her with malice. "I will rip your goddamn throat out if you don't leave now." He snarled as the wolf sought to howl with Aric's vocal chords.

Swallowing audibly, fear reflected in her gaze. The scent of it wafted toward Aric as she lowered her eyes in submission. Cautiously, Selene stepped backward, out of his reach, then she turned and fled the trailer.

Now, he could focus on his mate. Satisfied the female presented no further discomfort to Divina, Aric turned.

Coiled in the navy sheets of his bed, he found Divina had paled during the altercation. Staring wide-eyed at where the woman had stood, she looked right through him.

Quick to her side, he wrapped her in a tight hug. He attempted to pull her against his chest, but she resisted.

Whimpering at the rejection, his wolf didn't understand. Aric furrowed his brow holding her loosely.

"Divina?" he whispered.

Vacant pale blue eyes stared off as if she didn't even see him.

Once more, Aric attempted to pull her to him.

Once more, she stiffened.

Aric squashed the urge to force her against him.

"What's wrong?" he asked.

With a slight shake of her head, the further silence amped up Aric's and his wolf's anxiety. His need to comfort her, to ease whatever bothered her, had him warring with respecting her boundaries. As much as he wanted to, he couldn't force comfort onto her.

Blinking, she slowly tilted her head and her eyes seemed

to focus on him. Good. She came back to earth. He could work with that.

"It's all a Vrăji," she whispered, "the witches," her voice cracked, "it's not real."

"No," he implored, wanting more than anything to make her doubt go away. "No spells. No witches. It's real. I know it. Mates aren't a spell. I can explain it to you."

Lowering her tear-filled gaze, her quivering chin dipped.

"This... this... this whole thing," she stammered and tried to pull away from him. "We have no say in it. The Ember Witches, they did this."

Aric's arms lingered around her, and his wolf snapped at him trying to get him to pull her back. Aric's heart threatened to beat out of his chest while the rest of him lacked the ability to move.

Divina stepped further away from him and his hands slipped from her. Taking the last three steps she had, before the back of her legs collided with the night stand, she tripped over the sheet tangled in her legs, then on a pair of pants, before she fell to the head of the bed.

As much as Aric wanted to follow her, he didn't. The knot in his stomach grew up to his throat. He couldn't move. Anxious within him, trying to urge Aric toward his mate, his wolf howled in his mind, making it hard to concentrate.

What his wolf didn't understand, but Aric the human did, was that his mate needed space to process. The more he crowded her, the less of a chance he'd have at keeping her.

"The prophecy. The council. The Ember Witches. Rori." Divina resumed staring at the wall. "You."

At the mention of the other male's name, Aric's wolf snapped. Tightening his jaw, fighting his inner animal with all he had, Aric took the three steps to Divina. Kneeling before her, in an attempt to convey he was no threat, Aric wouldn't reach for her. He needed to be in her field of vision.

"You're my mate," he reminded her. "I claimed you. From this day forth I will be by your side to help you in all the challenges you face."

"Don't I get a say?" she asked, finally meeting his eyes. "Don't I get to choose?"

Aric furrowed his brow. Choice? Why did choice matter? They were to be together. That was how mates worked. As much as the idea pained him, and he tried not to think of it, it had to be asked. "You want someone else?" he whispered. The wolf within raged within him. Every muscle in Aric's body tightened to restrain the inner beast.

Divina pulled the sheet around her tighter, hiding her perfect body from him.

"I don't know!" Her voice cracked. "But it should be my choice! You... you... you bit me!" Her hand went to her neck. "You didn't give me a choice! You just did it. We don't know anything about one another, but you did this thing! I have no control in any of this!"

Watching her face shift, Aric steeled himself for a physical attack from his mate.

With narrowed eyes, Divina's mouth set in a hard line. Her jaw clenched and her pale blue eyes clouded.

"You think you can control my life. You think you can dictate all of this," she shouted.

Her words lashed him as if she struck him with a whip. Unprepared for it, Aric gaped.

"I don't—"

Pushing to her feet, Divina knocked him back on his butt.

"Well, you can't! I choose!" Divina announced as she stepped over his leg.

"I never—" He tried again to scramble to his feet.

"You, and the witches, and Rori, all of you can bite my ass." She dropped the sheet and grabbed her panties. "I will decide when I am good and ready."

Momentarily stunned by her naked form, Aric's throat went dry. Even his wolf quieted as the two basked in the raw beauty of their mate.

Blinking to focus, Aric found his voice. "I don't want to force—"

Pointing an accusatory finger at him once she had her pants pulled up, she glared at him.

"But you did! You bit me! You said that was a claiming," she reminded him. "So where was my choice in all that?" she growled. "You just did what you wanted. Just like Rori, just like the witches. No one consulted me in any of this. Just because we fucked doesn't make me yours."

Bending, Divina snatched the shirt from the floor.

Aric watched his mate march down the middle of his trailer with purpose. "Where are you going?" he asked.

Whirling toward him, she yanked the door open. "Wherever I want."

Walls shook, the lock snapped, and Aric's door slammed shut behind her. Bouncing back open, Aric caught a glimpse of her angry stomping paces moving away from him.

Unable to move, Aric blinked. Sitting back, naked, on his heels in his trailer, the earthy scent of his mate dissipated. The small space of his trailer suddenly felt vast in her absence. Glancing around the room, at his bed, at the dark spot of blood which had dripped from her neck onto his sheets, he couldn't figure out what had just happened.

His wolf urged him to chase her, to make her see what she did.

Lifting the sheet she had wrapped around her, Aric brought it to his nose. Inhaling deeply, he took in her heavenly scent. Their joined scent from their coupling clung to his sheets.

An ache spread in his chest. He had no plan for what to do if his mate refused his claim to her. Flaring throughout his front, Aric rubbed at his sternum to ease the pain of the distance between him and Divina.

It wasn't supposed to happen like that. Even when one was human, mates felt a pull toward one another. He was sure of it, yet his mate had just walked out. She'd left him to deal with the fallout of half a mating bond. The only way she could do that would be if she didn't feel the pull but that was impossible.

Slowly, Aric lifted himself off the floor.

It would get worse the longer they were apart.

His wolf howled for her, and it rang in his heart. Frowning, Aric didn't know what to do.

The walls felt as though they closed in on him. The floor rose and the ceiling shrank. The air got thick and Aric choked to breathe.

Forcibly scratching at his insides, Aric's wolf wanted out. Pain radiated from his core outward. Aric fell back and writhed. Forcing the shift, the wolf took control. Aric gritted his teeth attempting to push the animal down. A snarl rose from Aric's chest as the burn covered his skin. Fur poked through his pores. Aric rolled to his side and banged his fist on the floor.

"No!"

Letting the unpredictable animal out in its emotional state wouldn't be good.

Spent from the multiple rounds with his mate, Aric was drained. Add Divina's rejection and Aric had nothing left to fight his wolf.

His animal knew he was weakened and the shift was inevitable. Tired of being on the sidelines, his beast wanted out.

The crack of his legs snapping hobbled him, and Aric let out a shriek. Bones shifted into their canine place. Skin tore and blood splattered on to his floor while Aric futilely resisted and pain consumed his senses.

"Stop!" he begged his wolf.

The shift took longer when he fought it. It hurt more. The veins in his neck protruded as Aric tried to stop the change.

"AAAHHHHH!"

Aric's back fractured, and a tail pushed forth from above his ass. Rolling onto his stomach in time for his arms to bend then break into their wolf shape, Aric gasped for breath spewing bile and spittle in the process. His fingers receded, and claws pushed out from his nails.

Aric gave in.

His jaw went next jutting forward, and his teeth grew in length.

Internally, Aric withdrew from the process finding a small corner of his consciousness to hide from the pain of the transition. Though, as hard as he tried, he couldn't lessen the ache of Divina's rejection.

He closed his internal eyes and allowed the wolf full control of their joined faculties. He didn't want to watch. The angry and impulsive wolf intended to cause some serious harm. Aric didn't have it in him to prevent it.

Where a man had once sat, now stood large brown wolf. Growling and sniffing the air, the beast intended to hunt.

Trotting down the center of the trailer, he pushed the half-closed door open and sprang out of it. Taking a moment to get a whiff of the breeze, the wolf didn't hesitate. Running full speed, into the woods, the animal had a mission.

Aric sat in his mind, in pain, plotting.

CHAPTER 33

Fuming as she stormed away from the trailer, Divina had had enough supernatural nonsense. They could push her only so far. They all kept telling her how strong she was yet none of them thought to consult her about her own damn fate. Fuck all of them.

Fuck Rori and his throne. Let the world find out about him. Maybe he'll learn how to treat people. Maybe it'll teach him to be more human. He had a heartbeat now, and thanks to Divina he should be more human.

Fuck the Ember Witches and their manipulative ways. Who did they think they were? If they wanted her at their table, they should have come to her. They didn't have to send Rori. They didn't have to work all secret-like. She was a big girl; they could come and ask her themselves. She didn't care if they didn't ask someone to be at their table, they should have been more forthcoming if the prophecy stated it.

Stomping her way through the field and trees surrounding Aric's trailer, she paused. Turning in circles, she realized she'd lost her bearings.

"Fuck," she muttered.

She hadn't paid attention to where Aric drove. Without a clue to where she was, she found herself unsure how to get back to her truck at the diner.

They were near the park, that much she knew. Where, near the park, was another thing entirely. Taking her phone from her pocket, she pulled up a map app. With no road in sight, Divina groaned. According to her screen, she stood in a block of green, with streets quite a distance away.

Taking in the tall grass and woods around her, she huffed. There had to be a street around somewhere. Trudging along, still angry, she had more immediate concerns than the prophecy and the men who weren't present. Divina needed to find a way to get somewhere, so she could think clearly.

Having chosen a direction, Divina could only hope it led to the park. As the trees thinned and grass transitioned to dirt, a hint of a path appeared. Praying she hadn't turned herself around, she pressed on.

An annoying buzz began in the back of her mind the farther away she walked. Sounding like a power line or something, Divina dismissed any sort of concern. However, the buzzing persisted, and further inspection of her surroundings, she found no power lines.

Mentally yelling and telling everyone she knew to fuck off worked initially to drown out the noise. A twinge settled in her chest, replacing the buzz, causing her to stop and rub it out.

Divina wasn't accustomed to so much walking and wrote off the ache in her chest to her non-athleticism. Dropping into a cross-legged position under a tree to enjoy the shade, she closed her eyes.

Inhaling through her nose she allowed nature to fill her senses. Where the warm sun had baked her skin, an occasional cool breeze eased it. Grass tickled at the tops of her exposed feet. The scent of dry grass and earth wrapped her in a tight hug.

Typically, the sort of meditation Divina practiced allowed her to connect with nature and soothed whatever ailed her. Unfortunately, the ache in her chest lingered. Resting wouldn't ease it. Something else was at play; another thing out of her control.

Ten futile minutes of meditation did nothing to ease the ache. If anything, it graduated from barely felt to mildly annoying. Rubbing her sternum, she refused to consider anything other than biology.

"Acid reflux," she said, making a mental note to get something to relieve it.

~

Reluctant to open his eyes, Rori woke from his heavy daytime slumber haunted by the previous evening's events. Every moment he thought he had found clarity was followed by a revelation or wrinkle that only served to cloud the waters once more.

The witches had planned for him to come into Divina's life. They had wanted him to show her the way of the witch. They told him to leave her.

The idea had been to leave her vulnerable and in need. In her hour of need, she'd seek out her coven. She'd go to the Ember Witches for instruction and protection. They'd teach her, or so they all had hoped.

Divina hadn't followed through on the plan made without her knowledge.

Rori broke her heart and his own for nothing. Lies and manipulations were his reward. Promises of a throne weren't an actual throne. Nor was a chair worth what he had given up.

Slow to get out of the bed, he ran his hands over the sheets. They hadn't been changed since he and Divina had made love the other evening, so her scent clung to them. If he closed his eyes, he could pretend she laid next to him again. It felt like a lifetime ago that they'd shared the bed.

Sighing, he glanced to the heavily curtained window. Though he couldn't see it, he sensed the night was young. Witch blood had faded from his system, leaving him famished.

With no interest in blood, he scrubbed his face with both hands. The gurgling of his stomach and the dry cracking of his throat indicated that, while he may not have an interest in blood, his body needed it. He had no choice when it came to feeding. To not feed meant weakness.

Rori's gaze drifted toward the bathroom door. Reminded of the shower, the last place Divina had been, he was tempted out of bed. The idea of her slick, naked body lathered just beyond that door caused the slow pump of his heart to skip a beat. Placing a hand over his chest, he closed his eyes wondering if she'd given him a gift or a curse.

Hunger pangs stabbed through his gut, reminding him to feed. Another reason he needed to get out of bed. To keep his strength, he'd need to face the night.

Even though he'd done it before, the idea of going out to face the dark world without Divina kept him in place. How could he go out there, drink, and play the part of a strong vampire when he'd squandered his chance at eternal love?

He'd had what others dreamed of all their lives, and never got, no matter how many centuries they roamed the earth. Love had been in his grasp, and he'd let it slip over the promise of a fucking chair. That's all it was, a gaudy—most likely—uncomfortable chair.

The manipulative cunt witches dangled the power of an old antique in front of him and he caved. He'd given up

Divina, his life of happiness, for a fucking velvet cushion. He'd have to go on without her because he'd been seduced by some old mortal hags.

Or did he? The thought crept into his mind too easily.

Choices. The word sprang into his mind like a bright beacon on a foggy night.

Esmine had said he chose power over his mate. They may have pushed him in that direction, but he should have chosen Divina.

Tiny tendrils of hope sprouted within him at the possibility he could rescind his previous choice. He could choose Divina. Thumbing his nose at the prophecy, meant he could have Divina. He didn't really want to be emperor, anyway.

Flinging the covers off himself, Rori swung his legs over the side of the bed and he sat up. Staring into the mirror, he locked eyes with his own image. His hair was a mess, skin graying slightly, and he felt cold. He'd need to do something about that.

The question about his ability to rule popped into his head.

In all the time he'd known of the prophecy and his role, he'd never questioned his ability to lead his kind, or all kinds. Chasing the throne since before Klaus met the sun, he'd taken the witches at their word and purposely ran into Divina. Rori had flirted with her and seduced her, all to do their bidding and to get himself on a throne.

Doubting a throne was worth the pain he'd caused Divina and himself fueled him. The first time, he justified it because the witches said if he didn't, the humans would find out about all the other kinds. All beings other than human would be persecuted, hunted, and tortured. Rori didn't want that on his head.

Now, though; now he wasn't so sure. He could protect Divina from humans. He could whisk her away to some remote place. They could live out her days together. No one else mattered to Rori, just he and Divina. If the time came, he could change her. Rori's heart once more skipped a lazy beat.

Dismissing Esmine's words of caution regarding the emptiness of a changed witch, Rori assured himself their love could fill any void. He'd be enough for her to feel whole. The chance at eternity with his Divina was worth any risk.

Renewed hope filled Rori. He could have Divina.

Let Perci have it. Let Selene take her seat at the witch table. Divina didn't need a damn coven. She had done well all on her own. Plus, she hated the fucking witches. Rori hated the witches.

He could have his Divina. Esmine confirmed it. It was his choice. He had the choice of the throne or his love. He picked his love. Damn it all to hell, he wanted his Divina.

CHAPTER 34

With the sun dripping, pink and purple hues painted the sky. Exhausted, Divina flung the old pickup into park when she pulled up to the vardo. After the long walk to civilization, she'd gotten a cab to get to the diner and her truck.

With throbbing feet, she stood before her wagon. Waiting for the relief of being home to take hold, she inhaled deeply. It had once been a source of great pride for her. She closed her eyes waiting.

Nothing.

Opening her eyes she peered at the wagon as if it were a stranger. She had restored that thing as a way to connect to her roots. The roots Rori had said were hers. Now, it only reminded her of the sham the concept had turned out to be.

Sure, she was a witch. That wasn't the sham part. Rori was. Their love was. Or, well, her love for him was real, but his for her, that was manipulation. Either the witches had spelled him, too, or he had played her for a heartbeat. Both ideas turned her stomach

She knew he was a bastard. She should have believed

herself this time. Tears filled her eyes as the pain thumped in her chest. Since he walked into her life nothing had been authentic.

Her emotions warred inside. Waffling from regret to anger to mourning, Divina didn't know what to feel. It all manifested into the tendrils of ache coiling around her heart since she left Aric.

Yanking open the door to the vardo, she scanned the inside. Never one for collecting things, she appreciated the minimalist nature of the tiny home. Stepping inside, she swiped at the tears on her cheeks.

Lifting the mattress of her couch/bed, she pulled out a large bag. Stuffing all her clothing inside, she swallowed more tears, preventing them from falling. She went toward the cabinet, undid the bindings, and sorted through the herbs. She would need those.

The only way to fight spells was with spells.

Divina was a witch—that wouldn't change. Practicing her craft was her priority. Everything else had to take a back seat.

Everyone told her about the power within her. They talked of her potential. Well, she had every intention of developing that power. Those bitches wouldn't know what hit them.

Taking a shopping bag, she emptied the herbs from the cabinet. The book Rori had given her sat on a shelf before her. It seemed like a lifetime ago. Pausing her frenzied packing, she lifted the book in both hands. Bringing it to her nose, she inhaled the scent of old pages and leather, and memories rattled through her threatening to fall, a new stream of tears.

Biting them back, Divina flipped through the old pages and found the picture. The two of them were together, happy, and with blue tongues laughing at her. Frowning, heat plumed in her aching chest and filled her cheeks.

There was a time she had pulled this picture out and felt sad at what she had lost.

Taking the picture from the book, Divina regarded the two blue tongues and the happy couple. The temptation to tear the picture up, burn it, and rid herself of the memory forever coursed through her.

Instead, she looked away and closed the book with her other hand, holding it by the spine. The picture fell from her fingers onto the floor to be forgotten. She planned on forgetting Rori and how she had been introduced to being a witch.

She didn't need to look back anymore. Divina needed to look forward. Forward didn't include a coven or a vampire. Forward included Divina dictating her own life.

After packing up the few belongings she needed, Divina left the wagon. Tossing the few bags into the cab of her truck, she climbed in the other side. Without looking back at her wagon, she closed the cab door. The past was done. No need to look upon it again.

Her gaze fell on the large tome given to her by Josephine. The book from the Ember Witches would be her guide now. She would learn all she could from it.

She'd take them down than by using their own secrets against them.

Turning the key in the ignition, Divina shifted her attention forward. The sky darkened to blue and navy with the setting sun. She needed to get moving.

Part of her believed Rori would come back. He had to. If he wanted the throne, he needed her. He needed her and the wolf. Well, he couldn't have her. He made his choice. Now, she made hers.

With the thought of the wolf, of Aric, her heart skipped. The pang of pain in her chest intensified. Rubbing her palm along her sternum offered no relief, yet she did it reflexively with each new ache. Gritting her teeth, she attempted to ignore the sensation.

Pressing her foot on the clutch, she eased the truck into gear. She was through with people making choices for her. She'd decide on Aric in her own time. Bite or no bite, her life was hers alone.

Turning out of the lot, she jammed down hard on the gas pedal. The roar of the engine gave her a thrill and the tears she had cried dried up. The excitement of forging on into uncharted territory replaced her grief with anticipation.

Peeling out of the lot was like peeling away from her old life. Turning onto the road and going who knew where presented her with a world of opportunities. She had potential all right, and she sought to fulfill it all if for no other reason than to spite Rori and the fucking witches.

Without a care where the road led, she forged on. The need to get away consumed her. She had to get out of New Orleans. Putting it all behind her and moving forward was more important than breathing.

Fuck the prophecy. It wouldn't dictate Divina's life. Not anymore. It was Divina's turn to do what was right for Divina.